Julie McCoy

Eye of the Storm

ISBN-10: 0992604206
ISBN-13: 978-0992604202

Disclaimer:
All characters, events and incidents appearing in this novel are fictitious. Any resemblance to real persons, living or dead or actual events or incidents is purely coincidental.

www.juliemccoy.info

About the Author

Julie McCoy is from Dublin, Ireland but is living in North County Kildare with her husband, two daughters and various four legged creatures. She began writing in secondary school when an A+ on a homework essay, along with some praise and encouragement from a wonderful english teacher, helped her to fall hopelessly in love with creating stories and poems. While many students groaned at the mere mention of having to do a five hundred word essay on being 'In The Dark,' she rejoiced.

After a long, dry spell of writer's block all through her twenties, she took it up again in 2009 when a story crept into her head and nagged her until she eventually wrote it down. A novel was born. Since then, she has joined creative writing classes, writers' groups and now writes a selection of poetry, short stories and various musings on life, as well as novels.

'Eye of the Storm' is inspired by a life long dream of hers: to chase storms across America's 'Tornado Alley.'

Acknowledgements

I would like to thank the following people, for without whom, this book would not be in your hands right now.

Firstly, to Patricia O'Reilly, for her invaluable feedback when I couldn't see the wood for the trees, or the book for the words. To Gerard Byrne, who designed the cover so beautifully, knowing exactly what I wanted. To my friend and fellow author, Audrey Kelty: thank you for being my writing sounding board, for Swedish cinnamon buns and for play dates that are supposed to be for the kids but are really an excuse for us to shoot the literary breeze. To the members of Cill Dara Writers' Circle, current and former: thank you for your feedback and support - I've found confidence I never knew I had thanks to you all.

An unending stream of thanks must be awarded to my family: my parents and sister - for always being there for me. To my two children, who suffered many a loss of my time during the construction of this novel: they are my reason for being. And last, but most importantly, to my husband. Were it not for his support, encouragement and technical expertise, I would never have even put pen to paper or rather, fingertip to keyboard. So, this book is dedicated to him.

Thank you.

CHAPTER 1

The pages of the magazine swished as Sam flicked through them mindlessly. She was looking, but wasn't absorbing either the high gloss, photo-shopped pictures or the indulgent words. There were ads for perfumes endorsed by a variety of skinny, airbrushed celebrities, a full page ad for anti-wrinkle cream modelled by a girl who couldn't be more than eighteen and pictures of an emaciated-looking celebrity on her wedding day, complete with glowing report of the occasion. Throwing the magazine back onto the table, she picked up another and repeated the flicking process, stopping when she got to an article about a woman who had overcome her husband's death by travelling to India. Sam began to read the words but when she came to where the author wrote about how Yoga had helped her come to terms with her loneliness, she sighed, tutted and dropped the magazine back.

The receptionist looked across and raised an eyebrow at her. It was a room of insecurities, with a tired décor and silent people waiting patiently on the upright, torn leather chairs. Sam lowered her eyes to her hands. Small and tanned with short oval nails, they were shaking slightly. She clamped them down onto her tightly crossed lap and cast a glance around at the three indeterminately aged women, one overweight man and a suited man who looked out of place. She tried to look cool and calm, picking up a newspaper dated from the day before. It was well read but would help pass the time until she was called and she couldn't face reading any more vacuous celebrity rags.

Feeling more than a little precious about how shabby it was, she gingerly turned the pages. The death notices: nobody she knew; the TV guide: these days nothing on television interested her, the inevitable ads, the jobs vacant section: loads of opportunities for waitresses..... Then a specific one tucked into the top right hand column caught her eye. She read it through quickly, then slowly.

"Storm chaser looking for fellow storm enthusiast to drive modified Ford truck. Must have full, clean driver's license and be available full time from months of March to August. Meteorological experience preferred but not essential. Applicant must be dedicated and a team player. Contact Jonah at 555 714 0440 8660."

Sam sighed as she closed over the page and folded the paper, replacing it alongside the magazines on the table. She hated this room with a passion. The early nineties pastel peach, flowery wallpaper and scratched wooden floor did nothing to foster calm into its anxiously waiting patients. For Sam, it served to make her more nervous. The portly receptionist tap tapped away at her keyboard. Sam wondered what she could be typing. Surely her job was mostly answering phones and scheduling appointments. Yet she was hitting the keyboard as though she was writing the last chapter of a novel and couldn't wait to get it finished. The sound of her Shellac nails on the keys was almost hypnotic. Sam looked at her own nails. They used to be long, sometimes painted, sometimes not, but they had always been manicured and cared for. Now, they were short, dry and unkempt. While her clothes weren't exactly girly, and she was a closet tom boy, at least with groomed nails she'd felt feminine. The last time she'd had them long was over a year ago. The day they'd gotten the bad news, was the day her fingernails had died.

2

The clack clacking continued. Sam fired the receptionist a dirty look and glanced across at the suited man. Perhaps he wasn't a patient, maybe he was waiting for someone. He was handsome, with a smart blue shirt and cheery striped socks. In an attempt to drown out the typing backing track, she invented a story around him. He was a widower who, after his wife died, had developed a penchant for hoarding, especially women's magazines and scarves and who was harboring a phobia of birds and pathway cracks. The man coughed, rattled his newspaper and looked up, causing her to blush. What if he was a magazine obsessed hoarder who could read minds? She shook her head and scolded her absurdity.

She stared out of the window, riddled with children's handprints. It looked as though it hadn't been cleaned in a month. The blue sky was littered with cirrocumulus clouds, little brush strokes across the azure canvas, a sign that there may be a storm system, or at least rain on the way. She hadn't bothered to check the forecast for days; she didn't see the point anymore. What would she be doing anyway? These days either sitting in this grotesque room or at home watching television. The weather wouldn't matter a damn. Although a storm today might be nice. It would break the stifling air and match her melancholy. Fine weather was such a social buffer: bringing people out and together, smiling faces turned to the sun. Storms made them run inside, leaving the streets for the ones who didn't care about their hair or their clothes getting wet: the hermits, who would walk, heads down, not meeting anyone's gaze, using the rain as an excuse. She was definitely the latter. For a fleeting second, she felt a pang of something: like home sickness, but it was for meteorology. She was meteo-sick. Desperately she tried to remember the little excited twinge she would get when she came across a deep low in the charts that foretold a strong storm in the summer or the chance of snow in the winter. But she couldn't embody the feeling anymore. Those days were gone.

She hated these appointments. They seemed so pointless but if she didn't go, her mother would nag her into oblivion. It wouldn't surprise her if Dr. Greenberg sent her a monthly attendance report. The type tapping stopped as the receptionist answered the ringing phone. Jesus, she thought, even the phone's ring tone was irritating. It had snapped her right out of her introspectiveness.

"Sam, you can go in now."

She took a deep breath, gathered her bag, rose to her feet and opened the yellowing, once white, door. Dr Greenberg was sitting, in the brown suit he always wore, writing up the notes of the previous patient. Looking up at her over his glasses, he beckoned wordlessly for her to sit. When did psychiatrists stop using couches, she wondered? She'd much prefer a couch than sitting face to face with this middle aged, passively disinterested man, not watching her while she talked and he took notes. It was very disconcerting.

"How are you, Sam?"

"Fine, thanks."

"How have the nightmares been?"

"Getting better. Only getting them a couple of times a week now."

"Good, good." His response was mindless as he recorded her replies in his notes, or maybe he was drawing pornographic sketches; it was hard to tell.

"I think I could probably give therapy a miss from now on."

"It's your own choice, Sam, but I recommend that you continue with our sessions for another while. Even though the nightmares are abating, the grief is still very much present, and I think you need to work on some other issues. How is the anxiety? You told me a couple of sessions ago that you were avoiding public places. Can we elaborate on that?"

Sam sighed audibly in the hope the 'good doctor' would hear. She didn't want to do this anymore. The only way to deal with her loss was to deal with it. Sure, she was having recurrent nightmares and her day to day anxiety was overwhelming, but she couldn't see what coming to this distant, emotionless man once a week was going to change. While he babbled on about social anxiety, she let her mind wander to the latte and donut she was going to treat herself to after the session. Now THAT was therapy.

"Have you thought about finding work again, Sam?"

"No."

"Do you think it would be a step forward to at least look? It might be good for your confidence to even just see what's out there."

"I can't imagine doing anything. Meteorology is all I know and there aren't many other jobs other than research. I just don't think I can do that again."

"What about a different career path altogether? You could do a course."

As was her habit while the doctor made vague suggestions on how she should live her life, Sam zoned out. Then she remembered the ad in the paper. Both of them being meteorologists, Bobby and she had often talked about taking a summer off from their jobs at the TV station and chasing storms across the country. She would drive; he would read the radar and navigate. It was a long finger plan of theirs but when Bobby had gotten sick, all that changed. Could it be fate that the doctor was talking about her career after she'd seen that ad? She shook her head with derision. Stupid. Of course not. Still, as she bid a muttered farewell to him when the hour was up, she discreetly took the newspaper from the waiting room table, casting a sideways glance to ensure Little Miss Olympic Typing wasn't looking and tucked it under her arm. It couldn't hurt to phone this Jonah guy.

She read the ad again as she sipped on her milky coffee. It had arrived tepid but she wasn't going to complain. She just needed the caffeine. She hadn't slept well the night before. The nightmare had been a vicious one this time. Some nights were better than others. Last night hadn't been one of the better ones. Bobby was a faceless ghost, standing menacingly at the foot of her bed, goading her and calling her names. Then he collapsed on the floor in agony, calling her name, his voice riddled with anguish as he begged for her to help him. Bobby's begging-for-help stage was when she'd wake up, in a sweat and not be able to get back to sleep, insomnia controlling her like it was her ill meaning friend, the devil on her shoulder. He was nearly a year gone but his face and voice were still as clear as ever. She had always loved his voice. It was deep and resonate, the first thing she'd noticed about him. She had been busy compiling the upcoming day's report and was staring at the imminent rainfall on the radar when her boss had come up behind her and introduced her to the new weather anchor. Without looking up, she'd greeted him half-heartedly, even a little rudely, but on hearing his velvety voice, she'd turned to face him. He stood, looking earnest and slightly nervous, hand outstretched and she instantly liked him. His eyes seemed soft and gentle, not like his predecessor who was a loud and obnoxious egomaniac. She could get to like this guy, she'd thought.

She made a face as she drained the now stone cold coffee dregs, picked up her paper and threw a two dollar tip on the table. Driving out of the stifling Midtown Omaha afternoon, she took a detour to Village Pointe shopping mall. Maybe some retail therapy was needed as the coffee and donut treat hadn't filled the void.

"That looks so great on you," the shop assistant drawled, not even looking in her direction. The green satin scarf draped around her neck brought her emerald eyes to life in the mirror before her. Her olive skin seemed somehow more sallow, her freckles more defined: a legacy given to her by her half Irish father. How could one simple, plain scarf change her appearance so drastically? She'd never been one for fashion, instead choosing to remain in a state of comfort, facilitated by her jeans, T-shirts, maybe a sweater and always Converse sneakers. The girls she'd worked with at the television station were always so glamorous, in their pant suits and dresses. Sam had no time for such frippery. But this scarf: it did something to her. She refused the carrier bag from the super helpful assistant and chose instead to tear off the tag and drape the scarf around her neck as she sauntered out of the store.

The brief but intrinsic rush she felt following her purchase, made her feel, for a second, happy. Just for a second though. Next stop was to buy a new pair of Converse sneakers seeing as her black ones had become grubby and old, the rubber of the sole beginning to make its escape from the canvas. In a departure from her usual 'safety in dark colours,' she chose red. As she handed the shopping assistant her card, a doubt flickered across her brain and she tried to suppress the urge to run back to the shelf and change the red ones back to black. This chromatic rebellion was out of character. Who was she, this woman buying red, RED sneakers? Was this a glimmer of healing or a sign of self-loathing? It was too late now, she sighed as she punched in her pin number. The momentary doubt was quashed and she resigned herself to being a scarlet shoe wearing widow. Walking out with the shopping bag perched on her arm, she stopped to pick up a Huskers jersey. She ran her hand down the cotton fabric, remembering how Bobby would proudly wear his while screaming at them to tighten their defense or attack the opposition. Football, or sports of any kind, did nothing for her. She'd roll her eyes when he would declare it game night. How she wished she hadn't. If he were here now, she'd let him watch as many games as he wanted, all day if that made him happy.

After stopping at the drug store for some of her usual shampoo and to treat herself to a new perfume, she dragged herself and her substantial shopping bags back to her car. A faint whiff of the Marc Jacob's *Daisy* that she'd purchased filled her nostrils as she reached over for the seatbelt. She felt a sliver of guilt at spending so much, but the little thrill it gave her made it worthwhile.

The traffic back to West Omaha was heavy and she became increasingly frustrated. Turning the radio up when Foo Fighters *The Pretender* came on, she envisaged that if the car in front of her didn't move soon, she'd get out and beat its driver over the head with an electric guitar. Maybe she was becoming too absorbed in the song. Angry, political rock was not what she needed to hear right now. She turned the dial to a classical station, of which she didn't even know the name of nor knew existed, but it was soothing in this sweltering, claustrophobic gridlock.

Eventually, the traffic moved and the streets opened up to reveal West Omaha's suburbs: long streets of freshly mowed lawns, white picket fences and large wooden frame houses in all colours of the rainbow. She pulled into her own, a cornflower blue two-storey with neglected flower beds and shrubs that had been left to their own devices for the past year. Should the neighbours dare to complain or whisperingly defame, she would tell them unapologetically that she was going for the organic, meadow look before telling them to fuck off and mind their own business.

Sighing as she entered the front door, she dumped the bags and dropped her keys on the hall table. Silence. As always. No one to greet her, to say 'Honey, I'm home' to. Not even a cat to snake around her feet in an egocentric way of getting food from her. No, it was just her. The sound of her keys hitting the Mexican pine echoed around her head. Not even turning on the television could dull it out. Wine helped, though. She had just downed her second glass of Merlot, when she remembered the ad. Rooting in the various shopping bags, she found it stashed with her newly purchased, berry red Converse.

Taking her phone from her pocket, Dutch courage flowing through her veins, she dialled the number of whoever this Jonah guy was, and tried to stop the butterflies rampaging around her stomach when he picked up and greeted her with a gruff, "Jonah."

"Em, hi. My name is Sam. I'm phoning regarding the ad you have in the Omaha Review, for a storm chaser."

"Yeah."

"Well, I'm..... um... I want to apply for it."

"OK, well tell me about yourself. Have you a full, clean license? Any weather experience?"

He sounded impatient and put out by the phone call. She wished she hadn't bothered calling.

"My license is spotless and I'm a meteorologist, graduated 2004."

"Oh?" She could hear his interest pique. "Would I know you? Don't think I know a Sam. I graduated in 2000."

"No, your name doesn't ring a bell either."

"Right, well let's see. How about you come on a chase with us, let's call it a trial period. Any problems driving a Ford F-150 pickup? It's fairly new so has power steering and most mod cons. It's been adapted to house a small doppler radar and anemometer but that doesn't affect the weight too much so you should be fine."

"No problem. My husband had one."

"We have developed a sensor pad that we try to put in the path of the tornadoes so we'll be spending the season trying to deploy those. There's a good chance of some storms firing over Omaha tomorrow if the predicted wind sheer and CAPE values come good so we were going to head down that way. We could pick you up. I presume that's where you live considering you saw the ad in the Omaha Review."

"Yes. I'll text you my address."

"Well, see you in the morning then."

"OK.'Bye"

Sam sat back to catch her breath. She couldn't actually remember breathing at all through that conversation. Jonah sounded bull ignorant. His tone of voice and impatient attitude were evident across the phone line. She wondered what the hell she had just gotten herself into: going on a day's chase with a guy she'd never met. What if he wasn't genuine? What if it was a way of picking up women so that he could take them to a remote motel, rape, pillage and murder them? No hang on, most storm chasers were male. It was very rare to see a female one, so if the guy was a sexual predator, surely he would have placed an ad seeking companionship or someone to clean his house/mind his kids. She never got his surname so she couldn't even Google him. All she had to do was tolerate this guy for one day and if she didn't like him, she would tell him she wasn't interested.

CHAPTER 2

Next morning, Sam woke into her usual momentary world of not remembering. Squinting her eyes, her first sight was the gap in the curtain, the bit that she always forgot to seal the night before, that was now betraying her with a shaft of blinding morning sunlight. That was Bobby's job: to fix the curtains after she'd gotten into bed as she always forgot to do it in her hurry to be the first under the duvet, so that she could snuggle into the right position before he got in and pulled the duvet over to his side, messing up her little cocoon. She reached over to take his hand as she always had done, but there was nothing there. That's how most of her mornings started these days, a few blissful seconds when she had no recollection of the loss and for those few seconds, he was still lying beside her, gently snoring himself out of a deep sleep. Then reality would dawn and she would feel the crushing weight on her chest.

Some days she would cry, others, sigh deeply and get up to face her day. Today she cried until her stomach clenched as she remembered what she had set herself up for. The clock showed six thirty. After she'd sent Jonah her address by text the night before, he had replied that he'd collect her at seven a.m. She stretched, rose and contemplated breakfast, soon deciding that her stomach would throw it back at her. She considered coffee but her stomach constricted in protest, so she took a sip of water and left it at that.

As if timed by the atomic clock, the doorbell rang at seven exactly. She absentmindedly smoothed her baby blue T-shirt and

11

jeans and went to answer it. A tall, red haired man, with freckled pale skin, his eyes wide, stood before her grinning impishly. She immediately calmed.

"Jonah?" holding her hand out to shake his. He reciprocated but shook his head.

"No, I'm Paul. Paul O'Malley. I'm Jonah's right hand man and navigator. You must be Sam?"

"Yes. Nice to meet you."

"Wow, OK. When Jonah mentioned a Sam, I assumed a man. How wrong could I have been?"

"Well, you know what they say: to assume, makes an ass of you and me."

Paul laughed as though in agreement but a slight flush crept across his cheeks. Sam felt the tension needed breaking. "So is there anything happening today? I meant to get up early to check the satellites and radars, but didn't get time."

"Well, there are some supercells forecast for the Central Nebraska region, so we'll head that way and see what pops up. Jonah says you're a fellow 'met head?'"

"You could say that, yeah!" She grabbed her rain coat, bag and pulled the door behind her. She could feel Paul's eyes on her as she walked in front of him to the truck, making her aware of how she was walking, and she felt her steps become forced and awkward.

"You want me to drive up there or do you want to start right away?" Paul asked. She appreciated his offer but felt it was better for her to get stuck right in.

"It's fine, best to start now rather than later."

Paul clambered into the back of the adapted truck and Sam climbed into the driver's seat. Sitting in the passenger seat was a muscular man, floppy brown hair and skin tone like a Mediterranean native. He was dressed in combat trousers, a black T-shirt and didn't move from his rather intimidating pose, his right leg pulled up, knee resting on the door handle, elbow resting on the cill of the door.

"Sam? Jonah. Nice to meet you," came his short response. He held out his hand for her to shake but the presence of sunglasses covering his eyes and his face turned slightly away from the direction of hers, seemed to her to be the epitome of indifference. His attitude of coldness set her on edge. While Paul seemed nice enough, she was filled with dread at having to spend the day with this Jonah guy. The conversation wasn't going to be stellar, she predicted.

Taking the steering wheel in hand, she was relieved to find the truck was almost exactly the same model Bobby had driven. It was so much better than her Nissan. She'd loved the height and sturdiness of the truck, like you could drive over anything or anyone that stood in your way. The wheel felt substantial in her hands. She stroked it, feeling the soft leather under her palm, and felt her mind being pulled back to another time, several years ago.

She'd watched Bobby ease the brand new, shiny black truck into the driveway and running out to see it, had almost knocked him over in her attempts to get into the driver's seat.

"Missed you too, honey," he'd joked, watching her delight as she stroked the leather seats and pressed the brake with her foot. "You can take it for a spin if you like. She's a beauty." Without going back to the house for a coat or bag, she slowly reversed, barely leaving time for Bobby to jump into the passenger seat and drove off to nowhere in particular - just drove for hours, listening to Pearl Jam and Grant Lee Buffalo. It was the perfect day. The sun was shining in a cloudless sky; she was with the love of her life and was driving this great truck to a backing track of her favourite bands. They stopped in a small town for coffee and cake, sitting beside the window so they could gaze upon the shiny new truck. Then it was homeward bound, Grant Lee Phillip's lilting tones singing praise to *Arousing Thunder*. She was driving again and Bobby smiled over at her, taking her hand as they sped down the motorway.

"So are we gonna go some time soon?" Jonah asked sharply, snapping her out of her sunny, happy, sepia-toned reminiscence and back to the dull, lonely present. She was still stroking the wheel. Embarrassed at allowing herself to daydream, she eased the truck away from the curb and took them along the neighbourhood road to the highway. The sat nav lady mumbled every so often, but the highway was stretching for a good distance before they would need to make any turnoffs.

"So where are you from, Jonah?" she asked, trying to fill the silence.

"New Jersey."

The short coldness of his reply made her wince. Could he be any less friendly?

"How about you, Paul?" At least he would be more forthcoming.

"I'm from Boston but I was born in the west of Ireland, as my name suggests. I couldn't really be any more Irish! Freckles, red hair and a name like O'Malley."

"Well, I had a suspicion but didn't like to say."

Paul laughed heartily. Jonah didn't react.

"So do you go back to Ireland much?"

"No. I've been back twice. Once when I was a kid and two years ago for my cousin's wedding. I would love to go once a year or so but I'm on the road so much that I don't really get time. Mom is a constant flea in my ear telling me I should visit my relatives, but it's hard, you know?"

"I don't hear you complain when you're shouting for joy while we're punching the core of a Supercell," Jonah interjected pretentiously, not turning around.

"That's 'cos I complain under my breath, you asshole."

The joviality and name calling surprised Sam. She had sensed that Paul was intimidated by Jonah when she'd first gotten into the truck, but this display of school yard teasing made her think otherwise.

"I have family in Kildare. My Dad is Irish Italian. It's a lovely place. Very flat and green."

"You don't look very Irish," Paul remarked.

"My Mom is Italian so thankfully I inherited her colouring. No offense!"

"None taken! Just count yourself lucky you won't have to slather yourself in sun cream when out on a day's chase."

"Yeah, he gets himself slicked up like a cream cake. And the smell, the flies love him," Jonah quipped.

"Well, at least I look after my skin. There's no need to be smug because you were born looking like a cappuccino."

Jonah threw an empty soda can behind his head at Paul and the jeering and jibing continued for another few miles. The horizon in front of them began to dull slightly, the azure blue turning to an orangey grey. In the distance, the peaks of a tower of cloud were beginning to billow up, like plumes of smoke. Paul, glued to the radar on his computer screen, guessed that the best way to head would be toward North Central Nebraska. There was nothing much showing up at the moment, but Jonah said the potential for convection would increase throughout the day. It was, after all, only ten thirty. They were heading for a town called O'Neill. The sparsely populated land began to yield more houses and farms as they drove along.

Sam's head began to thump. It was caused by two factors: lack of coffee and lack of food. Not that she ate much these days. There wasn't much point cooking for one. Coffee was her saviour but she'd been too nervous to have one this morning and her temples were now throbbing in protest. She was afraid to ask if they could stop for refreshments. Thankfully, Paul appeared to read her mind and suggested a coffee and muffin stop. He said there was a nice café in O'Neill. Directing her as they entered the town, she pulled into the curb. Jonah got out and stretched his legs beside the truck.

"What do you want, Jonah?"

"Just Joe and a banana nut muffin please."

"Sam? How about you?"

"Oh, I'll get out and get my own. I need to use the facilities anyway."

Cringing as she tried not to let any part of her body touch off the unhygienic cubicle, she crouched and her thigh muscles ached as she did the necessary. No way was she going to sit on the toilet seat. It looked like it hadn't been cleaned in.... well, ever. The thick smell of waste and damp filled her nostrils. The boys were obviously used to this kind of thing but she wasn't and would never be. At least there was an automatic soap dispenser, so she washed her hands twice, then taking some toilet paper dried them and helping herself to another few sheets, used them to mask her hand as she opened the lock on the door. She turned back and threw the paper into the toilet, thankfully walking out into the fresh, odourless air.

After ordering coffee and a banana, she made her way back to the truck to find the boys deep in conversation. She slowed down when she heard her name mentioned. The coffee was burning her hand and she winced trying to hold it and eavesdrop at the same time.

"Jonah, she's smoking hot. When she opened the door to me this morning, I was like 'Whoa, this Sam guy's wife is seriously cute.' You could have told me 'Sam' was a woman. I'd at least have worn something decent and put some aftershave on."

"What did you expect me to say? 'Oh, by the way, we're taking a woman on so pretty yourself up and make sure we've a stash of chocolate and sanitary products in the glove compartment.' Anyway, we're here to chase, not to get loved up."

"Jonah, you know what, you may be my best friend, but you can be a total douche."

Sam watched him slap Jonah on the arm jovially. Hauling herself up into the driver's seat again, she turned so she was facing both Jonah and Paul. The latter turned a suitable shade of crimson at her return. Jonah was non responsive. At least Paul had the decency to look embarrassed. She decided to be the bigger person and to ignore their childish whispering.

"So how long have you been chasing, Jonah?"

"About eight years. But I was off the road for a year back in 2006. So seven in all. Paul's been with me since the beginning. There was a guy with us, Jack, who drove, but he got offered a more stable job driving a rigid, so he left last week. That's where you come in." He turned to Sam and while he didn't look her in the eye, she managed to get a first flash of his blue eyes, his sunglasses having been abandoned on the dashboard. They were almost liquid. She couldn't help but to stare, although he didn't appear to notice. He was looking past her out the driver's window at the developing clouds. Mortification hit as she realised she was blushing under his indirect gaze. She cursed this reaction, a throwback from her teenage years, turning puce in any situation where she felt uncomfortable.

"Can we check the radar and see what's happening before we move off? I'm not getting a good feeling about today."

Paul hummed and hawed over his laptop for ten minutes before informing them that the convection wasn't as strong as forecast and that there was nothing really building up.

"It's up to you, Jonah, we could drive another while east and see or we could call it a day and head back home. We've already driven three hours. It'd be a shame to waste the day."

"Yeah but I don't want to go any further just for the sake of not wasting a day."

"The latest GFS model has wind sheer weakened."

"So really, there's no point. Let's head back. Yeah?"

"Sure boss. Whatever you say."

"Sorry about that, Sam. It would have been nice for you to have seen an excellent storm on your first day." Paul shook his head.

"It's not her first day. It's a trial," Jonah curtly interjected.

Sam discretely shook her head at Jonah's rudeness and began a battle of conscience in her mind. Even if he did offer her the driving job, would she accept? He was coming across as such a grumpy, rude man and she wasn't sure she wanted to spend her days with him. Sure, Paul was lovely and he seemed to be able to manage Jonah well, but she wasn't sure she'd be as proficient as him at not taking it to heart. She was still so raw that she didn't know if she could handle working for such an ass.

On the other hand, she had nothing else going on. She couldn't face looking for a job in a station or lab. There was something exciting and enticing about being on the open road, living off adrenaline rushes whenever a tornado was spotted. Maybe this was what she needed to remind herself why she'd studied for four years to become a meteorologist, give her back some of the passion she used to feel for weather before she'd lost it.

All the way home she considered the pros and cons. Even as she turned into her street back in Omaha, she still hadn't made up her mind.

Paul jumped into the driver's seat as she got out. An awkward silence hung in the air until Jonah broke it.

"So, will we pick you up in the morning, then?"

"OK," she heard herself say.

CHAPTER 3

The next morning Sam was prepared. The GFS showed a high possibility of storms over North Kansas. She presumed if they weren't going to chase, Jonah would phone her to cancel, but as yet, there was no word from him and it was almost eight a.m, so she got ready just in case. The nerves had left her so her stomach felt able to handle a good bowl of oatmeal and some banana slices. A breakfast like that would keep her going all day. Her coffee travel cup was on standby, ready to be filled as soon as the boys called. She had slept well the night before: almost satisfied that she had made the snap decision that she'd chase with them. It wasn't like she'd signed a contract so if Jonah got too much for her, she could always quit. Her new mantra was that she had gone through the worst thing she could possibly go through so now she must be strong and would be able for his snappy retorts and insulting comments.

Just as she was rehearsing some witty comebacks to match Jonah's predicted insults, the bell rang. She filled the travel mug with coffee, picked up her bag and keys and opened the door to a smiling Paul, with Jonah, once again perched in the passenger seat. She wondered if he ever got off his backside to do anything.

"Morning!" she said brightly to Jonah, heaving herself into the driver's seat.

"So we're heading to North Kansas today," he said coldly, not returning her greeting.

"Yeah, I checked the GFS and radar before you called. Some good potential today."

"Indeed. Paul, do you want to check the radar again before we leave?"

"But Sam said she just checked it."

"Yeah, well I want you to check it too, OK?"

Sam made a face out the driver's window and took a deep cleansing breath. She decided she needed to make up another mantra and repeated it in her head: 'I'm not going to let him bother me, let him be grumpy. It's his problem, not mine.'

When Paul confirmed what she had said, she noticed his apologetic look in the rearview mirror as Jonah gave her the all clear to move off, Kansas bound. It was going to be a long drive, and eight o'clock was a late start. She presumed they'd stay overnight somewhere, so she had packed some essentials in her bag just in case: toiletries, pyjamas and a set of fresh clothes.

Around lunchtime, they were almost there. There was a cell exploding just south of Wichita, so they headed there, planning to stop and get lunch while they waited for the storm to build before making their way north towards it. Paul instructed her to pull into a truck stop outside Wichita. Huge artics rested mightily on the forecourt, their drivers standing about, eating behemoth sandwiches, slurping on bucket sized drinks, their tattoos and long goatee beards shining in the early afternoon sun. The truck almost seemed like a dwarf in the company of such vehicular giants.

"You wanna stay, Jonah, and I'll get your lunch?" Paul asked.

"No, I need to drain the snake, so I'll go in too."

"Shall I check for any updates while you're gone?" Sam asked, dying to get her teeth into what could be a good day for storms, maybe even a tornado.

"Yeah sure, what'll I get you?" Paul asked.

"Oh, surprise me. I'm not fussy." She smiled at him. He was such a sweet guy. She busied herself with the radar. It felt great to be part of a team again and to be getting stuck into a project. She didn't notice the boys coming back. Jonah startled her, as he climbed into the passenger seat and Paul into the back. She handed him back his laptop and they ate their lunch in silence while watching the storm unfold on the horizon in front of them. She enjoyed the chicken bacon sandwich and it was a good feeling: most of the time, food tasted like sawdust. She stretched, arched her feet and her new red sneakers peeped up at her.

Paul was buried in his laptop, ear piece in his ear, listening to the weather reports. Jonah was leg up, arm resting on his knee, drinking his coffee and staring blankly, behind Ray Bans, out the window. He could at least try to make conversation, she thought. He didn't appear to have any social skills. Although, neither did she these days. It was such a chore to speak to anyone, to keep up a conversation that she really wasn't interested in. Most of her friends hadn't been in contact with her for several months, and she couldn't blame them. She wasn't exactly sparkling company. Most of the time when someone was talking, she would hum and haw, disinterested and evident that she wasn't really listening. Maybe Jonah was snagged on something that was dragging him back into the past too.

"Shit......... we've gotta go. There's a report of intense rotation. Let's head south," Paul said with a mouthful of chicken sandwich.

Sam rolled up her sandwich wrapper, put her coffee in the cup holder and putting the truck in gear, tore off down the highway, heading south of the city. The sky darkened as they approached the building storm. She could feel the hair on the back of her neck rising and the adrenaline being released into her blood stream. It would be such a rush to see a tornado today. The distant rumble of thunder led them to the cloud. Jonah shifted in his seat and rolled down the window.

"Do you hear that Paul? That is the sound of AWESOME! We're not far."

"Woo hoo!" Paul fist pumped the air, almost knocking the laptop off his knee. She drove on for another three miles until the wall of cloud loomed over their heads.

"Pull over here, Sam. This should be a good spot - hopefully it will move just east of us," Paul instructed.

Dutifully, she pulled the truck into the side of the road, marvelling at the menacing grey in front of her. A rolling shelf cloud tumbled towards them. Thunder rumbled around them.

"Whoa!" Paul exclaimed as a bolt of blinding lightning struck the field directly in front of them.

Jonah got out of the truck, leaned against the side of it and closed his eyes, seemingly savouring the wind on his face.

"There's a strong updraft, Paul. Can you feel it?"

"Yep. There's some intense rotation right above that field. If it organises, we could get something." Paul had an expression like a child on Christmas Day.

Sam couldn't help but smile, as the rush of adrenaline coursed faster through her veins.

"Jesus, it's organising, guys. Look at the funnel." Paul pointed excitedly. "There's disturbance on the ground. We have a tornado, Jonah."

While Paul rushed to get the camera, Jonah stood immobile at the side of the truck, as stoic as one of the trees that was about to ripped from the ground. Sam was mesmerised by his composure - he wasn't running around like Paul or the other storm chasers that had pulled up near them, he was just standing still, face into the wind, letting it ruffle and whip his hair.

She turned her attention to the developing twister. It snaked its rope-like body across the fields, sending hay and various plants and debris high into the air. It wasn't a particularly strong one, but its beauty far exceeded its strength, like the finger of Mother Nature, pointing in judgement.

As quickly as it formed, it dissipated, leaving a cloud of dust and hay floating back to the ground. A collective groan was thrown up from the storm chasers alike.

"Should we keep tracking it, Paul?" Jonah asked, sitting himself back into the truck.

"I don't think so. It's weakening on the radar. There is a cell behind it that's developing though. Do you want to hang out here for a while and see what that one does?"

"Yeah sure. Let's sit tight. How far out do you think it is?"

"About an hour."

"That OK with you Sam?" Paul asked earnestly.

"Yeah, sure."

"So your first tornado. How does it feel?"

"Amazing. I've seen one before but not on a proper chase. That was such a rush! I want to do it again!"

"Patience is a virtue for the storm chaser." Jonah sounded condescending, but Sam chose to ignore him. She was no giddy filly along for the ride. She was a bona fide meteorologist and was not about to be patronised.

"Do you want to see the shots I got?" she asked, producing her camera and handing it back to Paul.

"Awesome. I love that one where it's just behind the hay bale. Beautiful colours."

"Thanks. Jonah, you want to see?"

"No, thanks."

"Oh." She was dejected at his lack of interest, but repeated her anti-Jonah mantra in her head, and tried to forget it. She glanced at

Paul who was eyeing her with a confused expression. He shrugged and returned to his computer, leaving her feeling more than a little paranoid.

The afternoon passed, as did the second storm which although it came alive with lightning and a decent hail shower, failed to produce a twister. They agreed to stay in a motel overnight, so they could get an early start in the morning. There was more forecast for the same area the next day. Sam thanked her forward thinking self for packing an overnight bag.

Pulling into the motel parking lot, they stretched in unison, and agreed to meet at the restaurant adjacent to it for dinner in an hour. A shower was just what Sam needed after the long day of driving. She left the boys and made her way to the check-in desk. Her room was clean and modern. She'd had visions of a cockroach infested dirt box of a room, but this was not the case. The bathroom was freshly tiled, and she languished in the shower for probably too long, but it was heavenly. She put on the change of clothes she'd brought for the next day. She could wear them tonight and they would still be fresh enough for tomorrow's chase. She eased on the indigo jeans over her legs and dropped the black T-shirt over her head. Spotting herself in the full length mirror, she recoiled. She had lost weight. It was rare that she looked at her reflection at home anymore. She had no one to impress, but this image of herself caught her off guard. She was positively waif-like. Vowing to start eating properly again, she grabbed her handbag and made her way to the restaurant.

Scanning the restaurant, Sam saw no sign of the boys, so she chose a table in the far corner by a window. The place was half full, most tables occupied by couples. Some were barely speaking but one pair was only short of tearing off each other's clothes right there on top of their hamburgers and fries. She felt an ache for Bobby as she watched them kiss, fondle and play footsie under the table. They were young, probably first loves on their first mini break. Tearing her gaze from them, she took in the surrounds. It wasn't fancy by any means, but sure was nicer than the truck stops she'd visited in the last two days.

Moments later, she spotted Paul and waved him over. She watched him take Jonah by the arm and lead him through the slalom of tables and chairs. How odd, she thought. Perhaps, Jonah had injured himself. Paul pulled out a chair and taking Jonah's hand, placed it on the backrest, put his other hand on his shoulder and instructed him to sit down. Sam was just in the middle of processing what she was seeing when Paul commented on how well she looked. Eyes squinting, she thanked him while regarding Jonah. He asked Jonah if he'd like him to read out the menu, and then realisation hit her. Suddenly all the pieces of the jigsaw puzzle came together and formed a picture in front of her. The way Jonah never looked her in the eye; the way he always seemed to gaze out the windscreen; the way he never strayed farther than the truck door or stayed in the passenger seat. When he'd refused to look at her photos, she'd cursed his rude indifference. But she'd been wrong. He wasn't being rude.

"Jonah, you're blind?" She clamped her hand over her mouth as the words that she had intended to keep to herself spilled out like verbal diarrhoea.

Paul raised his eyebrows at her and the corners of Jonah's mouth flickered into the beginning of a smile - but a sardonic one.

It was Paul who broke the silence. "You didn't know?"

"No! I had no idea. Is it true?"

Jonah was smiling but in a way that would normally make her want to slap him across his patronising face, but she was too shocked to move.

"Yes. It's true. I'm amazed you didn't notice." His smile seemed to falter.

"How would I know? You could have said something."

"What was I going to say? 'Welcome on board, Sam. By the way, I can't see you. Or anything for that matter.' It's not something I advertise, exactly."

"But, but..... how?" She was gobsmacked at how she had managed to spend two days with this man and not know of his disability.

"You're stuttering, Sam. Take a moment." His tone was derisive and rude.

"So, so .....why.....?" She was falling over her words again.

"Why do I chase storms? Well, it's like this. I chased before my accident and the bug never left me. I just needed to create a supportive team around me, Paul being my right hand man. I couldn't do it if it weren't for him. I took a year off to recover after the accident and to be honest, was afraid to get back in the game, but Paul convinced me to go along with him one day and I just got sucked into it again, excuse the pun."

Sam stared at Jonah, unable to take her eyes off him. Those iridescent blue eyes, so broken and useless, were shining, curtained by long dark eye lashes. He must have felt her gaze as he ran his hand self-consciously through his unkempt, dark hair. It was the first time she had seen a sliver of shyness in him. He wasn't smiling anymore - he looked positively uncomfortable.

"So what are we eating?" He broke the tension.

"They have ravioli. You want that? Or just a hamburger?" Paul read from the menu like he was reading a story to a toddler at bedtime.

"Ravioli would be nice, with fries and salad."

"I'll have the same." Sam was too shocked to make any gastronomic decisions.

"My 'Spidey' senses are telling me you're in shock, Miss Di Matteo." Smug, patronising Jonah was back.

She ignored the tone. "You can say that again. So, how did it happen? You weren't always like this?"

"No, like I said, I had an accident. Six years ago we were chasing and got caught in the path of an EF4. The engine on the truck failed and we had no way to escape so just had to sit tight while it rolled over us. The windows blew in and I was struck by a piece of wood on the head. My optic nerves were badly damaged."

"Can you see anything? Light? Shapes?" She was too fascinated to restrain her questions but Jonah didn't seem to mind.

"I can make out basic shapes. Like you right now look like a dark person shaped blur."

"I had no idea. You hide it well."

"Oh, am I not wearing my 'Hello, I'm Blind' T-shirt today? Jeez, Paul, you could have warned me."

"There's no need for sarcasm. Were you always this narky, or is it just since you've been blind?" Sam snapped. She didn't care what condition he was in, he had no excuse for being rude. Paul stared at her wide-eyed and opened mouthed. She instantly regretted her comment. Mutually holding their breath, they turned to Jonah to witness the anticipated backlash.

"No, my ability to tolerate ridiculous statements was damaged in the accident along with my optic nerves."

Paul exhaled and Sam laughed in relief; she had been expecting a tirade of abuse. Perfectly timed, the waiter served their meal and they ate in silence for the next few minutes.

Wiping his mouth with a napkin, Jonah asked Paul if he could bring him to his room.

"You gonna turn in too or do you want to get a drink?" Paul asked Sam.

"I'd murder a beer, to be honest."

"Great. I'll be back in a minute."

"Remember you two, we've a day's chase tomorrow. One beer and that's it," Jonah ordered.

"Yes, boss!" Sam replied.

She watched Paul lead Jonah by the arm back through the tables and chairs and out of the restaurant and ordering two beers from the waiter, sat in a daydream. She ran over the events of the last two days and the clues of Jonah's blindness that she had missed. In fairness, he hid it well. Paul wasn't his lackey, fetching his coffee and lunches, he was his carer. When you thought about it, it was sweet really and said a lot about the type of person Paul was.

Just as she was thinking how good a friend Paul must be, he returned, smiling in her direction.

"Well, congratulations." He patted her on the arm.

"What? Why?"

"No one has ever spoken to Jonah like that and gotten away without at least a mild verbal lashing."

"Really? Probably because I'm a girl."

"No really. Fair play!"

Sam savoured the ice cold bubbles from the beer popping on her tongue. After a day being stuck in a humid truck, it was just the medicine. It numbed her to the shock of Jonah's bomb shell.

"You think you might stick with us?"

"This morning I thought I probably wouldn't. I didn't know if I could handle Jonah and his.... his... rudeness. But I feel like I understand him a bit more after today, and his revelation this evening. I've been through some stuff lately too so I get it."

"Oh?" Paul raised an eyebrow.

"Oh, nothing. So the beer is good here. I wouldn't mind another."

Paul summoned the waiter, ordered two more and turned his attention to Sam.

"So, what's your story?"

"Well, I'm a former meteorological researcher for KWON Omaha. I left and after a year of doing nothing, decided to do something different with my qualification, hence my applying for this job. So what about you? How come you ended up on the road?"

"Jonah lectures at the University of Nebraska, I do a few bits in his lab and during storm season we chase together. We met in college."

"You seem pretty tight. The way you help him is really beautiful." She watched him flush.

"Yeah, we're like family. He was like my big brother, always looking out for me. Now, I guess it's the other way around. It took him a year after his accident to finally come back out on the road. It took some persuasion but once he realised I was here for him and that he could manage a lot of things himself, he was back in the game. Although, he still moans consistently about my forecasts: thinks I can't forecast for nuts." A smile crept into the corner of his mouth as he dropped his gaze to his beer.

"So, do you guys live together?"

"No. He lives with his sister just outside Omaha, but we may as well live together during storm season. I'm usually around there or he's at my place. His sister is great, really mothers him."

"You must have a very understanding wife or girlfriend."

Paul laughed, but it wasn't a laugh of mirth. "I don't have a girlfriend. Well, I have been seeing this girl but it's not too serious. We've been on a couple of dates. That's it, really."

Sam nodded, not meeting his gaze. She ran her index finger around the rim of the glass, giving it all her attention, hoping that it would deter him from asking her the same question.

"So, how about you?"

"Me what?"

"Have you a significant other who is about to be abandoned for the season?"

"No."

She cringed at herself for being so clipped with him but he seemed to take it on board and didn't delve any deeper. Feeling guilty for being so curt, yet still not wanting to furnish him with explanations, she afforded him a half smile, catching his glance.

He was quite cute. His red hair was floppy and fell around his Irish green eyes. The conversation moved away from their love lives and they chatted easily over their second beers, deciding it best to retire to bed before a third was ordered or they'd be suffering in the morning, not just from hangovers, but from the wrath of Jonah.

The night was heavy as they walked the short distance to the motel rooms.

"I'm glad you're on board with us. It's always weird having someone new chase with us but I think you're gonna fit right in."

"Aw, that's so nice of you to say. Thanks. I did enjoy today." She touched his arm and then felt guilty as his cheeks flamed under the orange glow of the street lamps that illuminated the motel parking lot.

"Cool. Night then."

"Night."

Sam was grateful again for her forward thinking earlier in putting on the air con in the room. A blast of cool air hit her as she opened the door. She was asleep within minutes and slept for ten hours.

*

Knock, knock.

Sam opened her bleary eyes and forgot where she was for a minute. She looked around at the magnolia walls and by the time she had sat herself up, she remembered she was in a motel.

Knock, knock, knock.

"Just a minute," she called as she raced around, finding and throwing on her clothes from the previous night, before opening the door.

"You took your time. My, you are some sight in the morning."

"Thanks Jonah. I'll take that as a compliment! Where's Paul?"

"In the shower. He said you were the next room down so I thought I'd make my way down and wake you up from your drunken slumber. And anyway, you women take hours to get ready."

"I wasn't drunk." Sam spoke determinedly. "Come in and have a seat. I didn't know you used a cane." She took him by the elbow and brought him into the room, showing him to the armchair by the bed.

"You didn't know I was blind till twelve hours ago. I use it when I'm not wearing my 'Hello, I'm blind' T-shirts. Gets me to the top of lots of queues and stuff."

Rolling her eyes at his sarcasm, she told him to sit tight while she brushed her teeth. The silence hung awkwardly on the air between them but Sam couldn't think of anything to say to break it.

Knock, knock.

"COME IN," Sam shouted from the bathroom, the words muffled, toothbrush in her mouth.

"Have you seen...? Oh, you're here," Paul said, a little irritation spiking his voice on seeing Jonah perched on the bedside chair. "Since when did you start using your cane again?"

"Since we took a woman on to drive for us and since she slept it out. Someone had to wake her or we'll never hit the road."

Sam came out of the bathroom, shaking her hair out and rolling her eyes once again at Jonah, before they made their way down to the diner.

The waitress placed an enormous plate of pancakes smothered in maple syrup in front of Sam; she tucked in hungrily. Jonah sipped coffee and Paul was making light work of a mountain of toast while studying the screen of his laptop.

"I think we should head to South Oklahoma today. Lots of activity building up there," he suggested, as Sam looked over at the screen.

"There's some good potential up in Nebraska, see right here?" She pointed to the yellow/orange squall line on the radar. "Would it be better to head there? I think that dry line will be more definite than the one for Oklahoma. I'll bet there'll be a higher chance of strong wind sheer and the CAPE values are better." Sam traced the area with her finger.

"Do you think? My money's on Oklahoma."

"What does the GFS say?" Jonah interjected.

"Much the same for both."

"But the predicted wind sheer is higher in Nebraska. Could be a better chance for rotation." Sam said, looking over Paul's shoulder at the screen.

"I think we go to Nebraska," Jonah said.

"You're the boss," Paul replied.

Jumping into the driver's seat, Sam couldn't help but feel a little smug about Jonah going along with her forecast. Knowing her luck though, all they would get would be some rain and nothing much else. Oh well, that was the risk they'd have to take. They could easily head to Oklahoma and get nothing either. Paul helped Jonah in and jumped into the back to set up his equipment.

"Well, it looks like you were right," Paul said to Sam, later that afternoon, as they were parked along a roadside fifty miles from

Omaha, Nebraska watching a rope tornado snake its way through a field and over a line of trees about half a mile away.

Although, there had been a tornado reported in Oklahoma, this was their second one of the day in Nebraska, and Sam was pleased with herself. Jonah seemed to be taking her more seriously, asking her opinion on which direction she thought was best to observe from.

She felt a pang of pity as she watched him, face turned to the wind again, embracing the feeling of the violent downdrafts washing over him as the team observed the twister. It was a strange feeling: she hadn't felt pity or indeed any emotion other than sadness, anger and grief since Bobby's death. She walked over and stood beside Jonah, leaning against the truck, arms folded, enjoying the feeling of the wind whipping through her hair. Standing side by side, she felt dwarfed by his height. He had over a foot on her petite five foot three stature.

"It's about half a mile away, very thin but there's a powerful rotation on the ground. Lots of vegetation debris. It's about to pass over a thicket of trees, just snaking back and forth, not much of a path really. It's so long that it's almost doubling back on itself in an S shape. There aren't any buildings around which is good, and I don't think it will register too high on the Enhanced Fujita scale. It's a real beauty. It's starting to rope out..... yeah, it's dissipating now. And it's gone." Sam tried to describe the intricate details. She hoped it wouldn't annoy him, but she was sure he'd be the first to tell her off if it did.

Back in the truck, a successful day's chase behind them, they made their way home. Jonah cleared his throat.

"Your description was very vivid," he said matter-of-factly.

Was that a compliment? She glanced in his direction and as usual, his face was turned away.

Paul complained of hunger, suggesting they visit his favourite truck stop that housed a Chinese restaurant. Pulling into the forecourt, a cacophony of modified vehicles sporting anemometers, doppler's and various other scientific instrumentation sat before them.

"Look who's here! Everett's team."

Paul jumped out and ran to hug a gigantic man covered from neck to both wrists in tattoos. Jonah gingerly got out and the large man hugged him fondly too. Sam felt self-conscious and left out. She stayed in the truck, busying herself with tidying up the equipment and watched out of the corner of her eye as the boys chatted excitedly with the large man and the four other guys with him.

"So, I heard you took a woman on to drive? Did you not hear what they say about women drivers?" the tattooed man jeered, slapping Jonah on the back.

"Yeah, but we had no choice. We'll just have to make sure she doesn't have to parallel park!"

Sam felt her face heat. The bastard, she thought. He continued with his jeering and she fought the urge to get out of the truck and hit him with the laptop. Paul shifted uncomfortably on his feet, looking guiltily toward the truck.

"Hey Sam, get out here!" he called. She took a deep breath and sighed, nervous about meeting the rowdy bunch of men. Jonah was going to get the frosty treatment for this one. She forced a less than authentic smile and went to meet the group. Each one shook her hand as Paul introduced her. Everett was the big tattooed man who, Jonah told her, was an old college buddy and fellow chaser. She ignored Jonah, telling Everett it was nice to meet him.

"So, how long you been chasing with these crazy bastards?" he asked.

"A couple of days."

"And you're still here. Wow. You must have a real thick skin to put up with Jonah!" He came to her side, wrapping an enormous, inked arm around her and nearly crushing her as he pulled her to his side. A mixture of sweat and mustiness filled her nostrils.

"It's getting thicker," she said coldly and Everett laughed a hearty, fat man laugh, thankfully letting her go in the process.

"So, where did you guys chase today?" Jonah, unimpressed, changed the subject.

"Stayed around Nebraska. We just missed the EF2 rope that ran through Columbus. Didn't last long but she was a beauty."

"Yeah, we were just north of it. We were going to go to Oklahoma, but I thought we should hang out in Nebraska, better potential supercells." Jonah sounded smug. Sam snorted and wanted to slap him. Staying close to home had been her idea. She shook her head, biting her lip to refrain from saying something smart. Jonah could be such an ass. And as for Paul, he could at least have stuck up for her. Finally, they said goodbye to the others and made their way into the restaurant.

Sam didn't say a word except to the waiter to order a chicken satay. She ate in silence, reading nothing in particular on the countertop menu.

"You're very quiet, Sam," Jonah noted.

"It's nothing."

"Oh, Paul, woman hormones are taking over already."

"Shut up, Jonah," Paul hissed, looking nervously at Sam, but she simply pursed her lips, repeating her 'Jonah can't bother me' mantra in her head. She'd done a good job today, sending them in the right direction and was responsible for them witnessing two twisters. Jonah could suck on it. It was his problem if he wanted to be an idiot. She'd hold her head high and rise above any of his comments and put-downs. There was no point in being annoyed, as he hadn't the sensitivity to notice. She struck up a conversation, albeit a cold one, with Paul about supercell dew points.

They ordered dessert, which was as cold as the atmosphere at the table.

"So, Everett is building an intercept vehicle." Paul tried to break the awkward tension.

"He's a crazy bastard. I'm surprised he's decided to build a vehicle for intercept. It would not surprise me if he just drove his Sedan into a twister. Do you remember in college when he tried to make his own lightning rod at the frat house?" Jonah and Paul dissolved into hysterics.

"He decided to put it up during a storm and didn't get a chance to earth the damn thing. Lightning struck it and set the housing he'd made on fire. He was lucky he wasn't killed, or that the house didn't go up in flames," Paul explained to Sam, trying to gauge her mood for amusement. He seemed relieved when she laughed. "Right, I'm going for a whizz. Jonah, I believe it's your turn to pay!"

Jonah grunted as Paul slipped out of his seat and slapped him on the back. Sam signalled to the waitress with her hands, making the universal check sign, but she waved them over towards a cash desk.

"We've to go to the cashier, Jonah, do you want me to pay?" she asked, relenting somewhat on giving him the ice treatment, unable to see how he'd manage.

"No. It's my shout."

She got up, took him by the elbow, as she'd seen Paul do, and brought him over to the cash desk. He took out a bundle of scrunched up notes from his pocket and handed them to her.

"Don't run off with my millions now," he joked but she read something behind his tone of voice. Embarrassment? Humiliation? She couldn't decide. She handed over the correct amount of money, and uneasy at her feelings of pity, she put a guiding hand on his back as she led him towards the door of the restaurant.

"Thanks for dinner," she said quietly, trying to inject something other than awkwardness into the air.

"No problem."

No matter how sorry she was for him, she had to confront him about earlier and now before Paul returned was as good a time as any. She took a deep breath, sucking in some confidence.

"Jonah, I need to talk to you about earlier. The way you treated me was uncalled for....."

"FUCK," Jonah yelled and doubled over, holding his thigh with both hands. A sharp table corner had caught him.

"I'm sorry Jonah. I didn't see it. Are you OK?" She winced as she watched him grit his teeth.

He straightened up, leg bent, trying to stretch it out. Sam felt terrible. She'd been so busy planning how to berate him for disrespecting her, that she hadn't been concentrating on negotiating him through the restaurant.

"I'm fine. It's just a bruise. I won't be able to see it." He was trying to joke, but Sam didn't laugh. "Was that your way of getting back at me for taking credit for your idea earlier?"

"No, Jonah. Jesus, I'm not like that."

"I know, I know. I'm kidding. It's fine, really."

"No, it's not. I should have been looking where we were going."

"That makes two of us then!"

She coupled her apology with a hand on his back, feeling his muscles ripple under her palm. Opening the truck door, she showed him the seat and moved around to the driver's side. As she got in, he turned to her.

"You shouldn't apologise. If anyone should, it's me. I shouldn't have spoken about you like that back there. Nor taken credit for your forecast, which was spot on, by the way. Well done."

"Apology accepted. Is your leg OK?"

He nodded. There was glimpse of something, in the way his jaw softened and his eyes glinted.

Paul returned, jumped into the back and Sam revved the truck, merging onto the motorway, Omaha bound. The fields stretched ahead of them, gold and brown. They were passers-by, speeding along past people as they lived their lives, mostly farmers making hay, the odd house and very rarely, a factory. She was catching a snippet of someone's existence as she sped by and they were oblivious to her voyeurism. Life went on. Maybe these people were suffering loss like she was. But one thing was for sure, they were living. A sensation of self-satisfaction settled about her, to her amazement as she realised, so was she. She was taking charge of her life, taking things into her own hands. Straightening up, she smiled, watching the sun dip behind a thicket of trees, a field dotted with hay bales in the foreground. Shafts of light darted out from the sun towards them, pulling them along. She lay her head back onto the head rest, her arms outstretched as she steered. Finding the stereo, she twisted the dial and tapped her fingers on the wheel as *Sweet Home Alabama* filled the truck.

She waited for Jonah to complain, but he was silent. When she glanced across at him, his head was resting back, his eyes closed and his face sunward, absorbing the heat. Sam wondered if he was asleep. The orange glow made his skin look like bronze.

The sun had dipped below the horizon by the time they arrived at her house. When she bid farewell to the boys and opened the front door, the house didn't feel so cold; it felt as though the sun had heated it for the first time in a year.

CHAPTER 4

After two weeks solid chasing, without even one day off, the three storm chasers were exhausted. Some days involved up to fourteen hours of driving. The thrill and sense of purpose were getting Sam through, although she was dreading Bobby's first anniversary, but being so busy over the past two weeks had helped. When Jonah told her one night as they were dropping her home that they were taking the next day off, her stomach sank and she was filled with dread. She was exhausted and could do with a day's rest. However, a day to herself, particularly the day that was in it, would end up as hours of heartbreaking reminiscing, and she didn't want to face into that. Part of her wondered at Jonah's timing. Bobby's anniversary was tomorrow - could Jonah have known that and was that why he'd organised the day off? No, he couldn't possibly. She hadn't breathed a word about Bobby or much else in her life for that matter to them.

Letting herself into the house, she waved at the boys as they drove off and felt the loneliness that had abandoned her for the past two weeks wash over her again like an old, unwelcome friend. The house was cold again. While she'd been chasing with Jonah and Paul, she was either staying overnight in motels or it was home and straight to bed, so tired that she thought of nothing but sleep.

First on her agenda was to fix some food. While the grilled cheese was bubbling under the grill, her phone beeped. She prayed it was Paul telling her something big was forecast for tomorrow and the day off was cancelled but it wasn't. It was her best friend, Stacey. *'Hey babe, where've ya been? Can we do something tomorrow? Was thinking dinner and drinks. Love ya. x.'*

Sam was on the point of keying a refusal but something stopped her. What else would she be doing tomorrow? Sitting in darkness, drinking herself into a wine marinated stupor while she mourned for her dead husband? What would Bobby say to her? "Sammy, honey, get off your ass and go out with Stacey. What are you achieving by crying for me? Do something with your life. You deserve more than to be a widow pining for her husband."

It was easy for him to say.... or hypothetically say. He was somewhere else now. She was left here to fend for herself, pay the bills, suffer the loneliness. With Bobby, she was something. A part of something bigger than her and him. Now she was so alone. She missed his smell, his presence, the way he would pester her to make coffee for him, how he would groan when she'd put *Storm Chasers* on the television, the way he wore his suit, how fresh and dapper he looked while getting ready for work in the morning. As the weather anchor for KWON, he had to be smart, hair slicked back and eyes bright and shining. He was a hit with the female viewers. She smiled as she remembered one particular Valentine's Day, the day he'd proposed to her. No less than 23 proposals came in for him on the station's Twitter feed. He had thanked the viewers for such flattering offers but told them live on air that his heart belonged to someone else. As well as all that, he'd had a plan of his own, roping in the staff on his secret. A researcher came to take Sam from her desk and dragged her onto the red heart and Cupid adorned set. She'd looked at Bobby in horror, drawing her finger across her throat and pointing at him. He laughed and tears came to her eyes as he got down on one knee in front of the entire staff and thousands of viewers and asked for her hand in marriage. Of course she'd accepted at the same time as cursing him for mortifying her live on television. Now she tried desperately to remember his face that day. It was worrying that she was beginning to forget what he looked like in her mind's eye. On his wedding day, as reminded by the photo on the fireplace, he was clean shaven and short haired. That was an exception; he usually had a tidy goatee and floppy brown hair, gelled back for TV. But how she loved him most, was when he was unkempt: hair un-styled, when he'd have to blow it from his eyes, and when his goatee was untidy, usually at the weekend, when shaving wasn't needed. She'd laugh and complain as his stubbly cheeks would tickle and scratch her face.

Their wedding photo looked down on her as she sat hunched on the sofa, crying into her hands, her sandwich untouched on the white plate in front of her. In the photo, she was worry free, dressed in white satin, hair blowing behind her as her brand new husband held her in his arms and stared lovingly into her eyes. A beautiful moment caught on a beautiful day.

The sun was making its way to its highest point in the sky when Sam woke the next morning. The curtains remained open from the night before, giving no shade from the insistent rays of sunshine. Dazed, she checked her phone. Not only were there three missed calls, two from Stacey and one from her mother, but the clock on the phone told her it was eleven thirty. She had fallen asleep on the couch and slept solidly for fifteen hours. At no time in her life had she slept for that amount of time. The grilled cheese sat, looking sad and soggy, still untouched.

She'd slept through ten fifteen. She couldn't believe she'd missed his time of death, exactly one year ago. The sound of that ticking clock in the hospital room filled her head once again. That incessant tick tick tick.... like it was death tapping its long nailed fingers on the table with impatience, waiting to take its next victim - waiting to take Bobby away from her. She desperately tried to think of his face as it had been when he'd been cancer free, tanned, brown eyed, healthy. But all she could see was the ashen grey of his skin and his yellow, bloodshot eyes, toxic from the chemotherapy. The only blessing was that she had managed to tell him everything she wanted to tell him before his chest rose and fell one last time: how much she loved him, how sorry she was that she couldn't save him, how she regretted fighting with him over their choice of photographer at the wedding, how she desperately wanted to go back to Rome with him, how she wished she'd felt that lump in his testicle sooner rather than later. They had made a pact after watching a documentary about the rise in cancer: she hated checking her breasts and he hated checking himself, so they agreed that he would check her and she him. If only they'd watched the documentary two years earlier. That first time, she felt that lump, her stomach had dropped. She'd debated whether or not to tell him but only for a moment or two. She knew she had to. Anyway, most testicular lumps were nothing serious and even if they were malignant, they were usually contained enough to be treated successfully.

The specialist told them otherwise one month later. Bobby and Sam sat in his office, holding hands, trying to absorb the news under the deathly stare and scythe of the Grim Reaper. The lump, while small, was widespread and malignant and had spread to his liver and lymph nodes. Later, they would be told it had spread to his brain and bones. He was only thirty-six. Did this sort of thing not happen to men in their seventies and eighties rather than to someone like Bobby who was so vivacious, handsome and full of life?

When he'd finally exhaled that last lungful, his grip on her hand loosened and his body fell still. It felt like all the energy that had left him had somehow morphed into a freight train that slammed into her. She felt winded and thrown down. In her darkest of moments, sitting vigil at his deathbed, she would try to imagine

43

what his last moment would be like. Would she jump onto his body and scream for him not to leave her? Would she collapse in a heap on the floor? Or would she run from the hospital in a fit of insanity? But when the moment came, she did nothing of the sort. She simply struggled to regain her breath and composure and sobbed quietly along with Bobby's mother and brother. It surprised her to feel, among the overwhelming sadness, a flicker of relief. He was free from pain and sickness.

The support she'd received from not only her friends and family, but also the television station and its viewers, was incredible. Bobby's co-workers were devastated and the show was suspended on the day of his funeral so everyone could attend. It gave her comfort to know just how loved her husband was, not just by her, but by anyone he met.

A knock on the door broke her free from her melancholic reminiscence. Her mother, as short as she was wide, wearing a floral dress that covered her from her neck to her ankles, bundled in, laden with trays of Italian food, a bunch of flowers and a giant box of chocolates.

"You didn't return my calls. You haven't called to see me in two weeks. You say you're out chasing twisters. What is this about, Samia, huh?" Vittoria's Italian accent came through whenever she was worried or angry. Then, the more worried or angry she got, the language changed from English to Italian and she would spit out nags and insults in her mother tongue.

"Mama, I told you, I got a new job."

"Now, I made you a lasagne. Sit and I'll serve you some. I made it this morning and it's still warm. You are so skinny. If you turned sideways, I wouldn't be able to see you at all. *Mia bella figlia, lei svanisce nel nulla.*"

"I'm not fading away, Mama. I just don't have much of an appetite." Sam rolled her eyes.

The garlicky cheese smell turned her stomach. The thought of eating lasagne at eleven fifty in the morning was incomprehensible but she needed to pacify her mother. Choking on each mouthful, she forced an entire portion down her throat. She'd probably vomit it back up later but she couldn't face a nag fest from her mother right now. The satisfied smile on Vittoria's face told her it was working.

"You come home to stay with Papa and I later. I will not leave you on your own today of all days, God rest you, Bobby." She clasped her hands together, shaking them at the sky, eyes heavenward.

"I can't, Mama, I'm going out with Stacey."

"You are going out on the anniversary of your poor husband's death? You are disrespecting him by going out in such a manner."

"It's not like that, Mama. She's taking me to dinner. It's her way of being there for me. Anyway, you can't put a time limit on grieving. Everybody is different. What do you want me to do: sit around, fiddling with rosary beads, wearing black for another year?"

"Now, don't give me your cheeky tongue, young lady. When I was talking to Father O'Doherty the day of Bobby's funeral, he said God gives you all the time you need but it was usually two years to come to terms with a loss."

"Well, whatever Father O'Doherty says must be gospel," Sam muttered under her breath but not under the bat-like hearing range of her mother.

"Samia, it wouldn't hurt for you to come to church with me once in a while. It will help you to get in touch with Jesus Christ again. So tell me about this new job of yours." Vittoria was an expert at changing the subject when she knew she was onto a losing battle with her daughter.

So Sam regaled her with selected details of working with Jonah and Paul. She didn't divulge everything though. Her mother would burst into another Italian tirade if she thought of Sam taking data and photos in the path of a tornado. As far as Vittoria was concerned, they always stayed behind and watched from a safe distance. Also, she failed to mention the long hours, the lack of decent home cooked meals and the fact that her boss was blind.

Unfortunately for Sam, her mother stayed for most of the day until she eventually managed to shoo her out the door at seven-thirty. She'd sent a text to Stacey earlier in the day to say she would meet her for dinner. The hot shower washed over her, cleaning away the day's mourning and the salty residue of tears from her eyes. Despite her mother's insistence and intrusiveness, she was grateful for her visit and company. She twisted and turned in the mirror, checking on the black shift dress that skimmed her knee and nestled on her bony shoulders. She'd make a point of saying to Jonah and Paul that they must stop more often for food. Some days, they would forget to stop for lunch altogether. Her hair fell into loose curls around her shoulders and her make-up was dark, grey eyeshadow, which did nothing to hide her swollen, puffy eyelids. Getting dressed and fancied up had felt like such a gargantuan task, but Stacey deserved the effort.

The restaurant was bustling and vibrant, filled with young, stylish people chatting and laughing loudly. It was of minimalist design, white tables and chairs, the only colour being from a single blue tulip on each table, echoed in the blue modern art paintings on the walls. Stacey was there, waving madly at her from a dimly lit table in the corner. They hugged and exchanged pleasantries.

"Great to see you." Stacey smiled as her friend sat down opposite her.

"You too. Thanks for organising this. I didn't really fancy being on my own," Sam said sadly, staring into the glass of Prosecco that her friend had ordered for her.

"Oh, no problem." Stacey shifted in her seat. She was awkward around Sam when it came to Bobby's death. She didn't mention the day that was in it and Sam was grateful for that. Knowing Stacey, Sam suspected she didn't know what to say and she didn't particularly want to talk about Bobby and so it was a symbiotic silence.

"So, how are you? I've hardly seen you."

Sam regaled the same story about the new job to Stacey as she had done her mother, except she didn't leave out any details this time.

"You are crazy! Good for you, though. It sounds dangerous. Are you being safe?"

"Of course, Stace. I'm a professional. I know what I'm doing."

"Of course you do, Babe. You were always interrupting our games when we were kids to show me some cloud or other. I thought you were mad! I still think you're mad!"

Sam playfully slapped her hand. They were so different. Stacey was a beautician: blonde, sexy, flirtatious and great fun. Sam was serious, tom-boyish and a bit of a science geek. But they'd been friends since kindergarten so it was a friendship that wouldn't easily be broken. Despite being force fed lasagne for brunch, Sam was hungry and finished every bit of her poached scallops starter, along with the lemon sole in parsley butter and the chocolate fondant for dessert.

"Are you feeling up for some drinks or would you prefer to go home?"

Guilt was creeping back under Sam's skin. She felt uneasy being out and twice as guilty because she was enjoying herself. She relayed her reasoning, as well as the 'Grieving According to Vittoria' conversation from earlier in the day to Stacey.

"It's up to you, Sammy, but don't listen to your mom. You do what you need to remember Bobby, but you have to remember yourself too. You're still here and alive. He wouldn't want you wasting away on your own at home dressed in black and twisting rosary beads around your fingers."

"That's what I said!" Sam was feeling giddy on Prosecco and didn't want to go home to suffer the imminent wine downer if she stopped to think for more than a minute. She needed something to keep her mind occupied. "Let's go dancing, will we?"

"You sure?"

"Yup. Let's do it."

The nightclub was bustling with atmosphere. Base beats were hammering through her chest as she sipped on Manhattans and watched people shouting into each other's ears, trying to converse over the music. Out of the blue, she thought of Jonah. This place would be way too stimulating for him. If it were true and a blind person's other senses were more tuned, his head would be hopping from this noise.

Someone behind Sam caught Stacey's attention. She winked as Sam turned around and saw a tall, tanned, blonde guy walking towards their table. He grinned at Sam, raised his eyebrows at Stacey and came to stand beside Sam's stool, his elbow resting on the table beside her.

"Hey." His navy blue eyes mapped her face and she felt herself shift in her seat. Stacey was wide eyed, lips mouthing silent encouraging words.

"Um, hi?" She shrugged over at her friend, wondering what she was supposed to say to this stranger. He might be what Stacey would judge as 'gorgeous,' but she had always regarded herself as socially inept at the best of times, never mind with strange, good looking men.

"So, you been here before?" His smile was confident.

"No." The neurons in her brain fired desperately as she tried to find something to say. Thankfully Stacey broke her impending fall with a welcome interruption.

"Hi." She held out her hand. "My name is Stacey and this is my friend Sam. She's a meteorologist who likes music and storm chasing. I'm going to get a drink. Nice to meet you." Stacey sashayed off bar-bound in an indiscrete effort to get Sam talking.

"Your friend seems fun," strange blonde guy interjected while Sam, in dismay, watched her walk away.

"Yeah, she's great. So what do you do?" She silently congratulated herself for getting at least two sentences out.

"I'm a Lexus sales executive." His cocked eyebrow and flowered up job description was an immediate shut off for her. He was a car salesman, nothing wrong with that but saying 'Car Salesman' would have bought him at least her respect. "So you're a meterol..... metrological.... What is it exactly that your friend said you do?"

As she suppressed the urge to spit her drink across the table, Sam composed herself enough to explain to him what she did.

"Woah. So you like clouds and stuff?"

"There's a little more to it than that, but yes, I like clouds."

"Excellent. I like clouds too. Sometimes I can pick out different shapes, you know like a turtle or a U.F.O."

Sam imagined Bobby in convulsions of laughter looking down on the scene - his wife being chatted up by the nice but dim car salesman.

The conversation trundled on awkwardly about the weather. Sam began to zone out, foreseeing her life being chatted up by random guys whom she would have nothing to say to except to 'um' and 'uh huh' as they babbled on about themselves. She would sit, bored, staring into space, thinking about Bobby and how she desperately wished he could be here to rescue her from the ridiculously dull conversations.

"So, what kind of car do you drive? I could do you a good deal on a Lexus."

"Oh, that's very nice of you, thanks but I don't think I could afford a Lexus. My own car is a Nissan Morano, but I drive a Ford Pickup for work."

"If you like, I could talk to your boss about upgrading you from Ford to an RX. Beautiful car: high spec, metallic paint, heated seats, automatic rain sensor and parking assist.

Sam couldn't help but laugh out loud, then felt guilty when she saw the hurt look on the stranger's face. She could envisage driving the boys around in a luxury four by four, its sparkling metallic paint being pelted by debris, hail, rain and parking sensors beeping like crazy as giant planks of wood and branches fly past. She laughed some more and told him that his offer was very kind, but a Lexus wouldn't exactly suit her line of work.

Eventually, having nothing in the world in common except the fact they were both human, the conversation teetered off to silence and he excused himself, telling her it had been nice talking to her. Planting a toxic coloured drink in front of her, Stacey returned and commiserated that he might be gorgeous, but he was obviously totally wrong for her.

Stacey dragged her up to dance and while awkward at first, Sam eventually found her feet and marinated by cocktails, yelped for joy when Beyonce's *Single Ladies* boomed across the dance floor.

She sang the lyrics at the top of her voice. Twisting her left hand in the air at the chorus, her redundant wedding ring flashed, reflecting the blue and red lights from the DJ's booth. She stopped dead on the dance floor, her eyes fixed on her left hand. What was she doing here? She was supposed to be mourning the death of her husband, not dancing to R'n'B while drunk on cocktails. Stacey witnessed her begin to breakdown and pulled her back to the table, collected their bags and took her outside.

"I'm sorry Sammy, I probably shouldn't have brought you out tonight. We should have stayed in."

"No, no," she managed to say through sobs. "You did the right thing. I'm just - I just forgot for a second and it all came flooding back."

"Come on, let's get a cab and bring you home."

*

"You sure you don't want me to stay with you?" Stacey asked as the cab pulled up outside Sam's.

"No, thank you. I'm OK now. Anyway, I'm chasing tomorrow ... or rather, today... so I'll be getting up early." It was two a.m. and the boys were due to collect her in five hours. She'd be exhausted and the only way she'd be able to function would be to drink coffee all day.

When Paul called next morning, she was still wearing her black dress, having fallen straight onto her bed and slept through. Her make-up was smudged and her hair dishevelled. He stared at her openmouthed; then laughed.

"Shut up."

"Well, you had a good night. We're not in a hurry. Jonah said to collect you first because his nephew is three today and he wants to be there when he wakes up to give him his present."

"So, hard ass Jonah has a soft side?"

"Don't let him hear you say that! So have you seen GFS today?"

"Does it look like I was up forecasting?"

Paul chuckled and said he supposed she wasn't. She told him to make himself comfortable while she showered and changed.

When she came down, he was in the living room looking at their wedding photo. He started when she walked in, embarrassed at being caught snooping.

"Wow, that's some difference. You look more like Sam now and less like the Joker from Batman. Hey, I didn't know you were married. I saw the ring but you never mentioned your husband."

"I was married."

"Oh, I'm sorry. Divorces can be hard."

Sam couldn't hold back. Dropping onto the armchair, she hid her face in her hands and sobbed. It was the kind of sob where you can't catch your breath and can't imagine yourself ever not crying again. Paul held her tightly, cooing and shushing as he rocked her gently. After what felt like an hour, her breathing began to regulate and in mortification, she looked up at Paul, who unknown to her in her convulsions of crying, had gone to find her a tissue and managed to find the kettle to make her tea. She hadn't even realised he'd left the room.

"You OK now?" he asked as she nodded sadly. "I presume it wasn't amicable."

"No... I'm not divorced. He died. Yesterday was his first anniversary." She sniffled and blew her nose into the tissue.

"Oh shit. Jesus. Sam, I didn't know. Why didn't you say something? Did Jonah know? Is that why he gave us a day off?"

"No, Jonah didn't know. Yesterday was just a coincidence. I'd rather have been chasing. Would have kept my mind off things."

Paul looked at the wedding photo again. He shook his head.

"Bobby Notaro? I almost didn't recognise him. You were married to him?"

She nodded sadly, wiping her eyes with the tissue he had provided.

"I'm so sorry, Sam. I'd no idea. Do you want to stay home today? I can call Jonah. He won't mind."

"NO. I mean, no thanks. I need to be busy. And please, don't tell Jonah. I don't want him to pity me."

"Sam, he'd never think like that. He's not the most empathetic of people, but he's not a monster."

"I know. I'd just rather he didn't know, OK?"

"I won't say a word. Are you all right now? Can I get you anything else?" Paul was sitting on the arm of the chair now, his hand rubbing her back.

"I'm fine. Just needed to get that out of the way!" she joked unconvincingly and rose to her feet, brushing herself off. "Let's go get some tornadoes."

"You sure?"

"Paul, I'm fine honest."

"You need a hug?"

"OK." He moved toward her and gave her the biggest hug she'd had in quite a long time. It felt good and therapeutic. He pulled away, looking softly at her, and reaching up he gently tucked a stray tendril of hair behind her ear. "If you need anything, ever, you call me. Promise?"

As she nodded, she had the distinct feeling that Paul was thinking about kissing her. Maybe she was imagining it but his gaze was flicking from her lips to her eyes. She backed away, smiling politely and apologised for him having to witness her meltdown. She watched him self-consciously run a hand through his hair as he stood, keys in hand and told her he'd be in the truck.

Standing in front of her bathroom mirror, Sam washed her face in cold water, wincing as it stung her overworked, swollen eyes. Between little sleep, hangover and a mammoth crying episode, she felt like she'd been hit by a truck and could sleep for days. She guessed she could have told Paul to go on and then she'd crawl back into bed, but the temptation of the adrenaline rush, as well as the fear of being alone was too much to keep her under the duvet. After all, she was starting to enjoy something for the first time in over a year.

Half an hour later, they pulled up outside a large, Spanish style house, with manicured lawns and trees growing all around it. Children's toys littered the garden giving the pristine house a homely air.

"Would you mind getting him? I want to study this radar for a moment," Paul asked.

Sam made her way up the steps to the house. The door opened before she had a chance to knock and a stunning thirty something woman stood before her. She was a brunette, with the same striking blue eyes as Jonah.

"Sam? I'm Jonah's sister, Bella. It's so wonderful to finally meet you. He's told me a lot about you."

"He has? Nice to meet you too." She was enveloped in her second hug of the day. His sister obviously didn't share his coldness.

"Come in, come in." Sam followed her into the vast hallway with a sweeping staircase and marble tiles. Jonah was sitting on the floor in the living room, surrounded by three children, one of which was covered in birthday present wrapping and wearing a party hat.

"Hey Sam, I'm coming now," he said before his sister could announce her arrival. He stood up and she marvelled at the way he maneuvered around the graveyard of toys at his feet. He seemed to know his way around the house.

"No, Unkie Donah, don't go," the beautiful, blue eyed boy whined, grabbing his uncle's leg and wrapping himself like a boa constrictor around it.

Jonah bent down to the boy and in one fell swoop, disentangled him from his leg and lifted him up into a giant bear hug.

"You have a great birthday and I promise I'll be back later to help you with your cake."

Sam stood open mouthed watching the exchange between Jonah and his nephew. Never in a million years, had someone told her that her boss could be so soft and warm with a child or anyone for that matter, would she have believed it. The little boy giggled as Jonah tickled him and dispatched him onto the couch before he could reattach himself to his leg. Bella handed him his bag and placing a hand on Sam's shoulder, let her lead him to the truck. Paul was stuck into his laptop, studying the radar to make a decision on which way to head.

"Talk to me, Paul," Jonah barked. Sam rolled her eyes. No 'good morning,' 'how are you?' He was back to his usual self.

"We're not going to have far to travel today. GFS predicting some supercell formation right over our heads. I say we head slightly south and watch them build. We should only need to go about thirty or forty miles."

"Sounds good. Paul, have you been drinking?" Jonah asked as they all climbed into the truck.

"Eh no," he replied, throwing a look at Sam. She lowered her gaze guiltily and admitted she'd been out the night before.

"Are you fit to drive?"

"I can drive for a while until she gets some coffee," Paul offered kindly.

Sam shot him an appreciative glance and mouthed an apologetic 'thanks.'

"OK, you work the radar and Paul can drive. Don't let it happen again."

Good lord, she thought, he was particularly obnoxious today. By midday, she was coffee fuelled and feeling better, so Paul pulled over and hopped out while she jumped in behind the wheel. They were tracking a supercell that was due to head close to home. They decided to stay in front of it to see what exactly it was going to do so they could warn friends, neighbours and family.

"Sam, we've got a really big hook forming here on radar. Do you think we can get in front of it?"

"The GPS says there's a road going west then north. I can try to get ahead of it. Jonah?"

"Do it," Jonah said, abruptly.

So she sped off, overtaking car after car.

"Take it easy, Sam. Don't want to get us killed."

"Jonah, I know how to drive. Do you want to intercept this rotation or not?" Sam snapped. Jonah threw his hands up, muttering 'Jeez' under his breath.

"OK, Sam. Take the next turn right and it should lead us up ahead of it. There's a confirmed tornado on the ground. Keep going," Paul interjected, before Sam could rip into Jonah.

She put her foot down and turned right onto a dirt track that had her battling to keep the truck on the road. The rain was heavy and relentless until it turned to hail. Large hailstones bounced off the bonnet of the truck and all around them. The dirt road was starting to turn into a mudslide and the truck became almost impossible to control, slipping under her feet.

"Paul, this road isn't great. Is there an alternative?"

"Just keep going. We're almost ahead of it. It's rain-wrapped and is running alongside us on the other side of those trees but we can head it off if you keep that foot down."

Sam's arms began to ache from keeping a grip on the wheel. They had no idea how far away the twister was, thanks to a very inconveniently placed thicket of trees in the way. Suddenly, through the rain, it showed itself. It was moving away from them.

"It's outrunning us. Keep going," Paul urged.

She drove as fast as she felt comfortable with, which wasn't very fast. The road was uneven and unpredictable. Suddenly, a deep pot hole appeared and it was too late. She had to drive into it. The truck jolted forward, she lost control and they hit the ditch. It skimmed the hedge-like shrubs before coming to a stop. Thankfully, it wasn't a severe impact, the hedge acting like a wall of tyres at a race track.

"FUCK," Jonah shouted.

"Is everyone OK?" Paul asked, concerned. "Sam? Jonah?"

"Yeah, I'm fine," Jonah muttered, rubbing his forehead.

Sam, too shocked to speak, nodded her head.

"SAM? Is she OK, Paul?" Jonah barked.

"I'm fine," she muttered, still clinging on to the steering wheel.

Jonah's face turned red as he began a tirade of abuse directed at her.

"Jesus FUCKING Christ, Sam. Have you no fucking sense? Not only have you almost killed us, but we've missed out on tracking a twister that is possibly going to run through our home town. What the fuck were you thinking going out and getting drunk last night? Just because I gave you the day off, doesn't mean you could do something stupid like that, knowing you were chasing with us the next day. I thought you were one of us. That was a stupid stunt. You almost got us all killed or maimed."

"And YOU could have done a better job?" As soon as she said it, she regretted it. The air calmed in the truck, a moment's silence ensued.

"No, I couldn't," he said quietly.

"Jonah, go easy. The twister has dissipated and Sam's not........"

"Paul, leave it. It's fine." She shook her head at him.

"No. Sam's not what? Is there something going on that I don't know about?" Jonah spat as though vitriol dripped from his lips.

"It's NOTHING Jonah. Paul, can you take me home?" She fought back tears as she spoke.

"But Sam......." Paul protested.

"Paul, please. Just take me home."

He reluctantly climbed into the driver's seat as Sam got out and jumped into the back seat, slamming the door. He reversed the truck out of the ditch and turned on the dirt road. They weren't far from Omaha so half an hour later, they turned onto Sam's street. The ride there had been silent and fraught with awkward coldness.

"Sam, please don't go. There's a cell behind that one that's building. We could still get something from that. We need to stay on top of it so that we can warn people here," Paul pleaded but his words fell on disinterested ears.

She jumped out and slammed the door behind her. Not bothering to go into the house, she got straight into her car and tore out of the driveway and down the road, leaving Paul sitting open mouthed in the truck, watching as her maroon Nissan Morano sped away into the hazy distance.

"What was that?" Jonah asked.

"She just drove off in her car. That was totally uncalled for Jonah. She's having a rough time. Accidents can happen and we were pushing her pretty hard to catch up to that twister."

"What do you mean 'having a hard time'?"

"She asked me not to tell you."

"Is there something going on between you two?" Jonah's voice sounded strangled as though trying to hold back a torrent of anger.

"No. Nothing like that. Jonah, if I tell you, you can't let on to her that you know."

"OK. Spit it out."

"Yesterday was the anniversary of her husband's death. She was married to Bobby Notaro."

"Oh fuck. Fuck, fuck, fuck." Jonah's face reddened and he banged his head repeatedly off the headrest. "Are you serious? Bobby Notaro was the weather guy on KWON who died of cancer last year, wasn't he?"

"Yeah, that was him. I thought maybe you knew seeing as you gave us the day off yesterday."

"I had no idea. No idea whatsoever. I gave you guys yesterday off because there wasn't much forecast and we were all exhausted." He dropped his head into his hands. "Should we go after her?"

"No. Leave her alone. Anyway, I think we need to watch this supercell to the south. It's picking up and they've just released a tornado warning for the area. You need to call whoever needs to be warned. I'm gonna make some calls and then we need to hit the road to track this thing. Let Sam do what she needs to do. She'll cool down. We'll call into her tonight and you can apologise. Right now, we need to warn people about this storm."

Paul and Jonah made phone calls to their friends and neighbours warning them to seek shelter as there was a strong, potentially tornadic storm approaching the town. Paul kept his eyes on the radar, watching the orange turn red, then pink in the centre, and then seeing a hook form.

"This is a big one, Jonah. We need to move if we want to catch it."

Paul jumped up front and tore down the road southwards. Without Sam, they were at a disadvantage. Paul couldn't drive and watch the radar at the same time, so they were driving blind. Ten miles out, they were heading into the storm. Hail pelted the roof of the truck. Jonah stuck his hand out the window to catch one. It was the size of a golf ball. He rolled it in his hand until it began to melt, letting little streams of water trickle and drip down onto his combat trousers. "Shit Paul, this is a big one, all right. I felt some really strong updrafts out the window."

Paul, driving precariously with one eye on the radar, nodded. "We're gonna have to punch the core to get ahead of it."

"Do it," Jonah said.

"If it's rain-wrapped, we're in trouble."

59

"I know, but it's heading for West Omaha. We've no choice."

Suddenly the hail abated and in front of them was an enormous wedge tornado.

"Jesus, it's huge. I reckon it's about half a mile across. I'm going to go east and try to get ahead of it. Do you reckon we should deploy a sensor into it?"

"No, not this time, Paul. I think we just need to watch this one."

Tearing down the road heading east, Paul floored the accelerator, leaving them stuck to the back of their seats. He had the siren on to warn other motorists of the imminent danger. Thankfully, people seemed to be being sensible and were heading out of its path. The large wedge tornado ploughed through a barn, decimating it and flinging its remains all around. His head was swimming and stomach clenched. If this thing hit the town, there would be hundreds of casualties. The enormous twister bore down on them in the distance and an unspoken anxiety was floating around the truck between Paul and Jonah. It was heading straight for the suburbs of West Omaha. They tracked it for twenty minutes and just as they got ahead of it, Paul noticed on the radar that it was beginning to weaken. Visually, the rotation above was starting to break down. And before their eyes, the huge column dissipated and giant lumps of debris fell to the ground.

Jonah and Paul issued a collective sigh of relief.

"Shit. That was a close call, Jonah."

"Yeah? How far from the town are we?"

"About two miles."

"Woah."

Pulling the truck over, they both sat in silence and enjoyed the feeling of relief wash over them in waves.

"Well, I think that deserves a drink, don't you? Wanna check out the damage path before we head back?" Paul asked, turning the truck back onto the road.

"Yeah, you can tell me what it's destroyed and I'll predict the EF level. If I'm right, you're buying," Jonah joked uneasily, still shaken.

"Deal." Paul took his hand to shake. "But before we go out for drinks, we need to call into Sam, OK?"

"Yeah. I know. Maybe she'll come out with us."

'Doubt it,' Paul thought to himself. She was pretty mad.

The damage path was at least a half mile wide, but luckily, it was mostly open farmland. The twister had crossed the road at an intersection and Paul noticed several roadside fences down. It had bisected the road just at a graveyard.

"Fuck, there's a car upturned over there by the graveyard. Should we go and check it out?"

"Yeah, absolutely. Go."

Paul jumped out of the truck. Jonah listened to his footsteps as they got further and further away. Then he heard them coming closer again.

"Jonah. I think it's Sam's car. She has a red colour Nissan."

"Jesus. Is she in it?"

"No. But the graveyard took a direct hit. And I'm presuming that's where she was. Oh god, I hope it's not her."

"We've got to find her. Come on, help me out."

Paul took Jonah by the arm and they ran. He gasped at the devastation before them.

"Paul? Is it bad?"

"Yeah. It's bad."

They walked in silence among flattened headstones, flowers and grave ornaments in disarray. Neither of them had any idea where Sam might be. The thought occurred to both of them but was left unsaid that she could have been picked up and thrown somewhere. Paul instructed Jonah to wait by a giant crucifix in the centre of the graveyard. It stood erect among the felled headstones.

"Don't move. There's a block of restrooms up ahead. I'm going to see if she's in there."

As Paul's frantic footsteps and calling moved further into the distance, Jonah heard a noise unlike the distant downdrafts whistling. He strained his ears until he thought he could make out a whimper. It sounded like an injured animal. Moving from this spot was hazardous, but he felt he had no choice. He unhooked the cane from his belt loop and slowly began to follow the sound. Panic rose into his throat but slowly and meticulously he made his way around the obstacles at his feet; he was getting close as the sound was getting louder. He smelled the freshly torn up earth and greenery, victims of the recently passed twister. It was a short but perilous walk. Several times he almost tripped over fallen stonework or branches. Then he was upon the sound.

He knew it was her. He could smell her scent on the residual downdrafts. "Sam?" he called tentatively. His cane hit off something that wasn't a headstone or flowers - it was yielding. He gingerly put his hand down until he felt something soft: cotton fabric. 'Sam?' he whispered.

"Jonah?" came a confused response. Sam, sitting huddled on the concrete surround of her husband's grave, looked up from her hands, tears streaming down her face, whimpers catching her breath.

"Oh, god, Sam. Are you OK? Are you hurt?" Jonah bent down to her until they were face to face.

"Yes. Yes, I'm fine. What about you? How did you get here? Where's Paul?"

"He's the other side of the graveyard looking for you. He saw your car overturned."

"Oh no. Is it badly damaged?"

"Kind of."

Dropping his cane to the ground, Jonah ran his hands up her arms, over her shoulders and into her hair, feeling for injury, blood, bumps. Stroking her cheeks, he felt her tears on his fingertips.

She heard his breath catch and watched him hold his fingers to his nose. He was placated the wet wasn't blood.

She was paralysed, stuck to the spot, sitting on the little curb around Bobby's grave.

Jonah chewed on his bottom lip. He was riddled with a mixture of anxiety, guilt and relief. Their faces, inches apart, their breath, catching and mingling with the remnant winds of the passed storm.

"Are you sure you aren't injured?" His voice was soft, as though he was afraid to frighten her away.

"I'm fine."

"Sam...." He let her name hang on the air between them. "I'm so sorry about earlier."

"It's all right." She was dizzy and confused. Everything had happened so fast: the tornado, trying to hide, then finding Bobby's decimated grave once the winds had passed. And now, Jonah turning up out of the blue.

"Jesus. There you are." Paul came running up. "What the fuck happened? Are you OK?"

"She's fine. Just shaken up. Come on, let's get her to the truck." Jonah took her by the arm for a change. Although she was leading him through the debris, he was holding her up.

Nestled in the safety of the truck, she dropped her head back onto the headrest and closed her eyes, exhausted. The hum of the engine and motion of the truck as Paul drove made her feel sleepy but her mind was whirling with the events of the day.

CHAPTER 5

Paul drove Sam home, reassuring her he'd sort her car out tomorrow and she wouldn't have to worry about it.

"You want us to come in with you?" he asked.

"No. Thanks. I'm fine, honestly."

"You sure?"

"Yes. I think I just need some sleep."

"Well, if you're sure you're OK. You know where I am. Just call if you need anything."

"Thanks. And guys, thanks for...... well, thanks for coming to get me today."

Paul and Jonah nodded and bid her goodbye.

Safely ensconced in her house, she took a deep breath. Catching a glimpse of herself in the hallway mirror, she saw she was covered in splashes of mud. She made her way wearily up the stairs and stripped off the mud sodden clothes. They still smelled of freshly dug up dirt and grass. While the steaming water ran over her exhausted body, she wept as the enormity of the afternoon washed over her. The devastation she had felt once again at being so alone and powerless, sitting by Bobby's graveside, knowing that there wasn't anything or anybody on earth who could bring him back to her. That was when the nagging thought crossed her mind that maybe she could be with him, let the storm take her. She wasn't sure if she believed in an afterlife, but anything had to be better than this existence. And anyway, someone as wonderful and vibrant as Bobby couldn't just be extinguished from the planet, snuffed out so quickly and needlessly like a flame from a match. Surely he was living somewhere on another plain, in another form. Despite the heat of the water, bordering on burning her reddening skin, she shivered as she recounted how close she'd come to death. Maybe Bobby had been her guardian angel and had arranged it that she'd be safe. She winced as the hot water stung her burned skin and turned off the shower.

Dabbing at her tear-stained eyes with the towel, she looked at herself in the condensation streaked mirror. She had survived. She *had* survived. She wasn't sure how, why or for what - but she had. She took several deep, cleansing breaths and threw on cotton pyjamas and a towelling robe. As she was going downstairs, the sound of the doorbell ringing made her jump almost out of her skin.

Paul was on the other side of the peephole, pushing dirt around with his toe, hands behind his back. She opened the door and smiled, letting him in.

"I was on my way home and saw your light on. I wanted to check you were OK."

"This isn't on your way home."

"Sprung." He kept his gaze fixed on the ground. "I was worried about you. I didn't like the idea of you being alone."

She nodded appreciatively and instructed him to go sit down while she made coffee.

"So, tell me what happened," Paul asked, as she sat herself down beside him, handing him a mug. She took a deep breath and after a long pause, let the words fall out.

"Well, I got so mad at Jonah, I didn't know what to do. I just felt this overwhelming need to be with Bobby." She looked questioningly at him, waiting for him to judge her with a look, maybe even call her crazy. But he simply nodded. "I just drove and drove until I got there. I could see the rotation, could feel the updraft and knew something was coming but I didn't care. I was talking to him when I felt the wind pick up, heard it in the distance, and knew I should seek shelter but I didn't move." Sam paused to take a sip of coffee and sighed deeply. "When I looked up and saw it baring down on me, I thought about hiding, protecting myself but a big part of me just wanted to stay and let the twister do whatever it would with me, bring me back to him, I guess. I don't know. I've felt so different these last few weeks, maybe even happy, really like a part of something with you guys. But it makes me feel incredibly guilty, like I'm turning my back on Bobby. So when Jonah shouted at me, I thought maybe it was his way of saying, 'this isn't right for you, come to me.' I wanted that twister to pick me up and tear me apart so I could be with him again."

She was crying now, big heaving sobs that wracked her whole body. Paul wrapped his arm around her protectively, pulling her close to him. She could smell his aftershave. It was heady and musky.

"But you were OK. What happened then?"

"I got this overwhelming feeling that I had to survive. Just as the tornado was almost upon me, I saw a concrete mausoleum about twenty metres away so I ran toward it and found a little doorway. I ran like I don't think I've ever run before but it felt like I was moving through honey, that my legs would never get me there. But they did. I ran in, threw myself into the furthest corner and crouched down into a ball. It approached so quickly. I could hear things smashing off the walls, could see branches flying across the little doorway. You know the way they said in college that there's a freight train sound? I never quite thought much of it until I actually heard it. It really is like a train laden with logs or something barrelling over the tracks right next to you. It's remarkable. Anyway, I knew it was just on top of me as the air rushed out of the doorway like a vacuum. My ears started to pop. I prayed for Bobby to..... to," she started to sob again and Paul pulled her tighter to him, reassurance in his touch, shushing her. Another deep breath and she was able to go on. "I prayed for him to protect me. Then, it was over. The downdrafts threw bits of twigs and mud into the mausoleum. It took me a few minutes to get up. I think I was half afraid to see what it had destroyed. When I came out, it was like walking out into a different place, a different time. Everything was destroyed. Bobby's headstone was broken, it had been knocked over: there was a giant crack down through his name and the flowers I had put there were gone." She cried softly.

"Shhh. It's OK. You're safe now. I'll get you some more tissues." Paul jumped up and left the room. The sleeves of her towelling robe were becoming sodden as she shed tear after tear into them. Sniffing and blowing her nose in the tissue that Paul handed to her, she straightened up.

"What did NOAA say about it? It felt like an EF3. Was it?" Sam asked.

He laughed heartily. "Once a 'met head' always a 'met head!' You're right, it was a three. You're so lucky you found that mausoleum."

She closed her eyes, trying to block out the memory of the afternoon. Clearing her throat, she forced a weak smile. "You must be hungry. Want some food?"

"Yeah, I could eat something."

"I'll get the menus. Chinese or something else?"

"Whatever. You decide."

Sam came back brandishing menus of every description. After ordering Thai food, they sat back and recounted the storm, how narrowly it had missed the town. They agreed, storm chasing was exciting and adrenaline inducing, but that had been too close for comfort. Paul told Sam he'd stay with her but she refused, saying she needed space to think. She was overwhelmed by the day's events and needed to be alone, appreciative as she was of his offer. He left reluctantly, making her promise that she'd call if she needed anything. She agreed as she showed him to the door.

When she closed it behind him, she braced herself up against it and let out a sigh. What a day. Bed was the only place she wanted to be, so she locked up and made her way upstairs. She was just dozing off to sleep when her phone trilled, startling her into wakefulness.

"Hello?" she grunted.

"Sam. It's Jonah."

"Oh, Jonah, is everything all right?" Her voice was croaky.

"Did I wake you? I'm sorry. I just called to see how you were."

"I'm fine, thanks."

"Good. I think we're going to go out tomorrow. Will you be up to it?"

Too tired to think about the implications of chasing after the day she'd had, she yawned and agreed.

Hanging up and putting the phone on silent, she replaced it on her locker. She slept uneasily that night: tossing, turning, dreaming about the day's events. In her wakeful moments, Jonah occupied her head. She tried to figure him out, wonder why he had such a wall built up, why he was so lukewarm. The accident that had robbed him of his sight must have really messed him up, or maybe he had always been like that: gruff and arrogant.

Scolding herself for thinking about him, she knew she had to get more sleep. She was only annoying herself. Clearing her mind of all things Jonah and near death experiences, she fell back to sleep and didn't wake until sunlight.

She was up and showered by nine a.m. She wasn't sure what the boys planned, but she wanted to be ready just in case. Turning the TV on, she flicked to KWON. 'Good Morning, Omaha' was on, the show she and Bobby had worked on together. Nostalgia flooded back as she watched co-anchors Janie Wallace and Jack Logan joke with each other on the live morning show. Bobby had been very fond of them. Just as she was reminiscing over the good times they'd all had as a team, there was a knock at the door. When she opened it, she was greeted with a giant bouquet of yellow and orange roses, dotted with Stargazer lilies, behind which stood the smallest delivery man. She didn't know how he was managing to hold them up.

Thanking him, she relieved him of the heavy but beautifully fragrant burden and brought them inside. Gingerly she opened the card and it read *To Sam, just something to let you know we're all thinking of you and remembering Bobby, love cast and crew of 'Good Morning, Omaha.'*

The sentiment brought yet more tears to her eyes. Yesterday had been such a dramatic day, that she felt like she'd been crying the entire time. It was exhausting. But these tears were a mixture of self-pity and appreciation. What a kind gesture, she thought as she dipped her nose into one violently orange rose, it's perfume pungent and sweet.

Another knock at the door, and more flowers. This time it was a smaller bunch of gas station blooms, with two larger men standing behind them: Paul and Jonah. Paul thrusted the half-wilted bouquet rather clumsily at her.

"These are for you. Can you give me your car keys? My buddy is here with the tow truck. He's gonna head to the cemetery now to pick it up."

Taking the flowers, Sam led Jonah inside and showed him to the couch, then ran out to Paul with the keys.

"Paul, thanks for this. I really appreciate it. And also, thanks for yesterday. You guys were great."

"No problem. That's what friends are for, eh? So, did you sleep?"

"I did. Thanks again and let me know the cost, yeah?" She watched him nod and jump into the tow truck, waving as he drove away.

Back in the house, Jonah was patting his hand softly along the larger bunch of flowers, holding a lily to his nose and inhaling deeply.

"More flowers? You're a popular girl."

"What? Those? No, they're from the people Bobby and I used to work with. I got them just before you arrived. Jonah, about yesterday...."

"I know. I should never have yelled at you like that. It was completely uncalled for. I can be a bit brash sometimes."

"A bit? I don't mean the yelling, I mean..... it doesn't matter. Thank you."

"Hey, no need to thank me. I wanted to be sure you were OK. I don't want to have to advertise for another driver so soon."

"Oh, gee thanks."

She watched him, his faint smile fading. "I thought you were really hurt, Sam. I was....... I was really worried. I'm glad you're OK."

"How did you find me?"

"I could hear whimpering. Paul had told me to stay where I was but I couldn't just stand by and do nothing while he was the other side of the graveyard. I almost broke my neck over some debris, but managed to take my time and get around them. Then I could smell your shampoo, or something, so knew I'd found you."

Silence fell between them, Jonah clasped his hands, twisting his thumbs around and around, almost hypnotising Sam as she stared, desperately trying to think of something to say. Instead, she found herself analysing him. His shoulders were chiselled, his arms though muscular and strong, were gentle - she'd found that out yesterday when he'd held her up as they'd made their way through the debris littered graveyard. His jaw-line was sprinkled with day old stubble that accentuated his lips and his white T-shirt was stretched tightly across his body. She had an all-consuming urge to run her hand down his chest.

"You've gone very quiet." He shifted on the couch, now fiddling with the button on the pocket of his combat trousers. A tattoo on his forearm flashed under his sleeve. She hadn't seen it before. It was a spiral, loosely wound at the top, tightening as it went down - a tornado.

"Your tattoo is beautiful. I've never noticed it before."

"Thanks." He sounded embarrassed as he changed the subject, asking her if there was any chance she'd make him a coffee.

Pleased to have an excuse to leave the room, she went to the kitchen and flicked on the kettle. When she returned with the steaming mugs, he was in the same position and still fidgeting with the button. They sipped and talked for a while. He told her they weren't going to chase today, there was nothing on the radar. That wasn't true. She knew as she had checked the GFS earlier in the morning and there were storms forecast for Texas, but she said nothing. Talking about everything and nothing: weather, college, jobs, they passed a couple of hours, him talking about old chases, while she listened, enjoying the animation in his voice as he reminisced.

*

A week went by without hearing from the boys. There was nothing major forecast as tornado season was winding down, plus Jonah and Paul had been away at a climate change conference, so chasing was off for the time being. Sam rattled around her house alone most of the time. Some days she went out shopping, spending the time looking in store windows at nothing in particular, only to return home empty handed and lonely. She dreaded going out, only to have to come back to an empty, desolate house. Not having her car was a major disadvantage as the local stores could only be visited so many times. How she longed to jump into the car and head to the nearest shopping mall, so that, if nothing else, she could sip coffee amid the hustle and bustle of afternoon shoppers and browse the endlessly big department stores.

Eight days after she'd last seen the boys, she arrived back from a jog to find her car in the drive, fixed up and sparklingly clean. Paul sat on her doorstep, soaking up the sun.

"Paul!" she yelled, jogging up and throwing her arms around him. He stiffened, taken by surprise at her display of affection and muttered an awkward 'hey.'

"Oh, I'm sorry. I'm really sweaty. Have you been here long? You should have called."

"I've only been here a few minutes. Thought I'd wait and catch some rays." Smiling, not making eye contact, he held the look of a schoolboy whose high school crush had just asked him to the prom.

"Paul, I can't thank you enough for getting my car straightened out. How much do I owe you?"

"Oh, nothing. It's paid for."

"No, I can't accept that. It must have cost a fortune."

"Honestly, leave it. It's sorted. Any chance of a cold drink?"

Shaking her head, she made her way inside and re-emerged with a lemonade in each hand. Easing herself onto the step beside him, they clinked glasses and toasted each other's health. Sam felt the silence between them become increasingly uncomfortable, as Paul stared into his glass.

"So, how was the conference?" She broke the silence.

"Good, yeah. Missed being out on the road, you know?"

"Yeah, I've missed it too. It's been a long week."

Paul looked up from his glass, making eye contact.

"You glad you joined the team?"

"Yeah, really glad. You guys are great. Well, you're great. Jonah's still an ass."

"He's not really an ass, you know. You should give him time."

"Sorry, I know you guys are friends. I shouldn't speak ill of him."

"He can be an ass, I guess. I just know him better. We've been friends a long time."

"So, enough about Jonah. Are you seeing anyone right now?"

Paul blushed furiously and avoided her gaze, instead turning his attention back to his glass.

"Kind of. I went on another date with that girl I was seeing. I don't think it will work out though."

"Oh, why not?"

His gaze remained downcast while he twisted the glass around in his hands. "There's someone else I like."

Sam nodded her head, like she knew what he meant even though she didn't. "Why don't you get with the girl you like?"

"Because I have a feeling she's hung up on someone else."

"Oh, that's tough. Are you sure?"

"I think so." He coughed, highlighting his discomfort at the conversation and Sam duly changed the subject, asking him to tell her all about the conference. After finishing their drinks, Paul stood and stretched. He climbed into the tow truck and told her they'd talk soon. She couldn't help noticing the hint of sadness in his lack-lustre conversation and vowed to keep an eye on him.

Despite the blisteringly hot afternoon, she turned her attention to weeding the garden. Her phone rang and she jumped to answer it like it would explode if she didn't. She was surprised to feel her heart sink a little when she realised it was her mother.

"Samia, how are you? Have you been eating?"

Sam rolled her eyes.

"Yes, Mom. How are you?"

"Good. So, I told you about Maria Belloti's son, Luca? His wife left him for his best friend. He is devastated, poor boy. Maria says he is so lonely, so I say to her, why don't I ask Samia if she will meet him for coffee and Maria, she says 'You know Vittoria, you are the cleverest woman I know. That is a wonderful idea.' So I say to Maria that I will ask you. What do you say? He's a very polite boy. Goes to church every Sunday."

"Mom, are you mad? You said yourself, Bobby is only gone a year. Do you really think I should be going on a blind date with someone?"

"It's not a date Samia, it's just to meet this nice, poor man to cheer him up. Maybe it will do you good to make new friends. You are wasting away in that house of yours and if you're not doing that, you're chasing storms and I worry you will get hurt or worse. My only baby girl and she chases twisters and tries to get herself killed."

Sam thought of the graveyard, the previous week. Her mother would lose her life if she knew what had happened.

"Mom, calm down. I'm fine. I don't need to meet some random stranger."

"He's not a stranger, Samia. He is a good boy whose mama I owe a favour to."

"You know what Mama," Sam sighed in defeat, "give Luca Belotti my number and I'll arrange a coffee with him, yes?" Anything to shut her up. She could almost feel her mother's self-satisfied smile as they said goodbye and hung up. The heat was too much for her to weed anymore so she poured herself a glass of wine and made herself comfortable. If Luca sent her a text or called, she'd come up with an excuse not to go and he'd eventually get the message that she wasn't interested. She'd deal with Vittoria's wrath then. It was too hot to worry about that now. No sooner had she taken her first sip, than the phone rang again. She sighed and got back up to answer it. Probably her mother, with details of the date with Luca that she'd taken the liberty of arranging herself. It was Jonah. Her stomach jumped a little.

"Hello, Sam?"

"Hi. How was your conference?"

"Oh the usual. Climate this…climate that…global warming etc. Pretty boring, actually. How have you been, since, you know?"

"Fine. Keeping busy."

"That's good. So, I wanted to ask if you fancied dinner tonight? Thought it would be good to meet and chat about the chasing season before it ends. Do you have any plans?"

"No."

"See you at eight?"

CHAPTER 6

Sam rang the doorbell of Jonah's sister's house. As the door opened, her jaw dropped. Jonah stood before her dressed in a white shirt and dark indigo jeans, wearing proper black shoes. This was the first time she'd seen him in anything but sneakers and combats. His hair was slicked back with gel and somehow it made his sky blue eyes pop even more.

"So do you know 'Millie's Grill?' I got my sister to book us a table there."

"Yeah, sounds good." Determinedly regaining composure, she took him by the elbow. "Is Paul meeting us there?"

"He can't make it. Just us two, I'm afraid."

"Oh." Her heart skipped a little.

"You smell nice."

The comment, or was it a compliment, was so unexpected that she found herself grinning. While getting ready she'd sprayed herself liberally with her favourite Marc Jacobs perfume. Her cleavage revealing blouse was wasted on Jonah but it made her feel good. Somehow, even before she'd known Paul wouldn't be coming, she felt this was more than their usual truck stop meal in a dodgy service station. It felt like Jonah had an agenda, maybe something he wanted to tell her.

An hour into the meal, they hadn't once mentioned anything related to weather. Usually, making conversation with him was like walking on egg shells: one slip into a subject he didn't like and

76

he'd turn moody, freezing the atmosphere just as it was warming up.

"I have another conference on Saturday. I'm the keynote speaker. It's about severe weather..... and I was wondering, if you would accompany me. You've a significant background in weather forecasting research and it would be good to have you to look over my speech and be a friendly face, or rather voice, in the audience. And maybe to help me not bump into things. Paul was supposed to come but something has cropped up and he can't make it.

Sam thought about it for a moment. She had an empty diary. It would be a change and anyway, she thought, it might be interesting to see Jonah out of the truck and doing his day job.

"Sure. Where is it?"

"Paris."

"Paris, Texas?" The European capital would be too good to be true.

"No, Paris, France."

"Woah! Really?" Her eyes widened.

"No, only kidding. It's in Paris, Texas.... but I hear it's just as nice!"

She slapped him on the hand for dashing her hopes.

They sipped Pinot Noir, ate steak and fries. He seemed at ease tonight, not putting up his usual front. It amazed her how deft he was, despite his disability. He didn't spill as much as a crumb or a drop of wine. Any person watching them would think they were a perfectly normal, fully sighted couple. It was as though she was seeing him for the first time: his face was so handsome when he was relaxed and in a good mood.

"So? Will you still come with me?"

"I suppose I'll need to drive down?" She didn't want to sound too enthusiastic.

"No, for a change. We'll fly and the organisers are sending a car. You're off the clock."

"OK, I'll go." She feigned reluctance, but her heart was thumping like a steel drum and her stomach was clenched. And she didn't know why.

"Sorry it's short notice."

"It's not like I've anything else planned."

As Jonah reached for his napkin, his hand hit off his glass full of wine and sent it toppling down his front. He cursed as Sam jumped up and began patting the spill with her napkin. His shirt was soaked with a large ruby stain.

"You need to go to the bathroom, your shirt is drenched. Come on."

Taking him by the arm, she brought him to the door of the men's room. How was he going to find his way around in there, she wondered? She couldn't leave him. Looking from the women's door to the men's, she made a snap decision. Grabbing him by the arm, she took him into the women's rest room. Better that they go where he can't see rather than her going into the men's room with him and having to look at, well, men's bits.

"Where are we?"

"In the bathroom. Now take off your shirt. I'm going to rinse it and dry it under the hand dryer." He reluctantly began to unbutton, making suspicious eyes in the direction of her voice.

"Are we in the men's bathroom or the women's?"

"Jonah, just take your shirt off, hurry, before someone comes in."

"Yep, we're in the women's. Jesus Christ, Sam."

"I don't know what else to do. Hurry."

He hesitated but handed over the shirt and stood with his arms folded while she took in his bare, muscle-chiselled chest. Her eyes widened as she mapped his buff torso.

"I don't hear the water." His tone was deadpan.

"Just looking for the sink. There it is." She let the water run over the shirt, leaching the red stain from the fabric. Wringing it out, she then held it under the hand dryer. It wasn't going to be completely dry and would be creased, but it would have to do. Better creased and damp than a big red wine stain down the front. Eventually, it was dry enough. She handed the shirt back to Jonah, watching as he felt for the seam, finding the right way around and swinging it over his head, letting the sleeves slip down his arms.

"Wait," she almost shouted. His chest was still stained with wine. She grabbed some paper hand towels and before he could button the shirt, patted his chest down.

He was motionless, a statue under her gentle touch. If she hadn't known any better, she'd say he was staring down at her while she dried him.

He inhaled deeply, taking in every molecule of scent on her.

She gazed up at him, haphazardly still patting, his chest now thoroughly cleaned. His eyes, though blank, were wanting. A charge was building. The paper towel dropped to the floor, but she was unaware as she continued to touch his chest, running a finger lightly down the little patch of hair between his pecs. He hadn't moved, as though he was paralysed by her caress. His head was bent towards her, his stance like a frightened horse, being calmed by a single touch, trusting, allowing her to do what she wanted. Achingly slowly, the charge pulled them together, their faces inching towards each other. The spell was cast but within a nanosecond, it was broken.

A large woman in a loudly patterned dress entered the bathroom. "Oh my gawwwd, there is a big ol' man in here. I'm calling the manager," she announced at the top of her voice and stormed out.

"Shit, we'd better go." Sam took charge, buttoning up Jonah's now creased shirt while he remained motionless. Dragging him out the door and back to the table, she grabbed her bag, threw a fifty down and taking him by the hand, half walked, half ran out of the restaurant. As she showed him the car door, she noted his face was like thunder. The spell was definitely broken.

"Are you OK?" She started the ignition.

"What do you think? Not only did you drag me into the women's bathroom, but you made me strip too."

"What the hell was I supposed to do? You had red wine all down your shirt."

"We could have just left and gone back to Bella's, so I could change."

"Yeah but......" He was right, she had to concede. There was really no need for the embarrassment she had caused him. He must have felt mortified and completely undignified.

"I'm sorry, Jonah. I thought I was doing it for the best."

"Yeah, well, you meant well, I'm sure." He said it but his snarl told her he didn't feel it. "Did we leave without paying?"

"No, I left some money on the table."

"Well, here." He fumbled for his wallet and took out some notes, placing them on the dashboard.

"It's fine." He'd only left one five dollar note and some singles but she said nothing.

"Just keep it. Dinner was supposed to be on me."

Driving back to Bella's, silence froze the air around them. He thanked her coolly as he got out of the car, the couple of feet between them feeling like a mile. He whipped out the cane and found his way steadily up the path. She watched him become absorbed into the house and dropped her head back onto the headrest in frustration. She'd messed up. That she had embarrassed her boss by bringing him into the ladies' restroom was bad enough but worse was the muddle of her own feelings.

"Aggghhhh." She punched the steering wheel and berated herself for having just made life very awkward.

Her phone beeped from the depths of her handbag. She almost broke her pelvis trying to retrieve it from under the passenger chair. It was a message from a number she didn't recognise.

'Hi Sam, Luca Belloti here. So your Mom and mine have been plotting and scheming to get us to go for coffee so I told her I would just to keep the peace. If you'd be interested, let me know on this number. If not, feel free to ignore this message as I completely understand. Luca :)'

Against her resolve, she found herself smiling at the text. Even before she'd met this man, they already had the torment of an overbearing Italian mother in common. She typed a text while sitting in the car, still outside Jonah's house.

'So you suffer at the hands of a bossy 'Madre' too? I guess a coffee wouldn't hurt. Plus it might actually keep them off our backs for a while.'

Sam's thumb hesitated over the send button but she pressed it and stuffed the phone quickly into her bag before she could regret the decision to respond.

*

Luca wasn't going to give George Clooney a run for his money, but he was reasonably attractive with boyish dark curls and cute, deep brown eyes. They sat facing each other in Mario's café. Vittoria was in a tizzy when she'd phoned, full of advice on what to wear and how to act, but Sam had shaken off her mother's guidance. She was only meeting this man to keep her happy. She remembered the Lexus guy from the club, but Luca seemed different: shy, unassuming and to her surprise, easy to talk to.

"So, our moms are something else, aren't they?" He hazarded a shy smile in Sam's direction.

"You could say that, yes."

"Mom told me about your husband. I'm sorry to hear about him. You must have been devastated."

She nodded, stirring her latte with a long handled spoon.

"Mom's funny, you know? One minute she's telling me it takes years to get over losing someone and then in the same breath, she's setting me up on a date. I know her heart is in the right place but I just wish she'd leave me be sometimes."

"I know exactly what you mean. Ever since my wife left, Mother has been living in my ear: she's there first thing in the morning, last thing at night and most of the day in between. Giving her a key to my apartment was the worst decision I ever made, apart from marrying Sadie, that is." He flashed her a sardonic grin.

"I'm sorry." She didn't know what else to say.

"She slept with my best friend. That was tough. But I'm getting through it."

"When did it happen?"

"Three months ago."

"Woah, your Mom doesn't hang around then!"

"Nor does yours, seemingly. Would you like another coffee? Mine's gone cold."

"That would be nice."

Sam watched him walk to the counter to order more coffees. He was smart in a grey suit and blue shirt. He waved down at her, catching her staring at him. She waved self consciously and smiled back.

After two hours, and another two cold coffees, Sam decided it was time to take her leave. Bidding him farewell, they hugged awkwardly and she turned home bound, feeling a little lighter. She considered phoning her mother to tell her how well it had gone and what a nice guy Luca was, but she couldn't stand to hear her 'I told you so's.'

Sipping wine while ensconced on her couch, later that night, a text flashed on her phone. It was from Luca.

'Had a wonderful time this afternoon. Would you like to meet for dinner tomorrow night, you know, just to appease our mothers. ;)'

Sam chewed her lip. Dinner was a step further, and so soon after they'd just met. She didn't want to lead Luca on, but then again, maybe she should give him the benefit of the doubt and maybe he just wanted a friend to talk to. They had so much in common and Sam could do with more friends. She typed an acceptance in response and sent it before her doubting conscience changed her mind for her.

*

The next day, at a truck stop in South Nebraska, Paul and Jonah were eating meatball subs while Sam was studying the radar. The boys had decided to chase today as an outbreak of supercells had been forecast that morning. Sam had had to hastily dress and get breakfast after Paul called to see if she'd wanted to chase.

"Guys, I think this is a bust. That front just south of us is weakening with each radar update. I can't see any more serious convection happening so I say we call it a day."

"Are you sure?" Jonah asked, unimpressed with her call.

"I'm sure Paul can give you a second opinion." She rolled her eyes as she handed the computer to him.

"She's right, Jonah. Might as well head back. Best we'll see is some heavy rainfall."

Jonah threw himself into the back of the seat like a petulant child. Sam felt a flicker of realisation, like a little light bulb had come on. He needed this. He needed it just as much as she did. She dreaded the non chasing days. They were long, empty and she was a widow again. For Jonah, the non chasing days were the same: endless and dark. When they were chasing, all that mattered was the storm: the adrenaline inducing, awe inspiring storm. Any other day was just a vacuum of loneliness.

Paul, as always, the conversational Batman, swooped in to save the day with a change of subject.

"Jonah tells me you're going to the conference."

Jonah grunted.

"Yeah, I am. It'll be something different, you know?"

"It'll be boring as hell, is what it will be."

"So, grumpy ass over there and I are going to the movies tonight. There's a Scarlet Johanssen one on and Jonah can't resist the sound of her voice. Want to come?"

Sam laughed at the thought of Jonah in the cinema, melting under the tones of the actress's voice. "I can't. I, um, I have a ...... a dinner with someone."

"Like a date?" Jonah's tone was jeering but Paul just stared.

She looked away. "Yeah, maybe. I don't know. We're just friends so it's not really a date in the true sense of the word."

"Yep, it's a date." Jonah smirked in Paul's direction.

Paul said it was time to head home, which were the last words any of them spoke on the drive back to Omaha.

Answering the door, later that evening, toothbrush in mouth, Sam groaned as Vittoria pushed past her, laden with bags.

"I bring you things to make you pretty for your date tonight," her Italian accent so sharp, it sounded like she'd just gotten off the plane from Naples.

"Mom! How did you know? Oh wait, let me guess - Maria Belloti told you. It's not a date. Luca and I are just friends."

"Yes, yes, yes." Vittoria waved her hand dismissively at her daughter who was still wearing her bath robe. "I bring you new red lipstick and blusher. The girl at the Mac counter said these would suit your Mediterranean skin tones or some nonsense."

"Seriously, Mama. Why are you doing this? Weren't you the one who told me it takes years to grieve? Why are you pushing this?"

Vittoria took her daughter by the arms and stared sternly at her. "Because, mia bambina, I cannot stand to see you so unhappy. It occurred to me that you need a man to look after you. You miss Bobby so much, God rest him. I thought meeting someone could help you get over him. Luca, he is a good man, from a good family."

Sam shook her head. There was no point in arguing. Vittoria meant well. She hugged her mother as she led her to the door.

"OK, Mama, I'll wear the lipstick."

"And the eye shadow?"

"And the eyeshadow." Sam nodded.

"And you'll shave your legs?" Vittoria produced a packet of lady shaves from the bag.

"MAMA. Go, please." As soon as Vittoria was safely in her car and reversing out of the drive, Sam slammed the door and leaned her head against it. No doubt about it, her mother was a force of nature.

*

The piano plinking and jazz flute tooting filled the air and resonated off the plush red velvet couches. Sam felt underdressed in her, albeit, good jeans and black cashmere sweater. When she'd thought dinner, she hadn't anticipated somewhere so fancy. Luca was dressed in slacks, white shirt and a dinner jacket. She sat legs and arms crossed.

"So, jazz and tapas. Nice combination," she smiled.

"Yeah. This is my favourite place."

The conversation flowed as did the Merlot. She began to relax. He asked about her job, her family. He was an only child, as was she. A giant platter of food arrived: patatas bravas, chicken with chorizo, mini paella, garlic bread and prawns in their shells. She tried to eat with dignity and grace, but dropped chorizo on her jeans and dripped oil from the garlic bread all over them too. Luca laughed and told her not to worry, that there was nothing more attractive than a woman who liked her food. A little forward, Sam thought, but forgave him his mild cockiness.

As he polished off another bottle, minus the glass Sam had had from it, he became looser, a little less of a good listener, increasingly abrupt, cutting her off mid sentence and growing opinionated.

It was relatively early, nine thirty, when Sam yawned and made her excuses to leave. Staying out late with Luca might give him the wrong impression. He jumped up.

"I'll give you a ride home."

"Oh, no. No thank you. Should you be driving? You've had quite a lot to drink," Sam watched him sway slightly.

"I'm fine. I only had a few glasses. I've driven on more." His tone was vehement, forceful almost.

"All the same, I think it's best if I get a cab." Sam recoiled slightly as his face changed. The softness had hardened and his eyes were glassy

"No, no. I insist. Anyway, it's only down the road. I wouldn't see you in a cab when I'm driving right by your house."

He had insisted on picking her up for the date. She hadn't wanted him to know where she lived, but he'd been so adamant on the phone that she'd agreed to it.

As soon as they were in the car, Sam knew she had made a huge mistake. Luca swayed all over the road, broke a red light and failed to stop at a stop sign. Had she not been so close to home, she'd have made him stop and let her out. He pulled up to her curb, front wheels on the grass, back wheels diagonally on the road and cut off the engine. Sam looked at him, alarm beginning to flood her nervous system.

"So, it's early. Why don't I come in for a nightcap?" he slurred, leaning over toward her, his face illuminated by the dim light above the rearview mirror, sliding a hand up her thigh.

Sam pulled her leg away, wincing in disgust. "I don't think so, Luca. This was nice but I'm not looking for anything like that, right now. Thank you for dinner. Good night."

Luca's expression changed from jovial to anger.

"Who do you think you are, you fucking cock tease. What is it with you women? You play hard to get, then confess your undying love for me, yet you throw yourself at my best fucking friend. He was my fucking best man, you know." He was ranting incoherently to himself as Sam desperately tried to decide what to do.

She felt her meal rise into her throat. Her heart was beating furiously as she considered her options. Escape was the only one. She grabbed at the door handle, but Luca took her by the shoulders and pushed her into the back of the seat. She screamed as he tried to press his mouth to hers. The smell of his breath made her want to be sick: alcohol, garlic and vitriol. His previously pleasant face was pursed into an aggressive expression, like he hated her. Instinct took over and, grabbing her bag with one hand, she punched him in the crotch with the other. He crumpled and groaned.

"Fucking bitch," he spat and, as though in slow motion, Sam watched him ball his fist and braced herself as it came toward her, stinging and burning her cheek as it made contact, hard like a rock. In that second, she felt a warm trickle down her cheek and her lip tasted of metal and saltiness. She felt dizzy and lightness in her joints as adrenaline flooded her blood stream. It was fight or flight, now or never.

She gathered herself and threw her body at the door, just as it flew open. Her foot was entangled in the strap of her bag, causing her to fall awkwardly out. The back of her head stung as it made contact with an ill-placed fire hydrant and the last thing she remembered was the roar of the engine and the screech of tyres as Luca sped down the road.

CHAPTER 7

The twister was baring down on her, just as Luca was pummelling her like a punching bag. Bobby flew out of the tornado, grabbed Luca and tossed him behind like a superhero. The winds picked him up and threw him until she heard his body hit the ground and crunch like a packet of potato chips. Then Jonah was with her, holding her hand, telling her it was OK and pulling on her arm. Her mother's and Paul's voices came to her from a distance. They sounded angry or concerned. She wasn't sure which, maybe both. They were the sound track to the fog that was all around her.

"Jo..... Jonah," she whimpered as the scene changed. The cloud, Bobby and Luca's broken body disappeared, replaced by white. Lots of white. White ceiling tiles, really bright white strip lights. She felt a tremendous weight pressing down on her body and the back of her head thumped as blood rushed into it. She groaned. Her eyes began to focus, slowly. The tiles became more defined, sharp enough for her to make out the lines between them. Blinking in the stinging light, she moved her gaze down the wall where there were sockets and switches. There was a curtain rail too. The weight became heavier on her body as she felt herself occupy its space again. Her eyes were focused now and she shifted, feeling rough, crisp fabric under her hands.

"Sam?"

"Jonah? Did you see that tornado?" Her voice was no more than a croak as his face came into view. He looked upset, concerned.

89

Her head began to feel foggy again. Her eyelids felt heavy so she allowed them to close.

"What? Sam. You're in hospital."

She opened her eyes. Her head throbbed, her cheek stung. Jonah. He was sitting beside her, feeling his hand along the bed towards her shoulder. He patted along her arm, as if making sure she was in one piece.

"What's going on?" she mumbled, her throat feeling dry.

"You're in hospital, Sam."

Then, there was more movement as a doctor and two nurses came in. The former shone a light in her eyes, had her follow his finger as he waved it in front of her face, pulled out a stethoscope and listened to her chest. She could hear convulsive sobs somewhere in the room which she recognised as her mother's and then she heard Paul shushing her.

"Sam, my name is Doctor Jameson. You are in hospital. You had a fall and banged your head. We've done a CT scan and you're going to be fine, it's just a concussion."

"But Luca, he......." The memory of his attack on her flooded her mind and she broke into tears. Vittoria rushed to her side.

"It's all my fault, bambina. That terrible boy attacked you. Your neighbour, Mr. Kaplinski saw everything and rang the police. They arrested Luca. I am so sorry, Samia. You should never have listened to me......" Paul took Vittoria gently by the shoulders and brought her out of the room.

"Jonah..." Sam reached out to him. Her voice was shaky and meek.

"Shush, you just rest." It hurt to move her head but she craned to look at him. He was sitting in the bedside chair, a troubled expression on his face. She closed her eyes but the image of Luca's fist coming for her was persistent. She moved to speak again but a pain shot through her head and she flinched. Jonah came to her side and tried to comfort her with clichés but she felt anything but all right.

"I thought he was going to ...."

"I know. Shush now. You got away. That's the main thing."

"The bastard hit me." Her voice was pained, laced with anger and shock, causing her to crumple into tears once again.

"Hey, hey, hey. It's OK, Sam. Please don't cry." Having dispatched Vittoria to the canteen to get a cup of tea and to try to calm down, Paul was with her now, dispensing his own brand of caring, cooing comfort at her. He handed her a tissue and she winced as it hit off the centre of pain on her cheek.

"What did he do to my face?"

"It's just a bruise and a little gash, that's all. You didn't even need stitches. You managed to get away from him," Paul reassured.

"Where is he now?"

"He's in custody. The police are dealing with him under charges of driving under the influence, assault and dangerous driving. You don't have to worry about him."

"But why are you here? How did you know?"

"The police looked at the last call you made on your phone. It was Jonah's number so they called him and he called me."

"When can I go home?"

"Doc says tomorrow, all going well. They just want to keep you in overnight for observation. You were out cold for about four hours. You need to rest now. Your mom is going to stay with you. We'll call back to see you tomorrow." Paul squeezed her hand and Jonah muttered a passing goodbye as they left the room.

Feeling dopey and fuzzy on medication, Sam slipped back to sleep and slept the entire night. She was stronger on waking the next morning. The sting in her face had dulled. The throbbing pain in the back of her head and the associated lump were still there but the nurse informed her that they'd send her home with painkillers.

Vittoria was still apologising through tears when Paul arrived. Sam felt a pang of disappointment that Jonah wasn't with him.

"Hey, look at you! You look much better."

She knew he was lying. She'd begged her mother to give her a mirror before he'd arrived and gasped as she stared into the little compact, taking in the wound on her cheek. It was a large purple and red blob, ironically the shape of a misshapen heart, with a cut right at the top of her cheekbone. Vittoria assured her that the doctor said it would heal.

Climbing out of Paul's truck outside her house an hour later, she caught sight of the fire hydrant. Bile rose in her throat. Vittoria took her by the arm and pulled her inside, not wanting to have her upset. After filling her daughter with meatball marinara and pasta, she joined her on the couch.

"Samia, I just want to say...."

"Mama, it's OK. Please stop apologising. You weren't to know that Luca was like that. I shouldn't have gone out with him. It's too soon."

"I should have listened to you, Samia."

"Please stop, Mama. I'm fine. It was not your fault. He's just an animal."

The phone rang, a welcome interruption.

"Hello?"

"Sam. It's Jonah. I just wanted to ask how you were." He was curt and succinct.

"I'm doing fine, thank you. Feeling much better. The pain killers are giving me a nice buzz too." She gave a little laugh, but he remained silent.

"About the conference. I'm going to cancel it. You won't be able for it."

The conference. She had completely forgotten. But it wasn't for four days.

"No, don't cancel. I'm much better and will be even better by then. Please don't worry."

"Well, let's leave it for now and if you don't feel up to it come Thursday, then I can cancel."

"Perfect. Thanks for calling."

"Sam, I.. I....... are you sure you're OK?" he stuttered.

"Honestly. Nothing I can't handle."

"According to the police, you handled him pretty well. Let's just say, that guy won't be having kids any time soon." Jonah chuckled, giving Sam some comfort. He'd seemed so pent up, it was nice to hear him cheer up, if only slightly. "So, I'll call you Thursday and we can assess how you are then."

"OK, and Jonah, thanks."

*

Friday came and saw Sam packing, primping and preening as well as shaving and conditioning. After the last few days of having Vittoria hovering over her, it was nice to be on her own again and have the privacy to get back to her normal self. Luca was due in court sometime in the coming weeks and she was relieved when the policewoman who had called two days previously told her she wouldn't have to testify. She was feeling positive. Sure, Luca had been a monster and put her in hospital, but it also gave her a sense of being able to look after herself. Perhaps she was stronger than she gave herself credit for. She closed the suitcase and laid her plastic wrapped gown on top of it. She had to leave soon if she was to collect Jonah and make the flight on time. She checked her face in the mirror. The swelling was gone and the bruise almost invisible, thanks to good healing and Yves Saint Laurent concealer.

Navigating an airport was complicated even for a person with twenty-twenty vision, and Jonah became frustrated and stressed at the long line for check-in. His face was red, his brow damp with sweat and he shifted from foot to foot as they waited for the line to dwindle down. Every so often he would reach out to find Sam, who was always within reach.

"I'm not going anywhere, Jonah." This annoyed him and he huffed and puffed about being fine. She tried to imagine how overwhelming it must be for him to be out of his comfort zone and into a crowded, hot, clammy airport and not be able to see what was going on around him. Eventually they were checked in and were allowed priority boarding. He seemed to calm down once seated on the plane but remained quiet for most of the journey.

The Oasis Resort, the hotel hosting the conference, was enormous. A sweeping staircase coiled around the reception desk as they were jauntily greeted by the whiter than white toothed receptionist.

She handed Sam two keys, one for room 408 and one for 515.

"I think there's a mistake here. We booked adjacent rooms," she said.

The receptionist perused the computer screen for a moment.

"Are you sure? These are the rooms that reservations have allocated you."

"No. When the booking was made, it was specified that we would need adjacent rooms. Your reservations department has obviously made a mistake. You need to rectify it and give us the rooms we asked for." Jonah's cheeks were beginning to turn the colour of a boiled lobster.

"I'm afraid that's not possible. The closest I can get you both is about seven doors down."

"That's not good enough." The anger was rising in Jonah. He was feeling particularly vulnerable and this wasn't good news. "Do something." The receptionist took a sullen stance at Jonah's rudeness.

"One second." Sam smiled at the receptionist and led Jonah to one of the armchairs that sat around a fireplace. "Stay here for a second. I'll sort this out." His face was now purple.

"Listen, can't you sort something out for him. He's visually impaired and needs assistance. There must be something you can do." She forced a smile again to soften the girl who had suddenly turned from sickly sweet, to looking like she couldn't care less, far removed from her sunny disposition on their arrival. She instructed Sam to wait and she'd consult her manager.

"Don't do that to me, Sam." Jonah was angry still when she rejoined him at the couch. "Don't make me feel like a child."

"I didn't treat you like a child, although, now you're acting like one. You were getting mad and that wasn't going to get us anywhere. Sometimes softly, softly is the way to go."

"Just don't treat me like I'm disabled, OK?"

"It wasn't like that. You're being overly sensitive."

"Excuse me, Miss Di Matteo." Smiley receptionist was back, evidently because her manager was looking over her shoulder. She left Jonah to seethe and walked back to the reception desk. Everything was sorted out and they had switched some things around to get them adjacent rooms. The manager apologised profusely and promised that the reservations department's mistake would be noted.

Satisfied, Sam took Jonah by the elbow, who was beginning to calm down and brought him to the elevator.

They came to his room first. Sam hung his tuxedo on the bathroom hook and set his case on the case rack, opening it to save him having to fiddle with it later. Taking his hand, she led him around the room, showing him where his case was, the bed, the bathroom and his tux for the conference dinner tomorrow night.

"Do you need help with anything else?"

"No, I'm fine. What time is it now?"

"Six o'clock," she replied.

"Are you hungry? I could eat a whale."

"I'm not sure if they serve whale here, but just let me freshen up and we'll go down for a bite to eat."

Her room was the mirror of his: six foot bed, cream walls, Italian marble tiles and plush aubergine and silver bedding. It was beautiful and she would have loved to have gotten into bed for an hour to snooze, but Hungry Jonah made regular Grumpy Jonah seem like a kitten.

Slipping into fresh jeans and a satin blouse, she ruffled her hair, freshened her make-up and had a good spritz of *Daisy*. The hotel wasn't busy, as the conference wasn't starting until tomorrow, so the restaurant was quiet. Sam appreciated the simplicity in its muted decor and clean white table clothes and napkins. They ordered pasta and balancing on his forearms, Jonah leaned towards her.

"So, how've you liked chasing with us so far?"

"I've loved it. I really have."

"Even though I can be a grumpy asshole?"

"Your words, not mine."

"So you think I'm a grumpy asshole?" He was smiling at the corners of his mouth, while holding the glass to his lips.

"You're passionate and, let's just say, easily frustrated."

"That's probably the nicest thing anyone's ever said to me. So how have you been since, you know?"

"Oh, fine. I'm just trying not to dwell on it."

"I think it's admirable the way you're dealing with it."

"So, what do you want to do after dinner? Go for a drink? Or *Lost in Translation* is on the hotel TV?"

"Would you mind if I turn in? Airports kind of exhaust me."

Sam looked at her watch. Eight thirty. Maybe an early night would do her good too. She gestured to the waiter for the bill and stood, taking Jonah by the elbow.

"Just knock if you want anything, Jonah. I'm next door."

"OK. Thanks. Goodnight."

Climbing into her warm pyjamas, Sam jumped into bed, snuggling into the blankets. Catching a glimpse of her washed, make up-less face in the mirror, the bruise, although fading, was more obvious than when she had it artfully covered in concealer. To her dismay, her heart began to beat quicker. Faster and faster the beats came, like it would beat out of her chest. She could feel the blood pressure rising, evident in the residual pain in her head, throbbing like a bass drum. The walls of the room began to close in, the ceiling lowered menacingly. Her breathing became shallow and laboured, and she began to pant. These symptoms were all too familiar to her. She was having a panic attack.

She desperately tried to remember what her therapist had told her: was it, breath in for seven, out for eleven or vice versa? She sat back on the bed to concentrate on her breathing and to let the attack wash over her.

"I am in control of my feelings. Do what you have to do to me, panic because I own you and you can't hurt me." Re-plays of the night Luca had attacked her ran fast forward through her mind: the way his face had contorted from friendly to angry in a split second, how he'd been so insistent on driving her, how his fist had met her cheekbone, how she'd thought he was going to force himself upon her. She repeated the mantra over and over, hoping it would slow her heart rate, but it didn't. Her chest became constricted and sore; her vision tunnelled and she felt herself become faint. Placing her head between her legs, the woozy feeling passed but the other symptoms were relentless. She couldn't be alone. She was worried she'd pass out and be found by hotel staff unconscious on the floor the next day. It could happen. She knew enough to know she shouldn't be on her own.

Knock, knock. "Jonah?" She tried to keep her voice steady.

"Come in, it's open," came Jonah's sleepy reply. "Sam, are you OK?"

"No. I think I'm having a panic attack." Her breaths were short and rapid.

"Shit, OK. It's OK. Sit down here on the bed." He jumped up, not sure where she was, but when he felt her sink onto the bed, he felt his way to be beside her. Turning her body towards him, he took her by the shoulders.

"Sam, you are safe. You are with me and you are safe. That Bellotti asshole is not here and he cannot hurt you anymore. I want you to concentrate on your breathing. Breath in on my count of seven and out for eleven. Can you do that for me?"

Sam looked into his tired face, his eyes looking so intently at her that she could swear he could see her, and nodded. She closed her eyes and listened to him count. All she could see was Luca's face: the anger, hate and resentment he felt for women. His wife must have really fucked him up. It overwhelmed her and she crumpled into a sobbing heap. Jonah wrapped his arms around her and let her sob.

"You're safe, Sam. Let it all out. That's it."

Eventually, after twenty minutes of crying into his chest, she began to relax. Her breathing and heart regulated and the haze of anxiety began to lift. She realised how safe she felt, in Jonah's arms, so safe that a tornado could rip through the hotel right at that very moment, or Luca could come barging in and she would be perfectly safe in his arms: not a hair would be ruffled nor a fleck of skin injured.

"I'm sorry. Oh god, I'm mortified," she sniffled and wiped her nose on her pyjama sleeve.

"Please, don't apologise. I'm used to dealing with panic attacks. I used to have them myself after the accident."

She looked up in surprise. Jonah had panic attacks too?

"Wow. Well, thank you. You really calmed me down."

"I thought you'd said you were fine after what happened? I should've cancelled." He shook his head.

"I thought I was. I was trying not to think about it. I guess I just got overwhelmed what with being away from home and being on my own here."

"Hey. You're not on your own. I'm here. And if you feel like that again, you tell me. I can help."

"Thanks. I should let you get back to sleep."

"You sure you're going to be OK?"

"Yes. Goodnight." In a way, she wished she could stay with him. She'd feel safer. But she needed to face her demons by herself. Jonah said goodnight and Sam let herself out, getting into her own bed and falling straight to sleep, purged of her anxiety and visions of Luca.

The next morning, after sharing breakfast together and taking in the first lecture of the conference, Sam felt uplifted. She'd gotten through the night, sleeping like a log and it helped her feel human again. Jonah was in good form too, which made being around him pleasant. At lunchtime, he suggested a walk around the grounds for some fresh air and they walked in the scorching sun.

"You've been a real asset to the team, Sam. I want you to know that. Paul and I like having you around."

Grateful for once that he was blind, she didn't have to fight the pink that was crossing her face.

"Thanks. I must admit, I'm enjoying it. Bobby always wanted to chase so in a way, I feel I'm fulfilling something for him."

Jonah nodded without commenting. The birds were chattering over their heads as they walked through the wood.

"You must miss him."

She looked up at him, feeling tears smart but managed to hold them back.

"Yes. But I think it's getting a little easier to live without him. I don't think I'll ever not miss him. Chasing with you guys has helped me realise that life goes on and that I can be fine on my own. Obviously some days are better than others but I think I'm getting there."

"That's good. You know, Paul and I are there for you whenever you need it. I like to think we're friends. Spending as much time together as we do, if we haven't killed each other by now, then it's safe to say we can get along. I mean it though, if you need me, or Paul, all you have to do is shout, yeah?" He touched her arm, so lightly that she almost doubted she'd felt it.

"Thanks, Jonah, that means a lot."

"While we're on the subject of thanks. I just want to thank you for coming with me. I couldn't be here if it weren't for your help. And I'm...... I'm enjoying spending time with you."

Sam snapped her gaze to him, waiting for him to laugh or tell her he was joking. She waited, but he said nothing more. Her stomach jumped with a flutter of something. Was it excitement? Something else?

"We'd better go back. I've to practice my lecture before I get ready." Feeling self-conscious, she took his elbow and they walked back.

Back at the hotel, they parted ways at their room doors and agreed to meet in an hour for Jonah's keynote speech and dinner afterwards.

*

An hour later, she was twisting and turning in front of the mirror, admiring herself. She hadn't done a bad job. Her navy blue satin dress draped itself over her figure, a line of crystals from her neckline down her front highlighted the shape of her breasts. Her hair was caught up leaving little tendrils hanging down over her face and shoulders, eyes smokey, highlighting their greenness, bruise invisible. Inhaling deeply, she grabbed her clutch bag and pulled the door behind her. When Jonah opened his door moments later, she stood open mouthed, her eyes so wide that they started to sting. He looked like Don Draper - his hair slicked back from his face. He filled the tuxedo with his innate masculinity, as it hugged the tone of his arms and legs, the white shirt, crisp and clean, framed his face that was clean shaven and contoured with tan.

"You there, Sam?"

"Yeh huh," was all she managed to say.

"What's wrong? Have I put the wrong jacket on or something? Is my hair weird?"

"No.... nooo. You look.... great."

"Cool. Not like the time Paul packed the wrong suit for me and I ended up wearing a brown plaid suit for a dinner with some very respected college deans."

Instead of taking her arm, he reached out and took her hand. She inhaled sharply.

"You OK?" he asked, concerned.

"Yes. Come on or we'll be late." His hand felt like lead as it gripped hers tightly and she became aware that her palm was beginning to sweat. She processed the meaning of it over and over in her head, all the while trying to make herself seem nonchalant. He'd never held her hand before. It was always her leading him by the arm or elbow. This was new.

The room was packed when they arrived. Jonah gripped her hand tighter as she led him to the podium. A round of applause went up as the MC announced him. Sam bowed out discretely and sat in a free chair by the wall, close enough so she could get him after the speech, absentmindedly rubbing her hand that he had held onto so tightly. He spoke for an hour, articulate and interesting, throwing in the odd joke. The audience loved him. He was charismatic, his eyes lighting up when he spoke of the love of his life: tornadoes, and his passion was evident. She was in awe of him. It was especially courageous to suffer such a horrific injury, and still go back to storm chasing. Just being around storms was enough for him, despite what they had done to him.

He received a standing ovation and Sam rushed up to help him down. She sat him beside her and whispered into his ear that the audience had stood for him. He flushed and smiled. They listened to another hour of speakers

Finally, it was time for dinner. The starter of mushroom and truffle soup was divine and she had to restrain herself from inhaling it. Then on to fillet of beef in a whiskey sauce, followed by tiramisu. It wasn't a patch on her mother's recipe, but it was well known that only a true Italian could make tiramisu. Feeling slightly tipsy, she excused herself to go to the bathroom. While in the stall, she overheard some middle aged women talking about Jonah. They were complimentary and she smiled smugly, knowing that she was here with him, even though it may be in a professional capacity, it was her, not them or anyone else.

When she came out from the cubicle, they stopped talking, recognising her as being the girl who was with the object of their affectionate gossip.

"Aren't you Jonah Mason's wife?" The woman was stockily-built, dressed head to toe in cerise pink and less than discretely, she surveyed Sam's left hand, seeing her wedding band.

"Oh. No, we're not married. I'm his colleague." Sam unconsciously twirled the band around her ring finger.

"Really? How can you resist a man like that? He's terribly handsome and isn't he wonderful to have overcome such a terrible accident and to get on with his life."

She hastily agreed with them while washing her hands and rushed out of the restroom. She hated to leave Jonah too long but he had been fine in her absence, being accosted by his peers while he sipped on champagne. He introduced them to her as being friends from college and after chatting and reminiscing for another few moments, they discreetly left.

"So, it seems you have some admirers." She regaled the gossiping of the women in the bathroom.

"Really? Well, when you look like this......! Anyway, there's only one woman's opinion I'm interested in."

"Who's that?

"You."

"Huh?"

She was furnished with no further explanation as an amplified voice filled the room. Up at the podium, the MC from Jonah's keynote speech was in the midst of a monologue on the history of the conference and the audience cheered and clapped as he mentioned Jonah, pointing towards their table. Sam forced a feeble smile as the spotlight hit them. Jonah reached out a hand towards her. He pulled her chair closer, found her knee and rested his palm on it, squeezing just a little. The touch was a cosmic connection. The power from it like a pulsar, feeding her energy, flowing through her veins. She sat stiff and awkward, not sure whether to respond. She chose to sit motionless. While the MC prattled on for another twenty minutes, Sam felt like exploding. She was close to running on stage, telling him to shut up and taking his microphone off him when he finally wound the speech up.

"Hey, is there a dance floor here?" Jonah whispered in her ear as the MC finally left the stage and the audience chatter was once again dominant.

"No. Why?"

"Because I feel like dancing. Come on, there must be some room somewhere."

"There's some space between our table and the wall. Are you mad?"

"Come on."

"But there's no music."

"Shush. Listen."

He took her hand and gingerly made his way around the table. "Here?" he asked and she confirmed. Sam hadn't noticed the background music. As she strained to hear, she recognised Norah Jones' velvety voice singing *Come Away With Me*. Jonah took her left hand in his right hand and wrapped his other arm around her waist.

"I love this song," he whispered into her ear as he led her around the make shift dance floor. He looked down at her and she could swear he was looking straight into her eyes. Nobody noticed them, bar one or two who gave them admiring glances as they danced, slowly in the dark, discreet corner of the restaurant. Their eyes locked, like he could see into her soul, their bodies close.

"This dress is amazing," he said in a whisper, as he ran his hand down her satin draped waist. "You have an incredible body." She didn't say a word, just continued to stare into his vacant eyes. She desperately wanted to touch his lips with hers and as if reading her mind, he bent his head down, lifted her chin with his hand and kissed her with the lightest of touches. He tasted heavenly, sweet champagne flavouring his lips, the taste making her feel drunk and dizzy. Her head swam in the heady aroma of his aftershave. She pushed harder into him, afraid that if he let her go, she would collapse in a heap on the floor. He read her sign and pulled her closer. She felt that safe feeling again. His hips pressed into her and her limbs weakened. He released her lips and kissed her on the forehead. Leaning his head down to smell her hair, he sighed and she felt him press harder.

"Can you take me to my room?" he asked quietly, slowly, seductively into her ear, his deep voice resonating off her eardrum like a subwoofer.

They said goodbye to no one, just left, walking in silence, hand in hand up the stairs as there was a queue for the elevator. This time, she wasn't leading him, he was taking her, striding purposefully up the steps like he could see each one.

"Here you go." She placed his hand on the fob for the key card.

"Would you like to come in for a drink?" His voice was like she'd never heard it before: a soft, alluring barotone. Her heart and loins were screaming 'YESSS' but her better judgement kicked in and she declined.

"I'd better not. We're both tired." She wanted him more than anything, was aching for him but now that he was offering it to her, she felt a responsibility to restrain herself. She had to be sensible. They worked together and this would complicate things. Bobby kept flashing into her head, confusion wrapped itself around her like a weed.

"Oh. OK," he said icily, disappointment clouded his face, rang in his voice.

"Goodnight, Jonah."

"Yeah, fine. Night." He closed the door. Was she insane? No, she'd made the right decision. There was no point making things complicated. He was mad now, but he'd just have to get over it.

At one point, before she took her dress off, she was tempted to change her mind and knock on his door, but regaining control of her hormones, she slipped the dress off, leaving her in nothing but black lace panties and matching bra. The bed was warm and soft. Wrapping herself in the duvet like a caterpillar making a chrysalis, she snuggled deep into the fabric in an effort to cool the residual heat from the fire left in her by Jonah. The man did something to her that she couldn't comprehend. She wanted him badly, craving a touch or a kiss from him but it would all be tainted by the ever present guilt she felt over Bobby. Jonah was everything Bobby hadn't been and that was both good and bad. She berated herself for comparing them. It wasn't healthy.

An hour later, she was still tossing and turning, sleep evading her like a bold child slipping free from its parent's grip. All she could think of was how Jonah had smelled, how tight his arms had felt beneath her hands as she steadied herself while they danced, how he'd breathed whispers into her ear and the heat from that breath. Was refusing him the right thing to do? What would Bobby think? She cursed herself. Bobby wasn't here anymore. She was a grown woman and she had to step out of his shadow. But with Jonah? Not only was he her boss, but he was gruff, cantankerous and surly. She'd let her guard down with a man only last week and look what he'd done to her. No, she did the right thing sending him to bed. Her life was complex enough as it was, sleeping with Jonah would send it into a spin completely.

She needed to stop the tornado of thoughts in her head, so fumbling for the remote control lost in the tousled sheets, she found it and flicked on the television, watching mindlessly as Tyra Banks critiqued waif like young girls on how not to walk down a catwalk. There were tears, tantrums and drama as the girls fought and bitched. Her mind suitably numbed, she turned off the TV, closing her eyes in the hope sleep would envelope her but the thoughts crept back in, tormenting her.

Thinking tea would help she rose from the tossed bed and flicked on the kettle. Steam filled the room and the little kettle boiled and bubbled, making her yawn. She flipped through the selection of herbal tea bags, plucking out a sachet of camomile. The tea was soothing: she understood why people resorted to it in times of stress and trauma. She sat cross legged on the edge of the bed, hot cup in hand, blowing on the little whirls of steam that were creeping out of the cup and up into the air before her face, like mini vortices. She looked at her reflection in the mirror. She was pale with circles of exhaustion under her eyes. She wondered if Jonah was awake, tried to imagine if he was, was he lying naked, thinking about her? Or was he fast asleep, annoyed at her rebuff? Perhaps he was indifferent? She shook her head and scolded herself for thinking such things. Draining the cup, she climbed back into bed, willing sleep to come.

Just as she was drifting off, assured that turning Jonah down was the right thing, there was a light knock on the door. Groaning, she got up and made for a towel to drape around her almost naked body, but peeping through the hole, she saw it was Jonah and left the towel where it was. When she opened the door, he was standing, arm stretched above his head, leaning on the doorframe, head down. He was still wearing his tux but the bow tie had been removed and the top button of his shirt was open.

"You OK?" she asked, mapping the pained, troubled expression on his face.

"No." He reached out to find her, his fingers brushing her clavicle and ran his hand down her arm, pulling her to him. Stepping into the room, he closed the door and turned her, pressing her up against it, kissing her differently this time: like he wanted to taste every drop of her, absorb himself into her body.

The image of Luca trying to kiss her flashed into her mind. She tried to banish it, but it wouldn't abate. She put her hands on his chest and pushed him away. He looked down in disappointment.

"Jonah, I can't..... it's too hard. It's too soon, after Luca and ....."

107

"Sam, I'm not that other shithead. It's me. You trust me, don't you?" She nodded her head, child-like. "I'd never hurt you and you don't have to do anything you don't want to. But you're safe with me. You feel that, I know you do."

She couldn't disagree. She'd never felt as invulnerable as she did when she was with Jonah. She battled her resolve and reached up to kiss him. Their mouths moved in unison, tongues entwined, dancing. He shrugged off his jacket, not disconnecting from her at all, owning her, groaning as he ran his hands down her naked flesh and catching the top of her briefs. She grabbed behind his neck, pulling him closer to her. She felt every inch of his longing pressing into her, his hands were in her hair and she was completely surrendered to him. Running her hands down his torso, she opened his trousers and moved back up to attack his shirt buttons. One was tricky and she cursed, fumbling with it for a moment. He groaned again, taking his hands from her hair and ripping the shirt off himself. She swooned like a schoolgirl as the buttons clattered like hailstones onto the tiled floor, while the shirt floated down, revealing his toned torso. He stood up straight and took her hand, walking backwards as he led her to the bed, narrowly missing the dressing table but she pulled him out of the way. He lowered her onto the bed, and lay beside her, supporting himself on one arm and running the other hand down from her chin in a line down to her panties. She writhed, wanting him to touch her everywhere. He kissed all over her breasts and torso, slowly and teasingly making his way down until she gasped, pleasurable pulses radiating around her body. He kissed lower, lightly, making her squirm.

"Oh god, Jonah," she panted as he took her almost to the brink and let her hang. Suddenly he was inside her, making her feel absolute. He moved slowly, biting her earlobe, whispering into her ear: how sexy she was, how much he wanted her. They came together, bodies blended and lay entwined for a while before separating.

Lying next to her, he pulled her deftly on top of him so that she was lying on his chest. She ran her finger intricately down his chest hair, twirling some strands as she went and delighted in running her palm over his abs. She planted feather touch kisses on his pecs, then shoulders and down his arm, stopping at the tornado tattoo, which she traced with her tongue.

He buried his face in her hair, inhaling and groaning as the scent of her sent shivers down his spine.

"The first time I met you, that was the first thing I could smell. Your shampoo." She took his bottom lip in her mouth, so she could taste his words and vowed to herself that she would never change her brand of hair care. "It was the second thing that made me want you."

"What was the first?"

"Your voice. When you called me that day to apply for the job, I just thought you had the sexiest voice."

"Oh? You didn't exactly sound impressed, if I remember correctly."

"Sam, I have wanted you since that first day. You do something to me. You ignite my senses, make me see things that I can't see, give my life colour again. When I thought you were hurt that day in the graveyard, I couldn't think straight. I knew I had to find you. I was beside myself. I've never been so happy as I was when I heard you say my name. I thought you were dead or hurt really badly. And then when that bastard did what he did to you. I swear, if I could see, I'd have gotten into a car, found him and pulverised him."

Sam gazed at him in wonder. He was so animated, just like he'd been when speaking to the audience about wind vortices and suck zones. She had no idea he'd felt that strongly.

"Did you have an ulterior motive for bringing me here instead of Paul?" She scanned his face for a flicker of dishonesty as he chuckled.

"Of course! Plus, he's not as good a kisser as you."

She slapped him on the chest before pulling herself up so they were face to face.

"Kiss me Sam," he begged and she teased him for a minute, touching her lips off his before pulling away. He moaned as he lifted his head to reach her. She relented and gave him a kiss that made him groan her name. She was in charge now and took him into her once again, their bodies melding together like a potter's hands and clay, like they were made to fit, moving until he began to breathe heavily, losing control. He called her name and arched his back under her as he surrendered to her. 'Jesus Christ,' he muttered under his breath.

"Why does this feel so right?" She whispered into his ear, chewing his earlobe between words, as his breathing regulated once again, lying with her, side by side.

"Because it is." He turned to her, took her face in his hands and kissed her. Her eyes closed, head swimming in a sea of Jonah. She peeled away from him and lay staring at the shadows on the ceiling.

"Jonah?"

"Yes?"

"What do you miss being able to see most?"

After a lengthy silence, Sam began to regret being so forward and worried she'd overstepped the mark. Finally, he took a deep breath.

"When I was a kid right the way up until my teenage years, we used to vacation in Vermont. There was this lake behind the house. My favourite thing was to get up in the middle of the night and sneak downstairs. I'd throw a blanket around my shoulders and sit out on the jetty. It would be freezing but worth it to feel the peace and serenity. The sight I'll always remember and the one I miss most is the path cut by the moon over the water. It was like this silver road that I'd imagine walking over and it taking me somewhere amazing. The lake would ripple under its glow and in that moment, it felt like the world was a wonderful, beautiful place and everything was going to be all right."

He sighed sadly.

"If I had one wish in the whole world, it would be to give you back your sight for one night and I'd bring you back to Vermont."

"Or, you could just wish for my sight to come back for good."

Sam laughed, embarrassed at her frivolousness. "Of course."

"Hey," he turned to face her, "that was really sweet of you. And it would be the most amazing night ever."

"I wish you could see me."

"I can." He ran his fingers down her cheek, around her chin, over her eyes and forehead, running them through her hair and down her back. "And you're so beautiful." His touch was like a trail of electricity, firing every synapse he made contact with. She imagined that everywhere his finger traced, left a track of silvery blue light in its wake, like his moon lit lake. Their noses touched and he looked into her eyes again, holding the one sided stare for an age. They slept like that: bodies facing, stomachs touching, arms and legs entwined.

CHAPTER 8

"Morning, beautiful." Jonah stroked her face as she stirred. Confusion reigned as she squinted in the dim morning light, taking in the hotel room, and Jonah, shrouded in nothing but sunlight. It had been well over a year since she'd woken up to company and it made her feel slightly nervous and self-conscious, as the memory of the previous night's revelries came flooding back.

"Hi," she croaked. "You awake long?"

"No. Just woke up. I think it's about nine, is it?"

Her watch told her he was almost right: just after eight thirty. "How do you know?"

"I can tell by how bright the sun is. I can distinguish between different strengths of light." Yawning, he stretched his contoured body and she couldn't help but ogle. His blindness had its advantages. She could gawk at him as much as she wanted without being caught. He rose and made his way tentatively to the bathroom, finding it with ease, only having to put his hand out twice. She watched him move, his lithe body contorting as he stretched along the way. He was gorgeous. She'd thought he was good looking when she met him first but she had no idea that body was hiding under his T-shirts and baggy combats. Plus, his cranky attitude took the shine off his looks most of the time. She had seen an entirely new Jonah: tender, passionate and very, very hot. He climbed back into bed beside her and pulled her onto his chest.

"What are you doing?" he asked.

"Looking at you. Since when did you have this ridiculous body?"

"My sister and her husband have a gym at the back of the house, so I work out most evenings. Need to be fit for chasing, you know?"

"You're certainly toned."

He laughed and her head bobbed up and down, chin nestled in the concave between his pecs.

"You're making me blush. Come up here where I can *see* you properly." She climbed up his body and lay on him, nose to nose. He kissed her cheeks, then her ears, then neck until she was breathless with longing.

"What's the plan for today?" Sam asked, nibbling his ear between syllables.

"Languish in this bed with you and eat fruit off your body."

"Oh, now that does sound like a plan. Shall I order room service?"

Sam jumped up and finding the phone, rang down for a fruit platter, some croissants and coffee. He was true to his promise and ate strawberries and melon off many parts of her. After fooling around, they devoured the pastries and coffee. They weren't flying home until the next morning, so had all day to be together.

"So now that we've done that, what's next? Don't you have some lectures today?"

"Yeah, but I'm not speaking. I was just going to attend. Now let me see.... do I go to a lecture about measuring the updrafts of a storm system or do I stay here with this wanton goddess?" He moved his hands up and down, weighing up his options.

"Actually, I wouldn't mind hearing about measuring updrafts."

He aimed a pillow at her general direction and missed.

"Ha! I'm going for a shower."

"Me too. Could you show me where it is."

"You know well where it is. I'm not falling for that."

Turning her onto her back, he kissed her on the lips, pressing himself into her, then jumped up and led her into the bathroom, stubbing his toe off the bed. 'Shit,' he exclaimed, hopping around on his good foot, holding the injured one. She stopped him midway there and kissed him feverishly to take his mind off the pain.

"Better?"

"Yes, actually! That's amazing."

His vulnerability caused a flash of guilt in her mind as she remembered the scene she'd made in the restaurant after he'd spilled his wine.

"Jonah, I'm sorry about the other day, you know, at the restaurant. We should have left. It's just, I didn't know what else to do. I'm sorry if I embarrassed you. I don't understand how you manage. I mean, if you're not with Paul, how do you find your way about?"

"Most places have a special needs bathroom, and if not, I wait until I get home or back to my hotel room. Paul is with me most of the time anyway. I did have a stranger help one day when I was with Bella. She brought me to the door and asked this guy to lead me in, which he very helpfully did, but then stole my cell phone. So don't worry, you did the right thing and please, don't apologise. Anyway, it wasn't all bad."

"What do you mean?"

He pulled her to him and with his lips barely touching hers, ran his finger-tips gently down between her breasts. She closed her eyes to enhance the sensation. She shivered, eyes remaining closed, found his lips and kissed him hungrily as she led him to the shower.

"I need to shave. Could you find my razor, please?" he asked, drying himself afterwards with a fluffy white towel.

Kissing his cheek, she left the bathroom, wrapped herself in the white, waffle fabric robe provided by the hotel and slipped out and into his room, found his wash bag and returned without being caught in her state of wet, almost undress by any fellow residents. Jonah was wrapping a towel around his waist as she opened the bathroom door.

"Find them?"

"Yeah. I've an idea....Why don't I shave you?"

"Well, I don't know. I value my jugular."

"Oh, come on. I've a steady hand and it'll be sexy."

"OK, if you find a man bleeding to death sexy, then be my guest."

Sam pulled a chair in from the room and sat him on it. Standing between his opened legs, she lathered the heavily perfumed shaving foam in her hands, gently smeared it onto his face, dotting it onto the awkward places, avoiding his nostrils and lips. He looked a little terrified but succumbed to her gentle hand. She used to shave Bobby's face sometimes and he'd loved it. She tipped Jonah's head back and told him to be still. He closed his eyes, as she ran the razor gently down his cheek, wincing as it caught in a stubborn piece of stubble. He hadn't seemed to notice, so she continued. Long, gentle strokes down his face until she came to the awkward parts of his chin and neck. Eyes shut tightly, he flinched when the blade touched his Adam's Apple.

"You OK?"

"Yeah," he whispered. "It's nice." He grabbed her behind her thighs and pulled her closer to him. As she glided the blade in its final stroke, he ran a hand over his chin. "Pretty close. Thank you."

She washed the remaining blobs of white from his face and kissed his stubble free, smooth skin, tasting the bitter, soapy foam on her lips.

115

Afterwards, she fetched him fresh clothes from his room. As she was searching through his suitcase for underwear, she noticed his wallet on the floor. It must have fallen out when he'd gotten back to the room last night. It lay open and splayed. Inside was a photo of Jonah, dressed in a morning suit standing next to a woman in a wedding dress. Jonah was married? And why did he have a photo? Surely that was a bit pointless.

Not wanting to change his mood, she decided not to mention it. Having a photo was probably indicative of the fact that he had put it there before his accident. He'd never mentioned a wife and he lived with his sister so they were obviously long since divorced.

"Hey, what am I wearing? Don't put me in the clown suit."

"It's not a clown suit, it's another tuxedo, seeing as you looked so Bond-esque last night."

"Now I know you're lying, because I don't have another tux." He said, pulling the sweater on over his head and stepping into his briefs, then jeans. "Come on then, let's go see the sights!"

The hotel was a resort in the middle of nowhere. The nearest town was ten miles away, so they hadn't much choice but to take a walk around the grounds. Sam described each scene: the vast forest of oak trees and maples, the stream and the different types of flowers growing alongside it. They sat on a grassy bank, beside the stream, listening to it trickle along to a backing track of bird song.

"You see, you do something that no one has done for me in the last six years."

"And that is?"

"You describe things. Nobody really thinks to do that. It's not their fault, they just don't really understand. But you.....it's like you know how I feel. It's kind of lonely when everyone else is experiencing something you can't. I know I can feel in different ways, but it's nice to be able to build a picture."

She lifted his hand and held it to her lips: not kissing, just feeling the heat from it on her mouth, then un-wrapped the green silk scarf from her neck and put it into his hand.

"What is this?" He stroked it gently and held it to his nose, inhaling deeply, eyes closed, appreciating every layer of her scent.

"It's my scarf. I want you to put it on me."

He pulled his face in confusion, but clumsily found her and tried to tie it around her neck.

"Not on my neck, Jonah. Over my eyes."

"Oh." He tried again, finding her face with his featherlike touch and wrapped the scarf around her head, tying it at the back, trying not to catch her hair in the knot. "Is this some weird sex thing?"

She slapped him playfully on the arm, then took his hands from her head and held them to her, kissing his rough skinned knuckles.

"Now, tell me about where we are now," she whispered into his ear, as he shivered under the tickle of her breath on his earlobe.

"I don't need to tell you." Taking her by the hand, he pulled her to standing and began to take slow, measured steps.

"Careful now, this is literally the blind leading the blind," she joked but was a little worried they might be heading towards the stream. She was right, as he shook his shoes off and instructed her to do likewise. The grass was cold and soft on her feet, stray blades tickling between her toes as they walked tentatively streamwards. Every footstep was careful and given time. His toes searched first before he'd commit to a step, taking her with him. The grass gave way to pebbles and stones, which weren't pleasant to walk on. She winced as the little rocks dug into her feet. Feeling with her big toe, she leaned into him as she took her first step down into the cool, crisp water. They stood, millimeters apart, face to face and let the water wash over their feet, the stream bubbling and gurgling over this new interruption in its path. While it was freezing at first, her feet and ankles adjusted, suddenly feeling warm. She stumbled over a large stone but Jonah had a firm grip on her waist, catching and steadying her. They stood close, their toes touching. She could feel the heat from his toes under the water.

Then suddenly, her senses were jolted into life. She could hear more distinctly. The birdsong was louder, as was the trickle of the stream. She felt the sun heating her face and the intermittent breeze. She could feel his heart beating against her chest and the softness of his sweater against her bare arms. He leaned down and kissed her, pulling her hands up to his face for her to trace with her fingers. She did so, gently and carefully, feeling what he looked like. Her fingertips tingled as she plotted his jaw line, smooth now, thanks to her careful shaving, his soft lips, flinching under her ticklish touch, his eyelashes flickered as she ran her thumb over his eyelids. His intoxicating scent filled her nostrils and she tried to take big lungfuls to commit to memory. The world was still a beautiful place, even without being able to see it.

He went to take the scarf from her eyes but she pulled his hand away.

"No. Leave it. Let me stay in your world for a little longer."

She heard him choke back something in his throat as she led him back to the grassy bank, or at least where she thought it might be and lay him down. Easing herself down beside him, she rested her head on his chest. His breathing was irregular, like it was caught in his lungs, as they lay surrounded by the warmth and gentle noise of the day.

After some time, he cleared his throat and sat up, shaking his head as if to clear his mind, discarding the momentary lapse of manly composure. Sam wrapped the scarf around her neck again and they walked hand in hand in silence back to the hotel.

"I'm going to take a nap in my room, if you don't mind. Why don't you go get a massage or check out one of the lectures?" His voice was hoarse and flat.

118

"Um, yeah, sure." Sam was taken aback that he so blatantly wanted to be on his own. Was he embarrassed about sleeping with her. Did he regret it? Sure, they'd only known each other a month or so but still, they'd been getting on so well. Had it scared him off? "I'll be back in a while so. Have you got your cell phone in case you need me?"

"Yeah but it's OK. I'll be fine. Take your time," he muttered, opening the door of his room.

Her stomach sank as he lay down on the bed and said goodbye without as much as kissing her. She closed the door slowly behind her and took a deep breath. That man was like a tap, running hot and cold. They'd been inseparable not an hour ago. She wandered, dejected and deflated, down to reception and checked the lecture list. There was one starting now about new advancements in wind measuring instrumentation. Might be useful, she thought and made her way to the conference room. Leaving an hour later, armed with notes that she thought might be of interest to Paul and Jonah, she decided to run back up to the room to drop them off. Then she'd get a massage. It was tempting to check on Jonah, but she didn't want to wake him if he was sleeping, so she decided to leave it.

She should have been relaxed and chilled as the masseuse ran her hands over her tight muscles but she was the opposite. The knot in her lower back since Jonah had gone cold was resisting under the masseuse's forceful hands.

"You're very tense," she stated the obvious, trying her best to work the knot out but couldn't, leaving Sam to walk back to her room like John Wayne. She'd be sore in the morning. Again, she contemplated knocking on Jonah's door, but, pride prevented her. She threw herself onto her bed and stared at the ceiling. She'd leave him be. If he wanted her, he knew where she was. At five thirty, two hours later, he eventually came knocking.

"Want dinner?"

"Sure."

They walked, in silence, Sam holding his elbow, down to the restaurant. Once seated, the atmosphere between them was awkward and uneasy. Deciding she needed to break the tension, she began to talk about the lecture, the weather, current affairs while he threw her the odd 'yeah' and 'um hum.' Eventually, she felt like she was talking to a brick wall so after dessert, announced she was going back to her room for an early night.

"Do you want me to bring you up to your room or are you all right here for a while?"

"Oh. I thought we could go for a drink."

"What's the point? You've hardly said two words to me this evening."

He remained silent for a few moments, his expression pained, like he was trying to find a way to verbalise his thoughts.

"I'm sorry."

"Yeah, fine. Goodnight." Her chair scraped off the tiled floor as she stood.

"Sam, don't leave, please. Sit down and have a drink." He held his hand out to her which she ignored.

Reluctantly, she took him by the elbow and led him to a table in the bar where she ordered a bottle of Merlot.

"Maybe after this, we could go back to the room and you could read out those notes you got me."

"I'm tired, Jonah, I'll probably just go to bed."

"Sam, please don't be like this. I'm sorry. I'm just in a bad mood. I just..."

She cursed silently as the waiter interrupted Jonah's explanation and poured a taster for Sam. She agreed it was fine and watched him liberally pour the ruby liquid into the glasses. Thanking him as he left, she took Jonah's hand and placed the glass into it.

"Thank you."

"Don't knock it over this time," she said icily, taking an appreciative sip and sitting back as that first hit of alcohol filtered into her blood and made her feel delightfully fuzzy.

"So listen. As I said, I'm sorry. I just needed some time to myself today, you know? Lots of new things happening and I needed time to process. I feel.... I feel confused."

"What do you mean, new things?"

"You know, being with you."

"So was it a good or bad thing?"

"Oh good..... very good." He groaned and smiled. She wasn't buying it.

"Oh really? So how come when we came back to the room this afternoon, you completely shut down on me?"

He sat forward, took a deep breath and cleared his throat. "Is there anyone else here?"

She looked around, saw no one except the barman over at the bar, shining glasses with a cloth. He was well out of earshot so she told him no.

"This is hard to explain. Today, at the stream, you brought something out in me that I didn't think existed. Since the accident, I haven't let anyone get close to me. Bella, Paul, even you having to care for me makes me feel so useless and needy. I've always been independent, always. So relying on people is hard for me. But that's what I have to do every day. I've managed to find a way to distance myself from it until now. Today, I opened up to you in a way that I haven't ever before. I let you in, let you see and feel what I feel and while it was wonderful, it scared me senseless to make myself so vulnerable."

Sam closed her eyes and nodded her head. She knew exactly what he was saying.

"I was frightened," he continued. "It was all so overwhelming."

"Jonah, you've no reason to be frightened. I understand. You're worrying over nothing."

"I'm not. You make me.... different."

"Again, in a good way or a bad way?"

"Oh god, a wonderful way. I knew I liked you that first day you came on the chase with us, but I had no idea you could make me feel the way you did this weekend."

She couldn't help the Cheshire cat smile that had situated itself on her face. The knot in her back magically vanished and she felt herself relax.

"You there?" he asked, Sam's silence made him uneasy.

She took his hand. She didn't need to reply, the reassurance in her touch translated to him.

"I am sorry about earlier. I just needed time to think." He twisted the wine glass around between his fingers.

"Hey, don't worry about it. It's me you're talking to. I understand you needed to think. And I'm sorry I called you a grumpy bastard."

"When did you call me a grumpy bastard?"

"Never mind." They both laughed and sipped wine. The bar filled up quickly and the atmosphere changed in the room from quiet and serious to jovial and lively. The atmosphere between Jonah and Sam had thawed too and they chatted happily while polishing off the wine.

"Want another?" she asked.

"No. I want to hear all about the latest in wind speed diagnostics."

"Oh, you are a party animal."

Back in Sam's room, after carefully peeling each other's clothes off and making love slowly and gently, they lay side by side, holding hands, while she read her notes to him. He was naked, covered only by the sheet and she was wearing her bra and panties, her hair tussled and sprawled across the pillow, some of which had strayed onto his chest and he played with it, intertwining it between his fingers. After she'd finished reading, she rolled onto her front, gazing up at him.

"Do you think we should get one of those new anemometers?" he asked, leaning down to kiss her neck.

"Jonah... can we not talk about this right now? Let's save it for Monday."

"You're right, sorry."

"Can you imagine if Paul knew what we were doing?"

"About that. I think we should keep this to ourselves. If we tell Paul or if he finds out, it will change the whole dynamic of the team, you know? It could make it awkward and I don't want him to feel left out of the loop."

"That makes sense. So, does that mean I'm not just a weekend stand?"

"Oh Sam. Absolutely not." He kissed her until she felt weak. He was right, this was a completely different man than the one she'd spent the last month chasing storms with. It was the same thing he'd described, but for her. The day she'd gotten caught in that twister and then in the restaurant bathroom, when she'd felt herself attracted to him, it opened something inside her, something that had been closed tight when Bobby died: her ability to feel something. Was it passion? Lust? She wasn't sure, but whatever it was, she liked it.

Jonah got up, stretched and felt his way to the window, opening it wide.

"There's something I want to show you. Get dressed and come with me."

"Jonah, it's ten thirty. We've to get up early for the flight. What are we doing?"

"Just come on and bring your scarf."

They walked down to reception and out into the fresh air. "Take me someplace quiet," he asked, as she scanned the hotel car park. There was nowhere really. She thought of the stream side but that was noisy with the water and the woodland sounds. They walked around for a while until he stopped her.

"Here is perfect. Can we sit down anywhere?"

They were out in the hotel grounds, near the golf course. He was right, it was silent. They sat on the grass and Jonah asked her to put the scarf over her eyes again.

"Is this gonna be kinky?" she asked.

"No," he laughed. "Unless you want it to be."

"No, well, not here anyway."

He laid her down, made sure her green satin scarf was covering her eyes properly and told her not to make a sound. As she strained her ears to ascertain what he wanted her to hear, she listened as a distant rumble rolled over the night sky. Crickets chirped intermittently but this sound was distinct. Thunder. Very much in the distance, but thunder without doubt.

"Hear it?" he asked. "I was listening to the weather channel when you were gone and they forecast storms for just south of here. I wanted you to hear what I hear and to appreciate the sound without being distracted by the lightning. Everyone gets excited about the lightning but no one ever appreciates the song it sings."

"That's beautiful, Jonah." Another rumble. This one angrier, more intent. Nothing to taint it, just pure sound. Then, getting slightly louder for a time, although still in the distance, the far away storm moved off to the north east and all was silent. It lasted an hour or so until Sam shivered.

"You've got goose bumps." Jonah stroked her arm.

"I'm fine."

"No, come on, let's head back."

"Jonah."

"Yes?"

"Will you stay with me tonight?"

"I have a date."

She punched him playfully in the arm.

"Of course I will." He wrapped his arm around her and pulled her tight to him. In her room that night, wrapped up in each other's arms, not speaking or moving, they lay and listened to each other breathing.

The next morning, they were at reception checking out when a large, jolly faced man approached them.

"Mr. Mason. How the hell are you? Loved your keynote speech. Say, we missed you at dinner last night. The receptionist passed on your message that you weren't well. We had a place for you at the head table. It wasn't the same without our guest of honour."

Jonah blushed slightly as he lied, saying he'd been feeling ill so had decided to stay in bed. Sam glared at him. He'd stood up his colleagues just to be with her. Afterwards, when the jolly man, who turned out to be the conference organiser left, she confronted him.

"What the hell, Jonah? Why did you go and do that? You shouldn't have passed up that dinner invitation, never mind have dinner with me in the same hotel. They could have caught you out."

"If you were me, would you rather have gone to a stuffy conference dinner filled with middle aged men and their boring wives or would you have rather spent the evening with a beautiful woman, listening to the sky talking and then having ridiculously good sex?"

"Don't do that again. I don't want to be a meteorological Yoko."

"It's fine, honestly." He placated her with a reassuring voice and a gentle pat on her shoulder.

Soon, they were Nebraska bound. The airport was busy but Jonah felt completely at ease. The weekend had been a turning point for him. He felt safe with Sam, trusted her implicitly. That day she had described the storm to him, compounded his suspicions that she was special, that she was on a similar wavelength to him.

*

Jonah asked where they were. When she told him they were just around the block from Bella's, he instructed the cab driver to stop. Sam regarded him quizzically. Taking her face in his hands, he kissed her long and hard. The driver raised an eyebrow in the mirror.

"What was that for?"

"I didn't want my sister to see. She's so damn nosy." He instructed the driver to continue on.

"She's probably just protective."

"Maybe. Look, I had a wonderful time. Really wonderful. Thank you."

"Me too." She discretely took his hand and gave it a little squeeze just as the cab pulled up outside Bella's. "Want me to help you into the house?"

"No. I got it from here. Check out the twelve and twenty four hour GFS and call me later. We can decide whether we'll get a few more days chase. Okay?" She agreed and said goodbye. Jonah asked the driver to get his bags. Sam watched him unfurl his cane and make his way deftly up the garden path which was cobbled and rough underfoot. She wondered had that been an intentional design feature or just a handy fluke.

Floating on a cloud to her own front door, she was weighed down only by her bags. What a weird weekend. Good weird, but weird all the same. Jonah was ...... wonderful. She sighed as she let herself in. It was going to be hard getting back to being chase partners after this. The house seemed brighter. Her magnolia hallway was almost luminescent as she dropped her bag and keys.

Taking a deep breath, she couldn't dampen the smile that was planted on her face. In the living room, she looked at her wedding photo and was alarmed at the pang of guilt that crossed her stomach. She lowered her gaze, the smile faltering.

The answering machine flashed, desperately trying to get her attention. She sighed and pressed play.

'Hello, Sam honey? It's Jim Krantz from KWON here. Hope you've been doin' ok. I want to talk to you about something so could you call me back on 555-2009.'

Sam dialled his number.

"Jim, hi. It's Sam Di Matteo. I missed your call."

Jim, her old boss at the station greeted her with delight in his baritone southern drawl down the phone.

"Sam, darlin.' How are you?"

"I'm good, Jim. You?"

"Oh, busy, busy. You know how it is. Now listen, I have a proposition for you and I want you to think about it."

"OK?"

"Our weather girl, Georgia is about to go on maternity leave. She's as big as a Thanksgiving pun'kin so not long left. I want you to come and fill in for her: you know, compile the forecasts, present on the morning show. Do you want to think about that?"

"I appreciate your call, Jim. Can I think about it and call you back?"

"Of course, my dear. But don't take too long, darlin,' Georgia's gonna be poppin' any day now."

"Sure, I'll call you back Jim. And thanks."

Sinking against the wall, her mind whirled. Weather presenter? Bobby's job? Could she really do that? Chasing was fun but there was next to no money in it and it wasn't going to last forever. Chasing season was almost over. What would she do when they were off season? Sit around as usual, feeling miserable. No, this new job was a sign from Bobby. She needed it and it had come along at just the right time. She wasted no time in calling Jim back and accepting the job. He congratulated her and told her he'd be in touch about a start date.

"Shit," she muttered as she realised she'd have to tell Jonah. She'd known chasing with him and Paul was a temporary thing, but would he still be upset? A thought struck her. What if Jonah freaked like he usually did and turned on her. He'd let his guard down for her, let her in and now she had to tell him that she was leaving the team.

CHAPTER 9

"Hello?" Sam put her phone to her ear, heart thumping when she saw it was Jonah.

"Hey. You got home OK."

"Yeah."

"Did you check the charts?" She shook her head in disappointment. He was straight back to business.

"Yep. Nothing much happening tomorrow but South West Iowa should yield some cells on Wednesday. Wanna head out then?"

"Yeah, I think we will. Definitely nothing tomorrow?"

"Nothing."

"OK. So, em, I was thinking. I was gonna invite you over here but my sister and the kids are here all evening. Why don't I get a cab over to your place?"

"I can't, Jonah. My Mom is here." She was whispering now. As much as she craved being with him, it was a small blessing that her mother had decided to make a surprise visit and that there was no chase tomorrow. It gave her more time to consider how to drop the news to Jonah about the job at the TV station.

"Jesus, it's like being a teenager again." He didn't sound happy. Shit. Not good. She needed him in a good mood before she told him.

"I miss you," she whispered, looking behind her to make sure her mother wasn't over her shoulder, eavesdropping.

"Yeah, I miss you too. See you Wednesday, OK?" he sighed.

"Bye."

As she hung up, Vittoria came up behind her as if on cue.

"Who was that?"

"Jonah. We're just arranging when to chase."

"Is he single? He's very handsome."

"Yes and yes, but he's my boss. Well, for now. I've accepted a job back at the TV station."

Vittoria threw her arms around her daughter and squeezed her into oblivion. She gesticulated and spoke in delighted Italian about how brave and wonderful her daughter was to go back to her old job.

"Do you think you will find it strange to be working where Bobby was?"

"I don't really know. I guess I'll find out. In a way, I hope it will give me some comfort."

"Of course, bambina. Bobby was such a good man, rest his soul." She clasped her hands together and shook them at the heavens. "Always loved my linguini putanesca. 'Mama Vittoria,' he would say. 'That was the best putanesca I have ever had.' Such a good man."

Sam smiled derisively at her mother. In truth, Bobby had hated Vittoria's cooking. The first time in her house, she had served him the putanesca and he'd been too polite to be honest. The dog was given most of the contents of his plate when she had her back turned. She'd gushed over what a good eater he was and how he was so good to empty his plate, that his mother must have raised him well. Meanwhile, Sassy, the shih-tzu was sauce stained and stuffed, lying flat out on the floor at Bobby's feet. Ever since, poor Bobby was served the one meal he hated and Sassy would wag her tail furiously when Bobby and Sam came to dinner, planting herself firmly at his heel, waiting for any scrap that he deemed inedible to come her way. But Vittoria was oblivious and Sam would leave her that way.

"So, Mrs. Belotti called me the other day."

"Mom, I don't want to talk about it."

"No, just listen. She wanted to ask how you were. He broke down and confessed everything to the police. She said he had a break down a few weeks ago and she thought he was doing well, but then.... well."

Sam listened, but refused to respond. She didn't want to talk about Luca. The hours she'd spent thinking about him and what he'd almost done to her were a waste of her time. Yes, he'd hit her but she'd ended up in hospital because of her fall. Who was to know if he would actually have raped her. Especially now hearing he'd had a breakdown. He obviously had some major issues. She wasn't angry at him anymore, she pitied him.

"Sam! You are daydreaming. Did you hear what I said? Mrs. Castanapolous said that if your father didn't trim the ...."

Sam nodded sleepily and zoned out again, reminiscing now about how she and Jonah had danced to Norah Jones in the restaurant. She laughed to herself as she remembered how one of the women from the bathroom had winked at her and given her a thumbs-up - like it was taking her advice had led her to bagging the subject of their idolatry.

"..... so I told her that if she didn't..."

"Mom! Let's get dinner, yeah?" Sam interrupted her mother before she could ramble on any more about the trials of her suburban existence and neighbourly disputes. She couldn't stand gossip and thought she'd crack up if she had to endure any more.

A belly full of lasagne later, Sam waved her mother off and got straight into bed to dream about Jonah some more. It would be hard in one way not to see him tomorrow but would give her the opportunity to come up with some way of telling him.

*

On Wednesday, Paul was at the door, bright and cheerful as always. He asked about the conference and Sam tried with all her might not to turn crimson, managing to stutter that it was fine. Her heart skipped when she saw Jonah sitting in the passenger seat. He was wearing a white T-shirt and jeans and singing along to the radio. Paul leaned into her. "He's in a really good mood. Normally we don't talk much in the mornings but he wouldn't shut up earlier. I'm worried!" He laughed and Sam laughed with him, a little too loud and forceful. Her face surrendered to the crimson, as blood pulsed into her cheeks. She shook her hair down to cover it as she locked the front door.

"Morning, Sam," Jonah said jauntily. Paul was right, he was in a good mood.

"Hey." She couldn't help the smile creeping across her face. "How are you?"

"Good." This cute, boyish smile, as he turned his head in her direction, was something she had never seen before. It was almost shy. She checked the rearview mirror to see Paul absorbed in his computer, so ventured to take Jonah's hand. He smiled again, squeezed and released, worried about being spotted.

Later that morning, in Harrison, Iowa, cells were building up from the south west but not yielding anything exciting. There was a stronger storm heading for them but it was about two hours out so Sam suggested they get lunch while things were quiet. They found a roadside diner that was like something from the 1950s. Red and white upholstered booths and waitresses dressed in short fitted uniforms. They sat down and Paul excused himself to use the restroom.

"Is Paul gone?"

"Yeah."

"I've missed you these past few days. I wish I could have seen you."

"I know, sorry. It's just my Mom was there and I had some things to do, you know?

"Sure. Did you hear anymore about that Belotti asshole?"

She took a deep breath. She couldn't lie to him. She reluctantly told him she wasn't going to press charges on Luca.

"What the fuck? That guy tried to ......" Jonah's voice was a little too loud for a quiet restaurant.

"Shhh. Keep your voice down, people are looking. He didn't *almost* do anything. He just hit me."

"Just hit you? That's enough for me to want to kick his ass from here to Mexico. You have to press charges for assault."

"Look, it seems he's been having a bad time of it lately and I was the unfortunate one he took it out on. I've made my decision and I'm sticking with it. It's my decision to make."

Jonah looked like he might kill someone, then after taking a deep breath, his countenance softened slightly.

"Of course, it's your decision. Whatever you feel is right."

"Hey, what'd I miss?" Paul asked, as he returned to the table, wiping his hands in his trousers.

"Just saying what a terrible driver you are," Jonah joked.

"Hey. I was good enough for you before Sam came along. So tell me about the conference. What did you two get up to?"

Jonah nudged Sam's leg under the table and made her jump. She kicked him back harder and he winced.

"You guys feeling all right?"

"Just thought I felt a spider on my leg, that's all," Sam lied.

When they'd finished their lunch, Jonah insisted on paying the tab.

"I'm really worried about you, Jonah. Either you got laid at the conference or you secretly went and had a personality transplant," Paul joked.

Jonah dismissed him, telling him he was delusional.

"I'm right, aren't I? You got laid! Sam, you should know, you were with him. Did he meet someone?"

"Em.... I.... I don't know," she stuttered but Jonah came to her rescue.

"Yes, Paul. Yes, I did meet someone."

"You dog! So what was she like? Will you see her again?"

"I don't know, Paul. Now are we gonna go chase this storm or not?"

"OK, OK.... you don't want to discuss your sex life. I respect that. Just tell me one thing.... how was it?"

"Paul!" Sam interjected, puce.

"Paul, she is the most amazing woman I've ever met. That is all I'm saying."

"Good for you, buddy. Good for you." Paul patted him on the back as they made their way out of the diner and to the truck. As soon as Paul's back was turned, Sam slapped Jonah on the arm and whispered 'you shit' into his ear. He shrugged and bumped shoulders with her, smiling like he knew the secret to happiness and was walking alongside it.

The storm was beginning to loom on the horizon. It was building up to be a monster on the radar. Setting the truck down on the freeway roadside, Paul jumped out to check the probe in the trunk to make sure it was operational. Jonah asked Sam to describe the storm to him.

"Well, the front is moving fast. It's very organised and there's a hook forming on the southerly aspect of the cell. The pressure has dropped to 966 hPa."

"No, not the technicalities. Describe what you can see."

So she told him how dark it was as it approached, how the hail curtain was visible at the cloud base now, above which was a very low wall cloud that was beginning to rotate and that it was heading directly towards them.

"You describe it to me." She leaned into him, discretely affectionate, whispering into his ear.

"I can feel the wind sheer and can hear the thunder in the distance. I reckon the wind speed is about thirty five knots? She's about two miles out. Am I right?"

"Pretty, damn accurate."

"Is the coast clear?" Jonah asked and she confirmed that Paul was still checking the probe. Jonah leaned in to give her a quick and teasing kiss on the lips. She kept her eyes closed, still swooning long after he'd peeled away from her. What she wouldn't do to him if Paul weren't here. Thinking of Paul made her feel a little guilty that they were hiding something from him. He'd find out sooner or later, but later was best. She'd be starting the new job soon and they could tell him then.

Paul shouted at them from behind the truck. There was a quickly expanding wedge tornado on the ground about a half mile out. Sam turned her attention to the radar and confirmed that it would cross their path.

Jonah yelled to deploy the probe, the chances of it taking a direct hit were good. He jumped out and felt his way to the back of the truck to help Paul place it.

"Guys, hurry. It's moving in fast." Sam glanced out at the boys trying to carry the heavy metal cone out into the road. Jumping into the driver's seat, she turned on the engine and brought the truck around, ready for a quick exit. Pulling up beside them, she yelled at them to hurry. Paul pushed Jonah into the back seat and jumped in himself, pulling the door closed with some effort as the twister thundered across the field behind them and crossed onto the road. Trees and bits of wood and metal flew around the truck.

"Sam, DRIVE," Paul called and she pressed the accelerator into the ground as far as it would go. The truck roared into life and sped down the road. The tornado was hurtling towards them faster than they had anticipated. Debris smashed around them. A sheet of metal swirled around the truck, falling down and then being sucked back up again as the twister was gaining on them. Then, a crash. Something had smashed into the back window. Jonah yelped in pain, then slumped down out of view. Sam watched in the mirror as Paul jumped across to him.

"What happened?" No response. "PAUL - WHAT THE FUCK HAPPENED? WHERE'S JONAH?" she screamed.

"He's fine. He's just lying down. Just keep driving, Sam. Don't mind what's behind you. Keep your eyes on the road."

Her stomach lurched and she swallowed down the vomit that had risen into her throat. Something had happened to Jonah. The wind tore in the missing back window and whistled around the truck. She did as Paul said and kept her eyes on the road. The twister behind them changed track, moving off into a field as the road meandered out of its path. When Sam was satisfied they were a safe distance away, she pulled into a gateway and turned around to see Jonah lying on the back seat, blood pouring from somewhere on his head. She screamed and jumped out and around to get to him at the back. He was unconscious and a thick stream of ruby blood ran down the cream seats of the truck. Paul instructed her to stay in the back, not to move him and to keep pressure on the wound as he took over the driving. There was a hospital nearby. He tore down the road, leaving a dust cloud billowing behind.

Sam's stomach was turning at the feeling of the warm, thick blood on her hand, oozing from Jonah's head, spilling his life across the seat in little red streams. She pulled her hand away for a split second. It was crimson and shiny. Whimpering, and desperately trying to suppress panic, she pressed as hard as she could while concentrating on not vomiting. His face was pale, eyes motionless. She noted how long his eyelashes were. If they were any longer, they'd be touching the top of his cheek. Women would pay hundreds of dollars for eyelashes like his. And yet, he had no idea how striking he was. All he was interested in was chasing storms and this is what they did to him. But he would still come back for more. If only he would wake up. Tears streamed down Sam's face and landed on Jonah's blood stained shirt.

"Jonah, wake up please. Please."

"It's going to be OK." Paul said rather unconvincingly from the front. She wasn't listening to him.

"Please be all right. I need you, Jonah. I need you to stay with me. Don't leave me like Bobby did, please," she whispered into his ear, kissing him and wishing it would work like Sleeping Beauty and wake him up magically.

Unknown to her, Paul was watching in the rearview. He looked puzzled, watching the scene behind him but Sam was oblivious. In a moment of reminiscence, she was back at Bobby's death bed, stroking his grey face, his skin dry under her palm. As he had breathed his final breaths, she'd felt moisture on her fingers. It had been her tears dripping onto his skin as she placed her cheek to his. It was no longer the face of her beloved Bobby. His once pink, stubbly, dimpled cheeks were now ashen, sunken and chilled. The warmth of her tears had felt like boiling water compared to his cold, cold skin.

As she emerged back into the present, the face that she felt under her hand was warm, scratchy with day old stubble and although paler than normal, was still sallow and sun kissed. Her tears mixed with Jonah's blood as she begged him not to leave her and pleaded for him to wake up.

Suddenly, his eyes flickered.

"S... Sam?" he croaked.

"JONAH!" Sam screeched. "I'm here, Jonah. I'm here. You're going to be OK. Paul, he's awake."

"Wha.... what happened?"

He tried to sit up but Sam shouted at him to stay lying down.

"Some debris came in the back window and you were hit on the head."

"Not again!" he tried to joke but winced in pain.

"Stay lying down. We're nearly at the hospital."

"No. I don't need to go to hospital. I'm fine."

"Jonah, you've had a head injury. You need to be checked."

"I'm fine, it's just my ear, I think." He touched his fingers to the side of his head as he sat up.

"But you collapsed."

"I felt the blood and passed out. I'm a bit squeamish." Sam kneeled up and checked his head over. He was right, there was a little shard of glass in the top of his ear. Pulling it out, a blob of blood bubbled up and fell onto his already stained shirt.

"Ouch! What did you just do?"

"Relax, you wuss. I pulled the glass out."

"Will it need stitches?"

"I don't know. It's pretty superficial. I think it just nicked a blood vessel, that's why there's so much blood. It seems to be stopping now though. Paul, what do you think?"

Paul pulled the truck over to the side of the freeway and turned to Jonah, analysing the wound.

"He's fine. It doesn't need stitches. Jesus Christ, Jonah. You frightened the shit out of me."

"Sorry, bud. I've always had a thing about blood, I didn't mean to frighten you. I got a shock."

"You don't look so good. Are you sure you're all right?" He was almost green in the face.

"Actually, I think I'm going to be sick." He went to jump out of the truck and Paul jumped out with him for fear he'd step out into the lane of traffic. Sam surveyed her blood stained hands and sighed. Her heart was still racing. She'd thought he was a goner. The sound of Jonah purging was beginning to turn her stomach. She needed to calm down.

A few minutes later, they were back on the road and looking for a truck stop. The wind was whistling in the broken window behind them and Sam shivered. A few miles on, they found one and Paul pulled in. Sam brought Jonah to the bathroom to wash the blood off. He'd stopped bleeding and they decided he didn't need stitches. Taking a paper hand towel, and soaking it in water, she gently ran it over his face. He winced as she touched his ear, washing out the congealed blood.

"You had me so worried back there."

"I'm sorry. It just felt, you know... familiar." There was an ache in his voice as his words faltered.

"I know. I know. But you're fine. Thank god it was just glass. I thought that sheet of metal that was floating around us had hit you."

"If it had, I'd be dead."

She nodded in the silence of what could have been as she dried his face.

In the parking lot, Paul was busy taping an opened up cardboard box he'd gotten from a sales assistant to where the back window had been.

"My friend who fixed your car, is gonna fix it up tonight," he said to Sam.

"That reminds me Paul. I never thanked you for getting that done for me."

139

"Oh, don't thank me. Jonah paid for it."

"You did?" She turned to him and throwing her arms around his neck, careful not to hit off his ear, kissed him on the lips, long, hard and full of the relief she felt knowing that he was going to be fine and gratitude for being so generous in fixing her car.

"Em, can Paul see us?" he whispered in her ear, then straightened up, pulling away from her.

"Yes, I can see you. And I'm not deaf or stupid!"

"I can explain."

"No, it's fine. I know all about it. You and Sam hooked up at the conference. It doesn't take a genius to figure it out."

"How did you know?" Jonah asked, perplexed.

"When you passed out and I saw how beside herself with worry Sam was. Plus, the scene she made: begging you not to leave her, kissing you, mauling you and saying how much she needed you. It almost made *me* cry."

Sam burned Paul with a look. He didn't have to tell Jonah everything.

As if taking a moment to absorb what his friend was saying, Jonah stood stock still for a second, pensive. Sam was mortified, her gaze fixed anxiously at him. He reached his hands out to find her, touching her face.

"You were worried about me?"

She nodded slowly, her face cradled in his hands and wished that if ever a sink hole were to open up under her feet, it would be now. He bent down and brushed his lips off hers, then pulled her closer, kissing her with such longing that her knees began to weaken. He was locked onto her, telling her he wanted her through his kiss, completely ignoring the fact that Paul and whoever else was in the parking lot watching them. Paul rolled his eyes in mock derision, but he couldn't help the stab of envy that punched through his stomach. Jonah had gotten there before him. It was always the same, even in college. The girls always went for Jonah's ruggedness, ignoring Paul's Irish charm. And Jonah was oblivious to women, caring only about his course work. He turned away, busying himself with taping the back window. He was happy his friend was happy, but he wished it was with someone else.

Paul drove home while Sam and Jonah sat in the back. They picked up the probe on the way back and Paul was going to upload the data when he got home. The tornado had hit it directly so it had been a successful intercept, apart from the accident.

"So, I've an idea," Jonah whispered to Sam on the way home. "Why don't I stay with you tonight?"

Sam thought for second. Common sense and guilt told her it was a bad idea but thinking of sex with Jonah was the decider.

"Sure. Won't Bella mind?"

"I'm a grown man."

She shrugged but said nothing.

"Hey, Paul. Can you swing by my place first so I can get something then bring us both to Sam's? I'm gonna stay there tonight."

Sam watched Paul for a reaction. She was surprised to see his face tinted with dejection and maybe a little annoyance.

Bella gasped when she saw the condition her brother was in and scolded him like any mother would. She was twice as annoyed when he told her he was staying with Sam. She raised her eyebrow at him as he took the clean clothes he'd requested from her and stuffed them into his duffle bag. Hands on hips, she watched him climb into the truck and take off down the road.

"Is she OK?" Sam asked, concerned that he had told her about them.

"Yeah, she's just fussing. She still sees me as her little baby brother, you know? I just told her we were all having a team dinner at your place and that I might as well stay over."

Sam felt placated.

At her house, Sam thanked Paul and waved him off.

"You want something to eat?" she said, turning to Jonah as he stood behind her in the hallway.

"I want you." He reached out until he found her and pulled her to him. Kissing her, he led her backwards until his backside hit the couch and he lay down, pulling her down on top of him.

"Jonah, your ear."

"My ear is fine. Make love to me Sam. I want you ....so badly," he groaned theatrically.

She obliged, pulling him to standing and leading him upstairs, then tore the still bloodstained T-shirt off him and threw it on the floor.

"You are so fucking sexy," he muttered as she kissed him from his head down to his belly button. He groaned, moving his hips as she kissed lower, unbuttoning his fly. She teased and licked him until he was almost about to climax, just like he had done to her on their first night together and then took him inside her, moving up and down. His groaning intensified as they blended into one, becoming entire, then came together. She sank onto his chest. Exhausted, they slept like that until morning broke nine hours later.

Jonah woke alone. A panicked feeling clenched his stomach as he realised he wasn't in his own bed. It took a while for the 'just awake' fog to clear before he remembered he was at Sam's. The previous day's events flooded back. He looked vulnerable as he patted his hand along the wall, stepping carefully, one foot in front of the other. His foot stubbed off something denim and he bent down, picked up his jeans and put them on. He padded his way out the door, patting along the polished banisters until they ended with a ball adorned pillar and he slowly felt for the first step. Finding it, he tentatively made his way down the steps, calling her name. He got no answer but the smell and sizzle of bacon from the near distance reassured him she was nearby. As he stepped off the bottom step, the cold tile shocked his bare feet. He walked carefully, noticing each tile was the same size as his foot so he counted them as he went. Twenty two tiles later, his outstretched hand reached a door, which creaked open, producing a wall of bacon scent which stole his breath.

"Morning, sexy. How's your ear?"

"A bit sore today."

"Do you want some pain killers?"

"Please."

"Sure, just a sec." She reached up to plant a kiss on his lips and went to find her bag. When she returned, she popped two pills into his mouth and handed him a glass of water.

"How do I know these aren't roofies?"

"You don't. If you remember what I do to you in the shower after breakfast, then you'll know they weren't roofies. If you don't, then they were!"

"You vicious minx." Grabbing her by the waist, he spun her around and pressed her hips into the worktop, pushing himself into her lower back. "Want me to help?"

She handed him a whisk and a tray of eggs. "Crack these in here," she instructed, putting his hand on a glass mixing bowl.

"You sure you want me to do this. It could get messy."

"You can do it. I trust you."

So he cracked each egg, almost perfectly but for a few shards of shell, into the bowl and whisked. She stood and watched his biceps constrict and flex as he deftly moved the whisk up and around. Taking his hand, she placed it on the handle of the frying pan. "Put the eggs in here and stir with this spoon. It's hot, so be careful."

He cursed as he burned himself off the side of the pan, but persisted and in the end, had perfectly scrambled eggs.

"See, I told you, you could do it."

He held her to him. "Sam."

"Yes?"

"I just want to say, I'm really glad we met. You make me feel so..... so.... good, maybe even happy. I didn't think I could ever feel like that again."

She wrapped her arms around his neck. He smelled so masculine: yesterday's aftershave mixed with sleep, mixed with testosterone. Man smell, Jonah smell.

"You know what? I feel the same. I could never have imagined liking someone after, you know, Bobby and especially after what Luca did. You know you make me happy too."

Meeting Jonah had shown her that she could overcome her grief, that it didn't define her and that she had the ability to move on, that she was more than just Bobby's widow. She was Sam again. Jonah made her feel like her old self, like things were beginning to fall into place. She reached up to kiss him. Gentle, tender and familiar. Safe and secure. When she was with Jonah, nothing could hurt her. Showing him a chair, she sat on his knee and they ate breakfast, feeding each other.

"So you mentioned the shower earlier. Am I invited?"

"You, my dear, are the guest of honour."

CHAPTER 10

"Should I check the forecast and radar? Are we gonna chase today?" Sam asked, watching Jonah dry himself after their long, steamy shower.

"You know what, maybe we should give it a miss. And anyway, the Ford is having the back window replaced this morning, so it wouldn't be ready in time for a day's chase. I've been thinking and maybe we should sit the rest of the season out. It's winding down anyway and we got a direct hit on the probe yesterday so that's enough to keep us going for a while."

"Shouldn't we discuss this with Paul? If we talk about it without him, he'll feel left out."

"You're right. Let's meet with him first."

It was now or never to tell him about the job. She took his hand and sat him down on the side of the bed. Her stomach clenched as she tried to think of the best way of putting it.

"Jonah. I need to tell you something."

"Oh? Sounds ominous."

"Well........." She took a deep breath and began. "You know the way I told you how happy you make me, earlier..."

"Oh god. Here we go.... 'you got caught up in the moment, didn't really mean it, etc.' Don't mess me around Sam. I thought I knew you better than that." His voice was getting higher and louder. She put her hand on his shoulder to stop him from getting up and losing it altogether.

"Jonah. I meant what I said. End of. This is something else. Now get off your high horse and listen to me without freaking, please. This is hard to say but I need to do what's right for me." She felt anxiety creep into her abdomen.

So she explained to him about the job offer, how she'd accepted, how she started on Monday and wouldn't be able to chase with them, if they did decide to continue with the season.

He sat silently for a moment, absorbing what she was telling him.

"That's wonderful. Congratulations," he said sadly as he rose from the bed, patted around until he found his jeans and put them on, then felt around for the door and made his way to the living room. Shit, she thought. Maybe it would have been better if he'd shouted. Seeing him so sad was ten times worse. She followed him down the hallway and finding him on the couch, sat beside him, placing a hand gingerly on his knee.

"You could try to contain your excitement a bit," she said, feigning sarcasm.

"Sorry. It's wonderful, really it is."

"But?"

"No. It's nothing. Really."

"Aren't you happy for me?"

"I am....."

"But?"

"It's just that we've only just gotten to know each other."

"Are you worried that I'll move on and not see you anymore?"

"You see," he said quietly, face downcast. "That's why I like you. You seem to know exactly what I'm thinking."

"Jonah, for fuck's sake." Anger rose into her throat. "Do you think that little of me that I'll just sail off with my new job and new life and forget about you?"

"I don't know. Why wouldn't you? When you start working at the station, you're going to meet new people, you'll be the glamourous weather anchor, you'll be living your life. And where will I be? Still at my sister's, working with Paul, chasing without you."

"You'll go back to doing exactly what you did before, except you can cuddle up to me at night, we can have amazing sex and go and do nice things at the weekend. You had a life before me. It was always going to go this way - after the season ended, you'd go back to what you did before, and I'd do something else: probably go back to sitting here mourning for my dead husband. But now it's different. We have each other."

"It won't be that easy. Where will we spend time together? If you come to me, you'll have my sister and her husband around, three kids jumping all over us. I can't exactly drive to your house so we don't have many options."

"Well.... how about you move in with me?"

"Isn't that a bit sudden? We've only known each other for a month."

"Well, it's the only option I can think of. Look, we're grown adults. We know what we're getting into."

"I don't know, Sam. You're still mourning for Bobby and I'm.... well, I have needs, you know? It's not easy living with someone who has a disability like I have."

"How could it be any different? You've already gotten to know your way around here. I could drop you to the university or Paul's on my way to work. I mean, what does your sister do for you that I can't."

"Yeah, I guess you're right. I suppose it does make sense, logistically. But it's a huge step to take. What if we find it's too much, too soon?"

"Well then we've found out sooner rather than later. Jonah, I want to be with you and if it means you've to live here so I can see you more often, then so be it."

"Can you handle my being so dependent though? It's not easy, having someone with such special needs around."

With both hands, she pulled his face to hers until they were nose to nose. "You are not my dependent. You will be my boyfriend/ lover/partner/sex slave, whichever way you choose to label it."

"Oooh, I like the last one!"

"Listen to me. We will work hard to find a way of living together that helps us both. You are not dependent. You will learn to cook, clean, do laundry by yourself. I know your sister means well, but I think she's babied you a bit, would I be right?"

"Yeah. You are, but it's just her way."

"Of course it is and isn't she wonderful for it but if you're going to live here, it's going to be different."

He sat back away from her, pensive and quiet. She could almost see the thoughts, like a whirlwind in his mind.

"It's just..... well, I'm scared. I'm not sure I can learn to be so independent."

"Did you or did you not find out how to get around this house, despite the fact you'd only been here a handful of times?"

"Yeah."

"And did you or did you not manage to make breakfast this morning without burning down the house?"

"Yeah, although I did burn my hand."

"Little steps, honey, little steps. Come on, let's do this, OK?"

"All right. I'll move in. But why don't we make it a trial period? Say a week or a month and then reassess."

"Great. That sounds like a reasonable idea."

"Oh god, my sister's gonna freak!"

"So is my mother! Let's not tell them."

"Well, I'll have to tell my sister. I think she'll notice that I'm not around."

"Good point. So I just won't tell my Mom!"

"Can you get my phone so I can call Bella?"

Sam refused, telling him he had to find it himself. He made his way to the kitchen where he'd left it last and she heard him command it to 'phone Bella.' He asked her if he could have someone over for dinner that night, as he had something to tell her. She agreed and said she'd do a pot roast, to be there at six. Sam came in behind him, put her arms around his waist and hugged him tightly. He spun around, and tilting her head up to meet his, kissed her delicately.

"I can't wait to wake up to you every day."

"In a way, I'm glad you can't see. I'm not very pretty in the morning. Hey, I'd love some tea. Why don't you make me some?"

"Because I can't see where stuff is," he said, flashing her a sarcastic smile.

"Well, let's do some orientation then."

Standing behind him, she took his arm and held his hand up to show him the kettle and where it was situated. Then, she traced his hand along the counter to the tin with the tea bags in it. She left him to find the sink and watched him as he slowly and cautiously filled the kettle, turned on the switch, then found the tea bag tin again and two mugs. He popped a bag into each mug, feeling all the way and when the kettle had boiled, poured the water slowly and careful into each cup. He did spill some on the counter but she didn't tell him that.

"Voila," he said, thrusting a hot mug in her general direction. "That's the first time I've done that in six years."

They sat at the table, sipping the tea he had so proudly made and discussed how they were going to tell Bella that he was moving out.

*

Sam sat on the pristine cream couch, while a beautiful blond child sat on the coffee table opposite, staring suspiciously at her. He then ran off, leaving her alone to look around the beautiful room. For a woman with three young children, Bella's house was immaculate. Everything was cream and spotless. There was the odd toy on the ground, but it was still tidy. She noticed how all the walkways were rugs of the same cream colour, but they were different textures - one was made from seagrass, another was extremely plush carpet, there was a tight knit pile and a sheepskin. Of course, she thought, for Jonah to find his way around. He'd know where he was by the different textures on the floor. Genius. She made a mental note to herself to buy some different rugs the next day.

"Uncle Jonaaah! Where was you last night? I missed my nighty cuddles."

Jonah came in with a five year old girl, again, blonde, wrapped around his leg. He tried to shake her off but when that didn't work he bent down and tickled her until she came loose.

"I was at my friend's house."

"Why?"

"Because my ear was a bit sore and my friend had the proper medicine."

"But Mommy has lots of medicine. Why couldn't she give it to you?"

"Because that's illegal in some states and a bit weird."

'JONAH!" Sam scolded and he laughed, coming to sit beside her.

"I'm going to tell Mommy what you said." The little girl, April, ran off to divulge her uncle's incestuous implied comments.

"She doesn't know what I mean."

"Yeah, but Bella will, and we're trying to keep on her good side, you know?"

"JONAH - STOP CORRUPTING THE CHILDREN," came a call from the kitchen, and they both dissolved into laughter.

Bella's roast melted in the mouth. Her gravy was delicious and Sam ate ravenously, nerves keeping her stuffing mouthful upon mouthful just to suppress the anxiety of her freaking out over their announcement. She watched in amusement as Bella poured the gravy onto Jonah's plate and then proceeded to cut his meat and serve him potatoes and vegetables. He was more than able to do that himself. When they had finished, Jonah suggested that the children watch a DVD. Nigel, Bella's husband, duly obliged, shooing them into the living room, then returned, offered Sam some more wine and sat back down. She refused as she was driving but another glass would have been nice to settle her nerves.

"So, Bell's, Nige. I've something to tell you."

"I think I know already, Jonah."

"No.... I don't think you do."

"Yes, you and Sam are seeing each other. I can tell. You both have this chemistry or something. I could tell the day she came to collect you."

"Hmmm. Busted. Yeah you guessed it but....."

"See Nige, I told you. Didn't I tell you? It was so....."

"BELLA. Listen. That's not all. I am moving out. I'm going to live with Sam."

Sam watched as Bella's fork stopped midway to her mouth and was left suspended there while she stared in disbelief at her brother. Nigel topped up her wine and deftly took the fork from her, whether he was afraid she was going to throw it across the table or not, Sam wasn't sure but she was grateful he had the foresight to play it safe.

"Jonah... this is the most hair brained idea you've ever had. You can't move out. Who will look after you? Who will cook, clean, do everything for you?"

"Bella, with all due respect, I need to learn to look after myself. You know how much I appreciate everything you do for me, but it's time I learned to adapt properly. And I won't be alone. Sam will be with me."

"But you've only known each other a wet week. This is ridiculous. How can she know how to look after you?"

"Bella, I've gotten to know Jonah pretty well and I know we can make this work," Sam said in placating tones, which fell on deaf ears. Bella looked like she might explode.

"Sis, we want to be together. And come on, that's not going to happen here. I need some privacy now. I've loved living here, but it's time I moved on and tried to become more independent. I'll never be able to thank you for taking me in after the accident and .... and Anna, you know.....?"

Sam's eyes widened..... Anna? Was that the bride in the picture? She wanted to know more but was afraid to ask. That was a conversation for another day when they were relaxed in their own environment and not in a situation where they were likely to be attacked by dining cutlery.

Sam took his hand under the table, more for reassurance for herself than any discreet show of solidarity. She felt a little offended that he hadn't mentioned his wife before. It was kind of a big deal, but she'd leave it for now. Bella seemed to have calmed and relaxed slightly as Jonah talked her around. Eventually, she reluctantly told him that whatever made him happy but that she'd always be there for him. Sam braced herself as Bella stood, took her napkin from her lap, placing it on the table and came around it to where Sam sat. She put her arms around her in a tight hug that

Sam wasn't sure was a warning or a genuine congratulatory embrace.

"I'll look after him, I promise, Bella," she whispered out of Jonah's super sharp earshot.

"So when are you moving in?" Bella turned to her brother.

"Well, straight away I guess. No point hanging around, is there?"

Sam was taken aback. He was right in a way, there was no point hanging around, but it did give her a feeling of imminence. She took a deep breath. It was fine. This was what they wanted. Later, while Nigel and Jonah put the children to bed, Bella took the opportunity to take Sam aside and give her tips on how to make life easier for Jonah: the rugs, plates at the front of the press and cups at the back so he didn't knock them over, keeping his clothes in a certain order that he was used to and various other tips and tricks to help him get on with things. She admitted to mothering him too much and agreed that it was indeed time that he gained some independence. Sam hugged her tightly when she went to leave. Jonah was going to stay one more night in Bella's and pack in the morning. She kissed him goodbye as she turned to go.

That night, she lay on her bed, staring into the open wardrobe of Bobby's clothes. She got up and stood among his coats and suits, inhaling his smell. He was always so clean and well groomed. As a TV personality, he had to be, she supposed. Not like Jonah, who was manly and although clean, had a ruggedness about him which was so appealing to her primeval self. She took out her wedding album, flicking slowly through each photo, savouring it for what felt like one last time.

"Bobby.... am I doing the right thing? I really like Jonah but is this OK with you? To move a man into your... our home so soon after you've gone?" The silence was her only answer. It was too late now. She couldn't let Jonah down because of her cold feet. It would always be Bobby's house. The little stream like trickle of doubts was beginning to surge into a river as she flicked through each wedding photograph, turning her wedding ring around her finger.

She had a fitful sleep that night, dreaming about a tornado sucking Bobby and Jonah up away from her and leaving her alone completely. She woke with tears in her eyes just as daylight broke.

CHAPTER 11

"Cheers."

They clinked wine glasses as Sam snuggled deeper into Jonah's side. He pulled her tighter to him and kissed the top of her head. A satisfied smile crossed her face: there was nothing in the world like lounging on the couch with wine, TV and a gorgeous man to hug.

"*Mad Men* is my favourite show. The writers are amazing. Close your eyes and listen to the script. It's genius."

"Yeah, but if I close my eyes, I won't get to see Don in his suit."

"Oh really? So you'll blindfold yourself to listen to storms with me, but not when Don Draper is on?"

"Pretty much, yeah!"

"Well, I can see where your priorities lie." He went to grab her, a punishment of tickling imminent, but she screamed and jumped up, running from him.

"Hey, no fair, you have an advantage. Come back here."

"You'll have to find me first!"

She ran upstairs, stripped and jumped into the shower. It was no time before he came into the bathroom, hand patting the wall. Opening the shower door, he reached his hand out to find her and she grabbed it, pulling him in fully clothed to join her under the hot stream of water. His white shirt and combats were drenched. She pulled the T-shirt over his head and threw it haphazardly on the shower floor. He kissed her until her knees weakened and she buckled and fell into him. His eyes closed, he kissed her hungrily, tasting her, needing her. She reached behind and felt for the shampoo bottle, the one she used that he loved and squirting some into her hand, began to massage his head, careful not to touch off the healing wound. He gasped and pressed himself into her, letting her feel what she did to him. She moved her hands down to his shoulders and rubbed them, loving the feel of his biceps as they flexed underneath her palms, when he pulled her to his lips. The kiss, saturated with water and some shampoo, was dizzying. She pulled her head away so she could look at him. His tanned face, shadowed by stubble that etched the shape of his jawline, strong and masculine. His river blue eyes sparkled like they were alive as they should have been. His lips, when clenched in pleasure, were like a strawberry that she wanted to take a bite of. He held her to his chest, letting the water run over them both until the heat left it and it began to cool.

"Come on, baby. Let's get to bed." He felt along the rail for a towel and wrapped it tenderly around her, then pulled off his saturated trousers, discarding them on the floor and got a towel for himself. They lay in bed, after Sam had gone back down to lock up and turn the TV off. Head resting on his bicep, they talked about everything and nothing, as she stared up at the ceiling.

"Jonah. Who's Anna?"

"What?"

"You mentioned Anna to Bella and when we were at the hotel and you dropped your wallet on the floor, I saw a picture of you in a morning suit with a bride."

He inhaled deeply and emitted a sigh that seemed to go on forever.

"Anna was my wife."

"I gathered that. Why didn't you tell me about her? It's kind of a big thing that you were married. What happened?"

"Sam, this is hard to talk about. I rarely mention her. I don't know if I....."

"But how can you be open and honest with me if you can't even tell me you were married."

"Yeah," he sighed, "you're right. It's just.... god, it's hard."

She rolled over onto her elbows so she could look into his eyes. Stroking his face, she reassured him that it was OK.

"We were high school sweethearts. Inseparable. Both each other's first loves. She stuck with me all through college, even though we only saw each other at weekends. We got married soon after I qualified as a meteorologist. One day, I was pulling into the driveway and my foot slipped."

"Oh my god, you ran over her?"

"No! No, I didn't run over her. My truck was fine but I damaged her car, tore the back bumper off. So, the next day, Paul brought it to his friend's garage while I brought Anna to work in my truck. Then, I collected Paul and we went on a chase. She finished work at four but we were still after a cell that was running up past the northern border of Omaha, so I collected her and we brought her with us to finish out the chase. She was thrilled she got to come with us. She'd been begging me to take her chasing, but I couldn't bring myself to put her in danger like that. Anyway she insisted and talked me into it. So we positioned ourselves in front of the twister, it was an EF4, mile wide base - a beast of a thing. We deployed a sensor pad that we were using at the time to record the base wind speed and when we went to get back into the truck, it stalled and we couldn't get the engine going again. We took a direct hit. The twister took the truck in the air for a couple of seconds then dumped us back down. The windows blew in. Paul was crouched on the floor, I was hit by a piece of flying debris on the back of the head, hence my injury and Anna........." The lump forming in his throat was so big by now, it was making it difficult for him to talk.

He choked it back and continued. "Anna was sucked out through the windscreen. They found her body in a nearby field an hour later. She'd died from the impact of being thrown by the tornado." His voice faltered.

"Fucking hell, Jonah. Jesus Christ. I had no idea. That must have been........ horrific."

"It was all my fault. If I hadn't damaged her fucking car and if I hadn't brought her on that stupid chase, she'd still be alive. I should have known it was too dangerous."

Sam could do nothing but hold him. So he knew the loss she felt too. They were kindred through tragedy. How hard it must have been for him, not only to lose his sight but to lose his wife too.

"I was in a coma for a week and when I woke up, I asked them to take the bandages off my face because I couldn't see anything. That's when they told me there was nothing over my face. Then when I said I wanted Anna, Bella had to tell me she was dead."

Sam felt her eyes fill and she held him tightly, hoping it would ease his pain. They dozed fitfully, the weight of grief pushing down on them as they twisted and turned in an uneasy sleep.

*

She rolled over in the shaft of morning light and reached across as always. Nobody there. The smell of bacon aroused her senses. Rising and throwing on Jonah's T-shirt, she made her way downstairs. He stood at the hob, moving bacon around the pan. She went to him, arms around his waist, resting her head on his back.

"Hey," he whispered, his voice croaky from the night before.

"Morning. Check you out! What brought this on?"

"I couldn't sleep and was starving." His eyes were bloodshot, eyelids heavy.

She was aware of her own eyes, swollen and stinging. She'd dreamed of Bobby. They'd had a fight and he wouldn't talk to her. He eventually died without her getting to make up with him. She worried it was a sub conscious reaction to the guilt she felt about moving in with Jonah.

He'd managed to make bacon and fried eggs. The eggs were pretty much raw. She poured him a coffee as they sat down to eat.

"So, last night was rough. How are you feeling now?" she asked, watching him closely for a reaction.

"You know what, I've never opened up about that. Not even to my sister or Paul. It feels kind of good. Cathartic. Thank you."

"Why are you thanking me? I didn't do anything."

"You did. You bring something out in me that I didn't know I had. I'm not quite sure what it is but it's there. It's like you see deeper into me than anyone else ever has, even, dare I say it, Anna. You understand some things about me that even I don't get. I can't explain it very well."

They remained silent, letting his words hang in the air. She didn't know how to respond, so staying silent was best. They had a connection, something on a different level than anything she'd ever felt before.

"So, are you excited about the job?" he asked, mouth full of bacon. The homeliness and simple domesticity of them both eating breakfast and chatting wrapped around her like a warm blanket.

"Yes and no. I'm really nervous, truth be told. It'll be nice to see everyone again but at the same time, it's going to be hard working with the same people and in the same room Bobby used to be in. I haven't been back since he died and I'm worried it's going to set something off in me."

"That's understandable, you know. You're allowed to feel like that. Everyone will understand if you get upset. Just give yourself time. It's a wonderful opportunity. How do you feel about being on TV? You were a researcher before, weren't you?"

"Yeah. I did one broadcast before, in Bobby's place, but I found it fine. You just don't think about thousands of people watching you. It's just you and the director and the camera. No big deal. Anyway, I'm only doing the weather - not exactly presenting the Oscars!"

"True. You'll be amazing, don't worry. I was due to have a lecture that day but Paul's going to do it for me so I can listen to your first broadcast."

"Oh, no. Don't do that. Please don't change your schedule. Anyway, I'll just be nervous if I know you're listening in."

"Hey." He put a hand on her knee. "I want to support you, OK? I'll be listening and you'll be great and if you need me, call me. I'll be here."

She smiled weakly, even though he couldn't tell. "Why don't you go back to bed and I'll wash up? I'm so proud of you for making breakfast. That was a really big step."

He kissed her and made his way upstairs. She heard the shower running and went to the living room to flick on the TV. With perfect timing, Janie Wallace announced it was time for news and weather. Jack sat beside her as always, bleached smile plastered to his face. After the newsreader, who Sam didn't recognise, had finished, he handed over to a very pretty, very pregnant blonde woman. She could barely stand. It made Sam feel slightly sad. It was hard seeing the weather graphics with someone other than Bobby pointing and clicking the button. She would do her best to make him proud: be strong, brave, confident, and try to be as charismatic as he had been.

The doorbell rang and Sam jumped. She looked down and realised she was only wearing Jonah's T-shirt. Then came the knock. That knock. Only one person wrapped heavily on the door like that, loud and with intent. Shit. Her mother. What was she doing here so early?

"One second!" She ran to the laundry room and grabbed a pair of dirty jeans.

"Why would you keep your mama waiting?" Vittoria pushed her way in, armed with yet more dishes of lasagne and meatball marinara.

"Sorry, Mama. I was just getting up."

Vittoria placed the dishes on the counter, shrugged off her coat and hung it on the back of a chair. She tutted and shook her head as she surveyed the kitchen, all while rolling up her sleeves.

"Look at the state of this kitchen. Have you no shame, Samia Di Matteo?"

"Samia? That's your full name?"

Shit. Sam cursed under her breath. Jonah appeared at the door, amused, arms crossed. She should have warned him, told him to hide upstairs or something. Well, here it was: now or never.

"Mama, you remember Jonah Mason? He's my bo........."

"Jonah? Your boss, Jonah? Yes, we met briefly at the hospital." If Vittoria's left eyebrow had been raised anymore, it would have been in her hairline.

"Yes, Mama." She stared at the ground, waiting for a chasm to present itself and swallow her.

"Well, he's here very early in the morning. And why are you wearing Bobby's clothes?"

"They're not Bobby's." She tugged the T-shirt self-consciously while her face reddened similar to her mother's. Vittoria opened her mouth and a tirade of Italian flowed out.

"*Mia figlia sta avendo sesso con il suo capo?*"

"I'm not having sex with my boss, Mama. Well, I'm not just...... oh god, this is awful. Mama, Jonah and I are together."

161

Jonah attempted to rescue the situation by offering Vittoria a beverage. She said she'd like a peppermint tea as she sat her substantial body down, dramatising shock at her daughter's revelation. Jonah panicked. He knew where the regular tea was but couldn't find the peppermint. He considered making a weak normal tea, hoping she wouldn't notice, but this woman seemed to be sharp as a shrew. Sam saw him feeling around desperately in the cupboards and came to his aid, finding the box and handing it to him. He slowly and cautiously made the tea and took his usual four steps to the table, felt for it with his left hand and put the tea down on it with his right. However, Vittoria was sitting opposite to where he placed the tea. She looked at him curiously, wondering if he was trying to be funny. Sam moved the cup to her mother and wished she would stop eyeing Jonah so suspiciously.

"Do you tell me nothing, Samia? A big change happens in your life and you don't let your own mother know? Say, Jonah. Could you put those lasagnes in the fridge. I don't want them to spoil on the counter like that." Sam could have killed her mother right then. As he was patting his hand along to find them, Sam jumped up again, announcing she'd do it and for Jonah to sit down and have his coffee. She pulled out a chair for him and he sat down, her guiding hand on his elbow. Vittoria narrowed her eyes, observing their strange choreography.

"Well, I suppose seeing as you two are together, I should officially welcome you, Jonah."

Vittoria held out her hand. Jonah sat still, doe eyed and confused. Sam cringed when her mother's hand was held aloft, her handshake unrequited.

"Jonah. Mama's holding out her hand."

"Oh, I apologise. Nice to meet you." He offered his hand out nowhere near Vittoria's.

"Sam, what's going on? Is this boy on drugs?"

"MAMA! NO! Jesus Christ, what a thing to say. He's not on drugs. He's blind."

Vittoria sat staring at Jonah for what felt like an eternity. Sam was still waiting for that hole in the ground to open. He took it in his stride, apologising, explaining that it sometimes wasn't obvious that he was. Vittoria stood up, walked around the table. Sam looked on in horror. Was she going to walk out? Instead, the large woman threw her arms around him and squeezed him until Sam was sure his optic nerves would be shocked back into life and he'd be able to see again.

"You poor, poor boy. What happened to you? I did not even realise this when we first met. What can I do to help?"

"Mama, it didn't happen this morning. He's been like this for six years. He's fine. Now will you please sit down. I've something to tell you."

"You're PREGNANT?"

"Jesus, Mama. I'm not pregnant. We're living together. Jonah has moved in."

"Samia Isabelle Carla Di Matteo..... don't you tell me you are living with this man. Your poor husband is only gone from this world a year and you have shacked up with someone else."

"But you set me up with a man. You set me up with Luca." Sam was irate now. Her mother was impossible and she was embarrassing Jonah, who had discreetly gotten up from his seat to seek refuge in the living room, out of verbal harm's way but still able to intervene, should the situation turn nasty. He laughed to himself as Sam's mother dived into a tirade in Italian. He had no idea what she was saying, all he knew was he'd rather intercept an EF5 right now than this tempestuous pair.

Standing at the door, he held his hand out. "Sam?" She went to him and as he felt her stand against him, wrapped his arms around her. "Vittoria, please. It's OK. I'm well aware that she is recently widowed. I too am a widower so I am very sensitive to the fact. Let me assure you, I will not hurt her."

Vittoria sank down into the chair. She remained silent, processing the information. After a few moments, she inhaled. "Very well. If you make her happy, then you have my blessing to be together. Now, I must go. I promised Mrs. Sambini that I would take her to the church. That lazy good for nothing son of hers refuses to go anywhere with her. I know she's loud but would it kill him to take his mama out sometimes? I said so to Mrs. Luciano the other day and she said......."

"Mama, here's your coat. I'm sorry I yelled at you," Sam said, kissing her mother on the cheek.

"Jonah. Make sure you look after my daughter."

"I will," he reassured, placating the portly woman as she bundled out past him.

Sam took a deep breath when she returned from seeing her mother to the door. "Come here, baby." Jonah held out his arms and she sat on his lap, straddling him face to face. "So, that's over with now. What did she say when she was shouting in Italian?"

"Oh nothing... just to not jump into something so quickly." That was almost a lie. While she had said something along those lines, there was no way she was telling Jonah that her mother thought she was just feeling sorry for this 'boy' and taking him under her wing as she herself was lonely. Her daughter deserved more than to be a carer for this man. Sam had shouted back that she wasn't his carer, she was his girlfriend and she needed to mind her own business and let her live her life. Jonah gave her a hug and suddenly the row dissipated from her mind and the vein throbbing in her head relaxed.

"Are you two going to be OK? It sounded pretty intense."

"Of course. We don't argue often, but when we do, the Italian in us comes out. I'm sorry you had to witness it."

"Samia," he whispered seductively, taking her earlobe in his mouth and sucking.

"Yes?" She threw her head back, beginning to lose control of herself.

"You're amazing."

He grabbed her around the waist and pushed himself into her. She gasped, kissing from the base of his ear, down his neck and to the top of his shoulder. He whispered her name again, turning her on even more. Grabbing at his hair, she kissed him feverishly, wanting him so much that she wished they could dissolve together into one.

CHAPTER 12

Monday morning came after a restless night. Anxiety, excitement and more anxiety had kept Sam tossing and turning. She spent much of the night watching Jonah sleep. His chest, toned and slightly hairy, rose and fell rhythmically, and she unconsciously found herself breathing along with him. His camel-length eyelashes flickered at the end of his eyelids that were draped over his beautifully blue, redundant eyes. His skin was smooth and sallow. She grinned to herself as he stirred and smiled in his sleep, revealing the dimples in his cheeks that she adored. His lips twitched and contorted as he mouthed some dreamland words that would never be heard and probably not remembered. His jaw line was strong and she resisted the urge to kiss along its outline. She settled with just gently holding his hand. He was exhausted after chasing a storm with Paul. They'd gone all the way to Texas and back. Sam hadn't gone as she wanted to be prepared and rested for the new job. When she questioned why they hadn't stayed over, Paul, when dropping Jonah back, had rolled his eyes and said that Jonah couldn't bare to be away from her overnight. That and he wanted to be around for the broadcast.

"Well, aren't you a big softy," she'd said, wrapping her arms around Jonah, who was wearing a shy, cute smile across his face and kissing his cheek until Paul begged them to stop, protesting it was making him ill. "Although, I suppose I'm happy for you guys though, you know. You suit each other."

"Is that a compliment or an insult?" she'd asked.

"Both!" Paul had said as Jonah bid him goodbye, announcing he needed to use the bathroom. Sam watched Paul stare intently at the ground, where he was shuffling dirt around with his toe. He raised his gaze shyly, making sure Jonah was out of ear shot. "I meant that. You guys are good together."

Sam had thanked him and couldn't help but pick up a sadness laced in through his words. She figured he was feeling a little left out and vowed to include him in more outside of chasing.

Her stomach lurched again as she smoothed down her suit and ran a hand through her hair while checking herself in the mirror. They'd dress her in wardrobe but she needed a confidence boost that only wearing good underwear and a power suit could give her. She was going to be late if she didn't get going. The station was about a half hour away and the traffic might be bad. She'd need to be in by six thirty as the show started at eight a.m. Jonah was still asleep when she left. She didn't disturb him, he needed his sleep after yesterday. The road was quiet and long, as the sun began to rise over the sleepy buildings of Omaha. As she pulled into the familiar parking lot, she found a spot and getting out, shook herself down, took a deep breath and made her way inside.

"Oh my god, Sam!" came the excited southern drawl of Bitzy, the ditzy receptionist she knew and loved. "You look amazing. So glad you're back."

"It's nice to be back, Bitzy. You look great."

Next to greet her was Jim Krantz. A big, gentle bear of a man, he took her in his arms and hugged her warmly.

"It's so good to have you back, dear. How've you been this past year? It's been hard, I'd imagine."

"Yeah, but I'm getting there, you know? Being back here is going to be good for me, Jim."

"It sure is darlin.' Now come on, I'll walk you to wardrobe. There're some new faces there, but they're all nice as cherry pie."

There was a new girl and man in wardrobe who seemed smiley and friendly. Sally was in her early twenties, pretty, very stylish and warm. Ed was about the same age, flamboyant and camp. They had chosen a cream pant suit with a pink camisole for her first forecast. Then it was off to hair and make-up to be primped and preened before checking in with the research department to get her new desk and look up the radar and charts for the day. It was surreal being back. They had given her the same desk she'd had before. She looked over to the desk Bobby used to have and there was a scruffy, post grad looking kid in it, studying the forecast models and looking confused. She smiled to herself remembering the times she and Bobby had had lunch and coffee at that very desk. Whenever he bought the coffee, he would bring her a mini muffin. It was his way of telling her he liked her. Of course, she hadn't realised this and needed to be told openly. At thirty minutes to air time, her phone rang. Jonah.

"Hey, you left without saying goodbye."

"I know. I'm sorry, it's just you were sleeping so peacefully, I couldn't bring myself to wake you. Yesterday was a long day for you."

"OK but I didn't know where you were."

"I didn't think Jonah, I'm sorry. I was just preoccupied, you know?"

"Of course, it's OK. I just rang to wish you good luck and to say I miss you. Do you know what time you air at?"

"Yeah, at eight and nine, after the news bulletin."

"I'll be listening. I'm so proud of you."

Jim came up behind her so she whispered a hurried goodbye and hung up.

"Almost time to air, Sam honey. You ready?"

"No!"

They walked to the studio and it was only then, that the reality of Bobby's absence hit her. The bright lights, the green screen and colourful studio pulled her right back to when Bobby was at his best: in front of the camera. He lit up the room, even without the lights. The way he used to do a stupid dance just as the anchors were about to introduce him. One morning he'd gotten caught out as the camera cut to him early and he was televised doing the robot dance, badly. It ended up on YouTube. But it didn't bother him much. He was just being Bobby.

Standing in front of the green screen, her nerves came to life. Her heart hammered uncontrollably in her chest and her breathing quickened along with it. Her palms began to sweat and her head swam. She cursed herself silently that now of all times, she was going to have a panic attack. And live on air. She tried desperately to get her breathing under control as dizziness washed over her. Just as she was willing herself not to faint, she thought of Jonah: the night in the hotel when he'd held her and reassured her that she was fine, safe with him, was replaying in her mind now. Her panic subsided as she regained control of her faculties, and watched the director count her in. This was it. She was back in the saddle.

"And telling us all about today's weather is our new weather anchor and former researcher, Sam Di Matteo. Welcome back, Sam. How does it feel to be this side of the camera?" Janie said straight into the camera, beaming like a Barbie on crystal meth.

"It feels good, Janie. Great to be back. So, today, we have an area of high pressure dominating the region so nothing except clear skies and highs of 90-95 degrees. A chance of thunderstorms along the southern half of the state tomorrow, but hopefully not turning too severe. This is Sam Di Matteo, with your weather for 'Good Morning, Omaha.' You have a great day out there."

"Thank you, Sam. So a good day in store folks. Keep that sunscreen handy."

Sam did another report at nine, identicle to the eight o'clock one and by then she was comfortable in front of the camera. She thought of Jonah. Had he listened? She imagined him sitting on the couch, listening to her voice. Then she thought of Bobby. Was he watching her from somewhere up there, shaking his head because she maybe did something wrong or delighted that she did well? She'd never know. One thing was for sure, she'd felt his presence today: in the studio, at her desk, the green screen. He was with her.

The team insisted on bringing her out to lunch. They went to their usual place, Wanda's Bistro, near the station. As she was just about to tuck into her omelette, her phone rang.

"Hey, babe. You were amazing. How did you find it?"

"You heard? Thanks. Yeah, I loved it. Hey, can I call you back? I'm just getting some lunch."

"Oh, sure."

"Is everything all right?"

"Yeah, it's just...well I thought you'd be home by now. Don't worry. It's fine."

"I'll be home after this, OK?" she whispered into the phone. "Bye."

"Someone congratulating you, Sam?" Jim asked, noticing her whispered conversation.

"Oh... just my mom. She's excited," she lied. She felt sick to her stomach, but couldn't bring herself to tell the crew she was with someone else, let alone living with him.

"Of course, she should be. You were great. Well done." They raised their glasses of cola to her and continued to chat about the morning.

When she arrived home at three, Jonah was waiting at the door, having heard her car come up the driveway. As she came through the door, he picked her up and swung her around telling her how wonderful she had been.

"Thanks," she said shyly. "I'm sorry about lunch. Just, the guys wanted to treat me for my first day."

"Hey, it's cool. Paul came over to fill me in on the lecture anyway so I ate with him. So what time will you finish at every day?"

"Oh, about twelve or one. We usually go through some stuff for the next day's show after the broadcast."

"Want me to make dinner?"

"Sure. You need a hand?"

"No. My treat to celebrate your first day." He put his arms around her waist and kissed her, then made his way to the kitchen, leaving her to have a shower and change. Exhausted, she revelled in the steaming water washing over her, sweeping away the events, anxiety, stress and excitement of the day. It was nice to be home and to feel so exhilarated and fulfilled. Chasing with the boys was good fun but it was never going to be permanent. Working at the station gave her a new sense of the future, despite the fact it was so closely associated with her tragic past. It felt like home, full of good and bad memories, but home none the less.

When she got out and dried herself, she heard cursing from the kitchen. Then the smoke alarm. She threw on a top and sweat pants and ran down. Jonah was panicking trying to find the sink, flaming pan in his hands.

"Jesus, Jonah, you're gonna burn yourself alive. Here..." She grabbed the pan and threw it under the tap, then swatted the smoke alarm with a towel until it fell silent. She watched, her heart breaking as he sat down, head in hands, cursing himself.

"Hey," she said softly. "One step at a time, OK?"

"Fuck it. I just wanted to make you a nice dinner to show you how proud I am. I couldn't even fry a fucking steak."

"It's not going to happen overnight. These things take time."

"How the fuck would you know?" he snapped and stormed off, banging clumsily into the half open door, bound for upstairs.

"You know what, I don't know," she said, finding him in her room a moment later, lying on the bed as she lay herself down beside him. "But all we can do is take our time. You've had Bella and Paul doing everything for you for such a long time, and now you're trying to stand on your own two feet, it's overwhelming." Despite the tense atmosphere, she couldn't help but giggle at his petulant expression. It broke the tension. He fired her a filthy look which made her laugh even more. She turned his face to hers. "Jonah, you're doing so well. Come on, let's go down and make it together. We'll take our time." The soft tones of her voice seemed to placate him, like a mother reassuring a frightened child.

"Sam, I'm sorry I snapped at you. It was uncalled for."

"Well, now, isn't that why I'm with you? My tempestuous storm chaser." She jumped off the bed and pulled him to his feet.

"Suppose."

"No suppose about it. We both took big steps today so we should be proud of ourselves. Come on, there's some more steaks in the fridge. I'll show you how to make home-made oven fries too."

The smell of incinerated meat was soon replaced by a heady haze of sirloin caramelising. Jonah left the pan to Sam as he felt his way along the counter top to the refrigerator. Taking out a bag of salad, he opened it and planting his nose in, decided with a grimace that it was gone off, confirmed by Sam who read the best before date as being a week ago. His hand crept over the shelves until he found another one, this time fresh and spilled out a handful onto the plates.

"That steak smells done, baby."

172

Sam, busy with de-corking a bottle of Cabernet Sauvignon, checked the pan and agreed. "You're good," she said, kissing him on the cheek.

"Hey, maybe I should jack in meteorology and open a restaurant. The menus could be in braille."

"Jonah, you'd be a lousy restauranteur, no offense. As soon as there'd be a whiff of convection outside, you'd be gone with Paul on a chase, restaurant forgotten."

"True. Oh well, it's good to keep one's options open," he said with a bad English accent, holding his glass aloft, pinky turned out.

Sam laughed, enjoying his lighter mood.

Jonah suggested they invite Paul over. He was beginning to feel excitement about his newly found, slowly building independence. He was starting to feel like a new world was opening up in front of him and he had one person to thank. He felt across the table until he found her hand. Taking it to his lips, he kissed it lightly, inhaling the scent of fried beef and onion from it.

"You're amazing."

Sam eyed him curiously. "Huh? No, I'm not."

"You are. You're just..... amazing. Sam, there's something I need to say." He took a deep breath and steadied himself. "I love you."

"Oh." She sat back, processing his words, tears spiking her eyes. He hadn't said that before.

Jonah waited but the silence was too much. "Sam?"

"Yes. I'm here. Jonah," she took his hand back, "I love you too."

"Wow, OK. I was getting worried there. Are you sure? You're not just saying that because I said it. If it's all moving too soon for you, then we can.... you know, take it slow."

"We're living together Jonah. Taking it slow is way back in the distance. But I meant what I said. I love you too."

Sam couldn't suppress the feeling rising in her gut. It was somewhere between happiness and contentment. She hadn't felt that for a long time. The guilt was still there, but for a change, it had pleasant company.

*

Friday came and Sam was in a tizzy of marinating, chopping and prepping. Jonah was on the task of cleaning the good dishes and cutlery that hadn't been used since before Bobby had died. They had been wedding presents, but she omitted that piece of information. At six thirty, right on schedule, the doorbell rang. As Sam was still in a cooking frenzy, Jonah answered. She heard Stacey's high pitched, excited tones greeting him, and him thanking her for the bottle of wine she'd brought. Sam's suggestion of inviting Stacey along was not without a plan. She figured her friend was the perfect match for Paul, who had been like a lost little boy the last few weeks.

"Oh my god, Sam, you never told me how gorgeous he was," Stacey trilled, coming into the kitchen behind Jonah.

"Jesus, Stacey, he's blind not deaf."

"Thanks anyway!" Jonah quipped, smiling smugly. Paul arrived soon after and when they were full of food and wine, they sat in the living room, reminiscing about chases and college.

"You know, Jonah, you're a different man since you got with Sam. I almost don't recognise you."

"Yeah, she brings out the best in me," he said, finding her hand and squeezing it gently.

"No seriously - cooking, cleaning. You couldn't even pour a cup of coffee before you moved in here. You had it easy back then, buddy. Maybe you should move back with Bella."

"No way! It's a new me. I'll be driving the truck soon!"

"Hmm, maybe not. Although, we will have to find another driver next season, seeing as Sam's abandoned us already."

"Yeah, sorry about that - I just couldn't stand the smell."

"More like you couldn't handle all the testosterone! Ouch!" Sam elbowed Paul in the side.

"See, I've said this to Sam before and I just don't get why you put yourselves in danger like that. I mean, no offense Jonah, but look what happened to you. And you still chase? I don't get it."

"It's about saving lives, Stacey. The more we learn about severe weather, the better prepared we can be to warn people. Too many people are dying from tornadoes every year," Paul replied.

"But in this day and age, surely there are more sensible ways to gather the information you need?"

"No, not yet. It's the only way."

"Well, I think it's stupid. Jonah is a perfect example of how your reckless behaviour can hurt people."

"Stace," Sam interjected, alarmed at the colour Paul's face was turning.

"You haven't got a clue. Jonah is the very reason why we should chase. We are trying to learn more so we can save lives. What do you do for a living?"

"I'm a beautician. What does that have to do with anything?"

"So painting nails and plucking eyebrows is just as important as gathering scientific information that will hopefully reduce the number of deaths from tornadoes every year?"

Stacey looked like she might throw something at Paul. Jonah hushed them while Sam stood and beckoned Stacey to follow her into the kitchen.

"That guy is a pompous ass. Are you sure it's the same person who you waxed lyrical about how wonderful he was?" Stacey bitched while slicing the cheese Sam had given her to keep her occupied and away from Paul.

Julie McCoy

"Stacey, I think you've had a bit too much to drink. Just calm down. He wasn't getting at you. He just hasn't been himself lately. Please be nice to him, he's a good friend."

"You sure? He seems to be an opinionated asshole, if you ask me."

She stood with her arms crossed and her lips pouting like a bold child.

"Please, Stace."

"Fine. But if he doesn't apologise......" She was interrupted as Paul came in, looking sheepish.

"Stacey, I'm sorry. I shouldn't have snapped at you like that. It was wrong of me."

Stacey nodded dismissively while Sam mouthed 'thank you.' She hoped he was OK. It wasn't like him to be so snappy. He was probably just having a bad day.

CHAPTER 13

"This seabass is good. Try some." Sam stretched across the table and took his chin in her left hand, guiding the fork into his mouth.

"It is good. Want to taste the beef?"

"No thanks. So I was telling you about Brett, the sports guy...."

"Oh yeah, is he the one who was flirting with you on air last week?"

"What? No! He wasn't flirting. He was just being friendly."

"Oh, come on. He was blatantly flirting. It was a bit embarrassing, actually."

"Jonah, please. He wasn't. Are you being paranoid?"

"Hard not to be when you're blind."

"Well, don't be. And even if he was flirting, I wouldn't do it back. I'm yours and nobody else's."

This seemed to appease him. After two months of living together, she was adept at reading his moods and anticipating him blowing up, although, he'd been in much better form, was less brash and snappy since they'd gotten together. She knew how to calm him. Brett had been flirting with her, but it was harmless. The guy was a walking bag of testosterone and he flirted with all the single girls. In work, everyone assumed she was single and she didn't put them straight. She was terrified they would judge her for moving on so soon.

"So, your Mom called me the other day. She has found a course on learning to read braille and has decided to learn so she can .... I don't know... read with me I guess?"

Sam laughed so hard she dropped her fork and it rattled onto the plate causing people to stare.

"Oh Jonah, I'm sorry. She does mean well. She just gets a little too involved."

"No, it's fine. Funny actually. She called to see how I was getting on with learning to cook. She also wanted to tell me that she had enquired about getting me a seeing eye dog."

"Yeah, it's official. You're her latest project. Last year it was Mrs. Phillips who'd had her hip replaced. She was only short of moving in with the poor woman. I promise her heart is in the right place, but she has no filter."

"I know. She's just trying to be helpful. I think if I asked her to be my guide dog, she'd gladly oblige."

Their convulsions of laughter once again drew the attention of the fellow diners and Sam warned Jonah they should tone it down or they'd likely be thrown out.

The late autumn sun was beating down with gusto when they left the restaurant. Jonah could feel its heat on his face and turned skywards. He was using his cane more and more as a result of Sam's 'Project Independence.' She didn't even need to hold his hand sometimes. He knew she was with him and that she wouldn't leave his side.

"We need to cross the road here, give me your arm."

She led him across and as they approached the other side, a young, awkward, acne ridden man stopped them.

"Sam the Weather Girl? Is it you?"

"Yes, it is," she laughed nervously, mortified.

"I'm a big fan, could I get a picture with you?"

"Sure!" She stood beside the man as he held up his phone before them and took a picture.

"Thanks! I watch your show every day." He walked away, beaming from ear to ear.

"Your first stalker! Are you excited?" Jonah joked, walking on.

"Shut up! I'm mortified. But he was sweet, wasn't he? That was really weird. You kind of forget people see you on their TV every day."

"You better not get big headed on me now."

"If anyone's big headed, it's you."

"True. Now come on, let's get home. I've to dictate notes for a lecture."

"Do you want a ride into the college tomorrow?"

"No, it's an afternoon lecture so Paul's gonna bring me in. Thanks though. I can laze about in the morning, listen to you on TV, think about you and whatever else!"

She bumped her shoulder off him, took his hand in hers and they made their way back to the car.

The next morning, Sam was being fussed over in the make-up artist's chair. She was going for smokey eyes again. The week before, the make-up artist Alicia and the style team had decided to give her a make-over. They cut her hair into layers so it looked like a long bouncy chocolate waterfall, cascading from her head. They dressed her in a black shift dress and gave her silvery black eyes and pale lips. The phone lines had hopped after she'd made her first bulletin. People liked this new, sultry Sam Di Matteo.

This morning, they were doing the same look on her. Except today, she wasn't only doing the weather, she was on the couch with Janie and Jack as a special guest, speaking to them about testicular cancer. They were having a show dedicated to it and were not only going to have an expert on to show men how to check themselves, but they were also having guests on giving their own personal experience and what better person than their very own testicular cancer widow, Sam. That wasn't quite how Jim had said it but she knew it was what he was thinking. After she did the weather bulletin, she rushed to the couch in time for the interview.

"So, Sam. We all remember the wonderful Bobby Notaro, our weather man here for quite some years who tragically passed away from this particular cancer last year. But what most people won't know is that Bobby was your husband. Tell us how you met."

Feeling strangely nervous, not just because this was out of her comfort zone, but also because there was a good chance Jonah was listening and she didn't feel right about him hearing her being interviewed about her husband. She told the anchors how they'd met, in this very studio, how they'd fallen in love instantly and gotten married after two years of dating.

Janie and Jack ooh'ed and aw'ed at the romance of it all. When the interview turned to describing Bobby's diagnosis and how it had affected her, she began to choke up. Janie passed her a tissue, telling her to take a second, while casting a slightly false, condoling glance at the camera. Sam felt the room spin a little as the memories came rushing back. The last few months of being with Jonah were wonderful for helping her to forget, but now she was on the spot in front of the crew who knew him and thousands of viewers who knew and loved him too. She felt like she was betraying them, talking about her beloved husband yet living with another man. It was compelling viewing for anyone watching, as she choked back tears and struggled to speak over the lump in her throat. Sam was sure Jim was wringing his hands thinking of the ratings. After another agonising four minutes, the interview was almost over.

"So to our male viewers, if you take anything from this interview, know this. Not getting checked can leave your loved ones in this situation, alone and grieving. Please, if you find anything, get yourself checked out by a physician. Now before you go Sam, we got a picture sent into us by a fan this morning who wanted to acknowledge what a good citizen you are. This photo is from a young man called Spencer who saw you helping a blind man to cross the road yesterday in the town. Isn't this a wonderful example of someone doing a good deed for a disabled person?"

Sam slid down the couch. This couldn't be happening. She knew she should say something, tell them that this was her boyfriend, but she couldn't bring herself to do it. She thought she'd be sick, so she pulled a saccharine smile, thanked the anchors as they went to a break and ran to the bathroom. If Jonah had heard that he would freak. When she'd eventually calmed down, telling herself that he probably hadn't heard, she went back to her desk to find her phone, on silent, vibrating like a demented insect. It was Jonah. 'Oh god, oh god, oh god,' she panicked. He was going to go ape. She wasn't going to talk to him over the phone so left it on silent and would wait until she got home.

Various members of the crew congratulated her on her interview and her 'good deed.' She couldn't even respond. She knew she should put them right and tell them he was with her, but couldn't stand seeing their looks of judgement, knowing she was moving on, accusing her of forgetting about their beloved Bobby.

All the way home, her stomach sat in her shoes. She tried to justify it to herself, tell herself that maybe he hadn't been watching. But she knew there was no justification. She should have come clean with them and he was most likely listening, if not someone would certainly tell him.

Pulling into the driveway, her stomach clenched. This was it. She opened the front door and called his name tentatively, half hoping he wasn't there, that he had been called into the college early or something.

He was there but didn't respond. She heard rustling from upstairs. The sight she saw when she got upstairs sent her stomach into a spin. He was packing his suitcase.

"Jonah," she croaked.

"Don't fucking talk to me."

"Please, let me explain."

"Explain? Oh, OK. Go ahead, Good Samaritan, helping a poor disabled man across the road. Aren't you great?"

"They didn't know."

"Yeah, that's the fucking point. They didn't know and how come they didn't know? Because you didn't bother to correct them. You let them believe that you are a saint who helps poor disadvantaged people, when in fact you were too cowardly to tell them that I am your live in boyfriend. You were too embarrassed to tell them that you are going out with a blind man."

"For fuck's sake, Jonah. It's not like that. I didn't get a word in with them."

"It didn't sound like it to me. There was plenty of time for you to correct them, but you just agreed with them and accepted their praise. How could you do that to me?"

"You're blowing this out of proportion. Honestly, it's not like that."

"Yes. It is. You are embarrassed. End of."

"I didn't tell them because they knew and loved Bobby and I don't want them thinking that I've moved on so soon."

"And you think that's a better excuse? You have moved on. You are with me now. Why is that something to be ashamed of?"

"It's not... well it kind of is because I work with these people and they would judge me."

"Who gives a fuck what they think? You said you loved me. You obviously don't if you could do that to me on live fucking television." He was shouting well above his normal angry decibel now. He was really mad. It frightened her. She felt bile rise in her throat.

"Hold on. You're not exactly 'Honest Joe' yourself. How long did it take you to tell me you'd been married? Only months." She watched him recoil slightly as her voice became higher and laced with aggression. "So, I don't think it's very fair that you're slating me for this."

"It's apples and oranges, Sam. Two totally different things. I didn't tell you about Anna because it was too painful and I needed to know I could trust you, be open with you before I told you. I never talk about her to anyone, never and telling you was extremely hard."

"It's not different at all, Jonah. It hurt to know that you would keep something so big from me."

"It wasn't about you. I just couldn't talk about it. Look, the fact is, you're embarrassed by me. That's what this is. It's purely and simply that you can't bring yourself to tell them you've moved on." He stood, flinging garments angrily into the case.

"Jonah, please - sit down so we can talk about this. And that's not your shirt, it's my pyjama top." She felt the bile subside and her voice soften. If there was one way to rile Jonah further, it was to match his decibel. She needed to calm down, in turn, hopefully calming him.

"Yeah, well it's hard to pack when you can't fucking see what you're doing."

She begged him to sit, but he refused, dumping random things into his case in the hope that he'd at least get something of his into it. She was crying now. She'd hurt him. She wanted to put her arms around him, to whisper soft reassurances into his ear, but she knew he'd push her away.

"Where are you going?"

"Bella's. Paul's on his way to bring me."

"You rang Paul? Jonah, can you please calm down and talk about this with me. I've tried to explain."

"Yeah, you've tried to explain. There's no point. You just can't let go of Bobby. You're back working with people who knew him, you're talking about him on the TV, you still have his clothes and I'm pretty sure you put them on. I can smell men's aftershave on you sometimes and it's the same one that I get whenever I open the closet door. And I know you still wear your wedding ring. You're wearing it right now, aren't you?" He tried to grab her left hand to feel but she pulled it away. "I'm not stupid, Sam. You are too worried about what people think and you haven't let go of your husband. I can't deal with that. It's not fair on me and it's not fair on you. You're not ready for this. So I'm going."

She sank onto the bed and discretely pulled out the clothes that she owned from his suitcase. "Jonah. Please. Don't leave. I love you so much. Tell me what to do to make this right."

"There's nothing you can do. I've made up my mind." His voice was almost a whisper.

Sam's stomach sank further. She'd have felt marginally better if he'd shouted. The resignation and defeat in his voice was worse than if he'd screamed abuse at her.

"Jonah... I'm begging you not to leave. Please. Surely you understand? You lost Anna, so you know what it's like to grieve."

"Yes, I do. But I also know what it's like to move on: to find someone you love more than anything, even when you thought you'd never love again. But you obviously don't."

"I do. I do. Please Jonah, don't go." She tried to take his hand but he whipped it out of her grip. There was a knock on the door.

"Paul's here. I'm going."

She could do nothing to stop him. She sank to the floor, and through her tear streaked eyes, watched him feel his way downstairs with one hand, clutching the ill packed suitcase in the other. Then she heard the door slam and seconds later, Paul's truck drive off down the street.

Her breath caught in her throat. She stopped breathing for a moment until a huge sob forced her to inhale and she sobbed until she thought she might pass out. She phoned Stacey. It was the only thing she could think of to do.

Stacey arrived half an hour later, laden with wine and chocolate and held Sam until the giant sobs had tired her out so much that she couldn't cry anymore. After Stacey left, she tried to call Jonah but his phone was turned off. She called Paul.

"Hey, Paul. Is Jonah there?"

"Yeah. He's here, Sam, but he doesn't want to talk to you right now. I'm sorry."

"Don't be sorry. It's not your fault. Just please tell him I need to speak to him and ... I miss him."

"Look, whatever happened with you guys, I'm sure you can sort it out. I'll talk to him."

"Oh, that'd be great. Thanks Paul."

She hung up feeling like the melancholic fog that was encasing her had lifted a little. Jonah listened to Paul. He would get him to calm down and then talk him around. It was going to be OK. This bit of reassurance helped her to fall into a heavy sleep.

The next morning at the studio, the testicular cancer/good Samaritan story had been forgotten and it was business as usual. Her plan was that if someone mentioned it to her, she would put them straight: that the man was her boyfriend, they were living together and were in love. Although, all of that was in doubt after he'd walked out. She had to rectify it. They couldn't throw it all away over one stupid act of omission.

Jonah was back working at the university as tornado season was just about over. She stopped at a little deli they'd visited a week previously to pick up some of his favourite banana nut muffins after work. Her stylist allowed her to wear the dress she had worn for the broadcast on condition that she dry-clean and return it. It was a red, chiffon summer dress with scoop neck and short sleeves. She felt really good in it, even though Jonah wouldn't be able to see it, he would appreciate the floaty fabric, if she could only get him to touch her.

She'd never been to the university before. It was a sprawling campus in which worried-looking students hurried around with haversacks that were almost bigger than they were and books in their arms. A large, main door loomed ahead of her so she headed that direction. A small, wizened old man sat on a stool at the door, wearing a cap and blazer and looking very official, so she thought he might know where to direct her.

She asked him where she could find Jonah Mason in the meteorology department. He directed her in a deep southern accent. There were three lecture halls and a series of laboratories in the physics wing. In the first one, a portly woman preached to a young-looking, eager audience. On the white board was a diagram demonstrating the fulcrum effect. Newbies, she thought, feeling sorry for them, their terrified faces plastered to the lecturer, pens moving at the speed of sound, for fear they'd miss a note. The next hall was empty. The last one, held a familiar voice inside talking about the various pressure values inside a hurricane. She closed her eyes and listened to his voice, although muffled, through the fire doors. His passion for weather was so evident in his speeches and lectures, it was contagious. She watched the students - some were bored rigid, others were mesmerised by their lecturer and what he was saying. She opened the door quietly and skulked in.

"Ah, a latecomer?" Jonah said, looking out indirectly into the audience.

"Sorry," she muttered, trying to disguise her voice. The lecture was almost over as it was just one o'clock, so she slipped into an aisle seat and tried to keep a low profile. She studied every movement he made. His hands, making a spiral in the air as he talked about the wind speed at the eye wall of Hurricane Katrina. His lifeless eyes flickered in the reflection of the cheap, florescent lighting whenever he looked up. His sinuous arms, covered only by a T-shirt, moved around hypnotically as he gesticulated, a choreography to his descriptions. Sometimes when he'd raise his arm up, the audience would get a flash of his tattooed bicep. She sighed audibly as she ogled him and thought him magnificent. The student sitting beside her, disgruntled and scruffy, shot her a dirty look.

Soon the lecture was over and the students filed out, some quickly, alone while others straggled, chatting aimlessly. Sam cursed them and wished they'd hurry up and leave.

Eventually, when the lecture theatre was empty except for Jonah, she tried to pick up the courage to speak. He took his cane, flexed it out and carefully stepped down off the podium, making his way to the door.

"Jonah."

He stopped dead in his tracks, head down.

"What are you doing here?" He didn't sound impressed. She flinched.

"I came to talk to you. I want you to come home."

"It's not my home. It's yours and Bobby's."

"Jonah please listen. I brought you muffins."

"Oh, well then, all is forgiven seeing as you have muffins. What do you fucking take me for, Sam, a five year old child?"

"No, I just thought....."

"Well, you shouldn't have bothered."

"Please just sit down here." She tried to take his elbow to lead him to a chair but he shook her off.

"Don't touch me," he snapped as he made his way out of the lecture hall, slowly and cautiously, cane tapping on the floor before each footfall.

He was still mad. She was going to get nowhere with him. There was no point in even trying. She had no choice but to leave and after watching him exit the lecture hall, she made her way out and down to the main door. A sob rose in her chest but she fought it down and took flight, running for the comfort and privacy of her car, where she relented and let the tears flow.

That night, Paul came around to collect the rest of Jonah's things. He was solemn and uncomfortable as Sam let him in and handed him the bag of various clothes and bottles of shampoos and shower gels. She invited him in, expecting him to refuse. However, he agreed to stay for a coffee. She asked him if there was any point in going to see Jonah tonight, to which Paul shook his head.

"He's still pretty mad, Sam. He told me what happened. He's really cut up."

"I know, and I'm so mad at myself for it. It was so stupid not to be honest about him. I got too caught up in people's opinion. Do you think he'll ever forgive me?"

"Just give him a few days. He'll cool down eventually. He always does."

Sam wasn't feeling too confident.

"Can you talk to him for me?"

"I'll try, but he doesn't always listen to me. Give it some time." And with that, he left, leaving Sam feeling slightly more confident. She'd do as Paul said and leave it a few days. Despite what he said, Jonah did listen to him. She had to have faith that he would talk him around.

The house was so empty without him. She would lie in the dark listening to Florence and the Machine: her sorrow so beautifully sung by someone who could say it better than she. Whenever

Cosmic Love came on, she would cry, the lyrics so profound and relevant that she almost felt they'd been written for her and Jonah. All their memories, although recent, were burned like embers into her mind: the storms, the sex, the nights they lay together just listening to each other breathe. She had something with Jonah she had never had with Bobby. It was a mutual connection, which she couldn't explain. It felt like everything in her life had been leading up to her finding him, that this was the pinnacle of her existence.

*

Days passed. She gave herself a deadline of four days before calling him. However, on day three, her phone rang just as she was getting out of the shower. It was Jonah. She jumped on it for fear his impatience would only allow a couple of rings before he would hang up.

"Hello? Jonah?"

"Hi. Listen, can we get together and talk today, please?"

"Yes. I can come over now if you like?" Her heart was singing and was ready to jump out of her chest with excitement.

"OK, see you soon. I'm in Bella's."

Feeling jittery, like she'd consumed a bucket full of espresso, she put back on the red dress she'd worn the last day she saw him. This time, for sure, he'd get to feel it on her. A spritz of perfume and she was away, down the road like a bat out of hell. She parked the car and had to restrain herself from running to the door. Deep breaths and act cool, she told herself, after knocking.

The door opened. The man she had been dreaming about the last three nights stood before her. Hair slightly dishevelled, wearing a shirt and jeans and looking as cool as a cucumber. She was on the verge of exploding into a million butterflies. He looked so good.

She couldn't wait to wrap her arms around him again and kiss his neck and his earlobe and everywhere.

"Come in." The cool air of his voice pulled her back down to earth. Not good.

"I'm glad you called, Jonah. I need to apologise for everything. I know that what I did was wrong. I'm sorry. I've missed you so much."

He left her words floating in the air as he gestured for her to go to the living room. Her stomach dropped.

"You've nothing to apologise for. It was an awkward situation and you probably didn't deal with it like you should have, but I get it, kind of. Why you don't need to be sorry is because it's not your fault. You haven't moved on from Bobby. You weren't ready. And maybe I pushed you into moving on and for that, I'm sorry. You need time to heal."

"But Jonah......" Tears came quickly. They spilled onto her red dress.

"Sam, it's OK." He was sitting with her now, arm around her shoulders, bracing her against him while she rocked but it wasn't the same as usual, it was colder, no spark, no chemistry. Just a friend holding another friend. "You see, you're not OK. You're still grieving. And I put too much pressure on you."

"You didn't. I love you, Jonah. I'll do anything. I'll get rid of Bobby's clothes and things if you want."

"No. I would never ask you to do anything like that. They're important to you and you should never have to get rid of them. But for now, it's not right for us to be together. And I've got something to tell you."

"What?"

"I've been offered a job at another University."

"Where?" She almost didn't want to know.

"Paris."

"Paris, Texas?" She asked, a hint of optimism in her voice, but she didn't feel it.

"No. Paris, France this time." He bowed his head, hating having to tell her this news.

Again, the tears came and he held her tightly until they ceased. When she could eventually form sentences, she asked when he was leaving. He told her it was next week. It was only for a couple of semesters but with a possibility of a permanent position. He'd met the university director at the conference where Jonah and Sam had first gotten together, and this man had been head hunting him since. How ironic, the event that brought them together, would tear them apart. He had offered Jonah the job two months before and had been hounding him since but he'd refused, until now.

"How are you going to manage over there on your own?"

"They're assigning me a carer. I prefer to call her a PA."

"*Her*? Oh."

"Sam, please don't be like this. It's a good opportunity for me and also for you. You need time. We will keep in touch. I'll have the latest in voice technology so I can email you. I need to do this."

"Oh god. This is it, isn't it?"

"No. We can be friends. I need for us to be friends. I need to move forward and you need to heal. I couldn't have done all this without you. You have taught me so much over the past few months. I can never thank you enough for it."

"I have to go." She got up slowly, her movements leaden. He stood too, reaching out for a hug. She clung to him, swallowing back the boulder in her throat and the waterfall of tears that were threatening. She tried to burn the memory of his smell into her mind so she could refer to it again when she needed to think of him, inhaling every molecule that would fit in her lungs. He bent down to kiss her. His lips tasted of coffee, honey and Jonah. Gently, sweetly, slowly, their lips moved, then all too soon parted, leaving her unsatisfied and wanting. She left quietly, sat into her car, took a last look at the house, hoping he'd still be standing there, but the front door was shut. She drove off.

CHAPTER 14

Sam sat in the waiting room, the peach colours making her feel ill again. The receptionist was back to tap tapping on her computer. She had to restrain herself from going over, picking up the computer and throwing it at her. Should she not have some more discretion when there were people sitting here breaking down inside? The last thing they needed to hear were her fucking fingernails.

"So, you're angry, Sam?" Dr. Greenberg was still no stranger to condescension, she noticed.

"No. Yes." The vortex of words in her head were rotating at a vicious pace, although they'd slowed down enough for her to form sentences. "I'm angry that Bobby died. I'm angry that Jonah left. I'm angry that that asshole, Luca, attacked me. I'm angry that my mother won't leave me alone and I'm angry that I'm back here. I thought I was better. Oh, and I'm angry at myself for messing things up."

"Can we talk about Jonah?"

"No."

"I think we should, but we don't have to talk about anything you don't want to."

"I don't want to talk about Jonah. It's just .... oh god, I miss him so much....." Tears again. At the end of the session, she could add to the causes of her anger: that she had paid out ninety dollars to spend an hour crying in front of a dissociated man who couldn't care less.

When she got home, feeling like she'd been hit by a train, her phone beeped with an email.

To: Sam Di Matteo
From: Jonah Mason

Hey.
How are you? I'm playing with my new voice recognition program. I speak and it converts it to text. Cool, isn't it? So I've been here a few weeks now. I hope you're doing well. How's the job?
It's lovely over here. The food is great and the university has s e t me up in a great apartment. They're very blind friendly! I have a PA called Sandrine who is indispensable. It's definitely different here but I like it.
I really hope you're all right, Sam. I miss you and hope you can come and visit me. Paul is coming over in a few weeks. Bella, Nigel and the kids came over to help me settle, which was lovely but it was nice to have some peace after they'd left.
I'm becoming so much more independent now, thanks in no small part to you. I'd never have done this if it weren't for the encouragement you gave me to do more things by myself.
I really hope you'll consider coming to visit me.

Love, Jonah. x

She slammed the phone down. He was enjoying himself and she was here suffering. She was right back to where she was after

Bobby had died. Alone, sad, angry, existing in the shadow of the men she'd loved. She drank an entire bottle of wine. Sprawling on the couch, she felt marginally better, although her head was swaying and her stomach felt sick. This room annoyed her. She hated this house. It was empty and lonely. And cream. Too much cream. Her sofa was creased and misshapen from years of lounging on it, snuggling with Bobby and then Jonah. She wanted to throw something, to smash something against the stupid cream wall. Maybe even hurt herself, just so she could feel something. The wine was making her feel numb now. Numb wasn't good. She needed to feel something cold, hot, painful. She dragged her nail along her forearm. It stung and left a red mark, but was still just a dull ache. There was nothing worse than that dull, numbness - in this cream, lifeless house. Something broke through the numbness, a feeling rising up from her stomach... more anger. She was angry at Bobby for getting sick, angry at Jonah for making her fall in love with him and angry at him for leaving her. If he knew what a state she was in, he'd come back. But she didn't want him to. She didn't want any more disappointment. She'd only fall too deep into him and get hurt again. She opened her computer and began to type.

To: Jonah Mason
From: Sam Di Matteo.

Don't contact me again.

Sam

The smug smile that she wore was forced and insincere. Was she taking a stand? Protecting herself? Or was she simply cutting off her nose to spite her face? Her stomach sank as her inbox beeped to inform her there was a reply.

To: Sam Di Matteo
From: Jonah Mason

What? Are you serious? Why are you being like this?

Jonah

To: Jonah Mason
From: Sam Di Matteo

I need you to not contact me again. Thank you.

Sam.

The next morning, her head felt like it might implode and her stomach was sick. Her mouth felt like sandpaper. She saw the empty bottle on the floor and the computer, still open but long since shut down and groaned as she remembered what had happened the night before. She jumped on the computer and opened it, shouting at it to boot up faster. Opening her email, her stomach turned in anxious expectation. Oh, how she wished there would be a response from him but there was nothing, just some spam about penile erectile dysfunction. In fairness, she had told him twice to leave her alone. He was only abiding by her wishes. But those were her wishes last night when she was drunk and upset after therapy. They didn't reflect how she really felt. Although, she couldn't exactly mail him back that she hadn't meant it as she'd been drunk.

Work beckoned so she vomited, showered and put on some semblance of an outfit. Alicia, the make-up artist, tutted and shook her head when Sam walked in and sat in her chair later that morning.

"What the hell happened to you?"

"I was out last night," she lied.

"Well, we're gonna need a pot of concealer to hide those dark circles."

"Thanks, Alicia." Sam was desperately trying to swallow the lump in her throat. If she cried anymore, she'd shrivel up like a dehydrated raisin. Checking her phone for the hundredth time, she saw there was still no response. The coffin that her relationship with Jonah lay in had taken its final nail.

Her broadcast was messy and disjointed. Jim called her into his office at eleven. He wore a concerned look on his face as she entered and shut the door gingerly behind her.

"Sam, honey. Is everything OK?" His eyes were kind but his words were stern.

"Yes."

"Are you sure? If there was something, would you come and tell me?"

"Of course, Jim."

"I know being back here must be hard on you but do not fuck up a forecast like that again. Viewers aren't stupid, they pick up more than you'd think."

She apologised to Jim and left his office, closing the door behind her, head lowered, thoroughly scolding herself as she made her way back to her desk.

That night, after her telling off from Jim, she opened another bottle of wine. She considered ignoring the knock at the door but nosiness got the better of her so she rose and answered it. Paul stood before her, holding the same facial expression Jim had done earlier that day.

"What are you doing here?"

"I saw your broadcast this morning. You didn't seem yourself. And also, Jonah called. He told me about the email. I just called to see if you're all right."

"I'm fine."

"Can't I come in?"

She reluctantly stood aside and let him walk in past her into the living room. He saw the almost empty bottle and looked at her. She was swaying slightly on the spot.

"Shhhit down," she slurred, struggling to keep her eyelids open.

"Sam, did you drink all of this?" He waved the bottle in the air.

"No, just... just a glass."

"Fuck, Sam. This is not good. I'm phoning Jonah."

"Don't you dare phone Jonah. What are you, his fucking minion?" She instantly regretted shouting at him, watching him wince as her words stung him.

"Don't speak to me like that, Sam. I'm just a concerned friend."

"You're Jonah's friend."

"I'd like to think I'm yours too. I'm worried about you. This has hit you hard and I need you to know you can count on me, OK? Drinking yourself into oblivion isn't going to solve anything."

"But it makes me feel better, Paul. I can't deal with losing him too."

"Oh, Sam." He wrapped his arms around her and let her cry uncontrollably into his chest. "You know he'll probably be back in the New Year. Surely you guys can pick up where you left off."

"I don't think so. He hates me, Paul."

"He doesn't hate you. He just thinks you both got in too deep, too soon."

"It doesn't matter now anyway. He's in Paris, not even the Texas one, with Sandrine and she's gonna fall in love with him like I did and they're going to lay out in the grass and listen to the weather, and they're gonna have sexy showers and lie all night long, naked together."

"That's a little too much information."

"Sorry." She managed a little embarrassed smile as she looked up at Paul. His green eyes were so inviting, as they smiled and twinkled at her, filled with concern and a little amusement. She felt her wine fuelled libido lift as she fixed her gaze to his. His countenance changed from jovial to serious, chewing his lip under her stare. She grabbed him behind the neck and pressed her mouth onto his, kissing him feverishly. He reciprocated, parting her lips with his tongue, finding hers and groaned as they both moved together, tasting, feeling. She pushed him backwards so he fell onto the couch and leaned onto him, kissing him more deeply. But just as she was fidgeting to find his belt buckle, he clasped her hand and pushed her off him.

"This is wrong. You don't want this."

"Oh, don't I? It seems it's you who doesn't want it." She slumped back onto the couch, sulking like a petulant teenager.

He shook his head, as if battling with his conscience.

"Sam, you're drunk. And more importantly, you're in love with Jonah. You don't want me." There was sadness in his voice, but he was right. "Now, you need to drink some water and coffee and sober up a bit." Fixing himself as he got up, he left the room. She groaned and held her head in her hands, berating herself for what she had just done. He returned moments later with a steaming mug of coffee and a large glass of water.

"Paul, I'm really sorry."

"It's OK. I'm used to women throwing themselves at me." He smiled half-heartedly.

"Well, you should be. You're a really good guy."

He shook his head, disbelieving her and himself a little for not taking what she had thrown at him. "Yeah, well, it hasn't gotten me very far. Anyway, I need you to drink this coffee and water and to promise me you won't drink anymore."

"I'm fine and I promise I won't drink anymore."

After he'd left, she drank another bottle of wine and passed out again on the couch.

The phone woke her the next morning. It was Jim screaming down the phone at her to get her shit together and get into the studio. She couldn't raise her head off the couch and cursed as she lifted her heavy arm to see her watch: seven thirty. It was as though a lead weight was sitting on her. She told Jim she had the flu and couldn't make it. Her absence from the show prompted worried calls from her mother, Stacey and Paul. The latter and former she ignored. Stacey's call, however, she answered. Stacey listened to her friend slur her words and speak in confused sentences, so she told her to hang up. She called back a short time later to say she'd made her an appointment with her own therapist and she would collect her in an hour.

*

This waiting room was much more pleasant. Everything was white except for three abstract, colourful paintings on the wall. The smell of lavender incense not only calmed her mind but somehow helped to clear it a little. The door opened and a smiling young woman dressed in jeans and a sweater walked out. Stacey squeezed Sam's hand as she rose to join the woman in the consulting room. Sam felt an instant connection with Dr. Levison. They were a similar age and the woman's casual appearance made her less patronising.

Sam told her about her recent drinking binges, Bobby, Jonah, missing work... everything. All too soon, the hour was up. Dr. Levison suggested she stay with a friend for a few days, to be sure she didn't drink again and gave her some exercises to do to calm her mind, along with some positive affirmations. This was a departure from Dr. Greenberg's apathetic humming and hawing whenever she spoke. His condescending disinterest only served to leave her feeling lower than she had been when she'd gone to visit him. And what was worse, he'd charged her money for the privilege.

She left Dr. Levison's office feeling lighter than she'd felt in weeks. She was going to stay with Stacey for a few days until she could get herself together.

CHAPTER 15

It was June and Sam had to blink to be sure she was seeing the calendar correctly. It seemed like Christmas had been only a few weeks ago. She was getting ready for her weather bulletin, the radar was alive with storms today. Tornado season had been quiet but was firing up just as it was coming to an end. She thought back to this time last year when she, Jonah and Paul were chasing, spending long heady days on the road, storms looming on the horizon, flashing and breaking in front of them, tornadoes stretching from the clouds.

"There's a warning for southern Nebraska all the way down through western Kansas. Lots of potential for tornadoes today folks so please take care and keep an ear on the broadcasts. Stay safe."

She had to race home as she was having some friends and family over for the evening. It was Bobby's second anniversary and she wanted to mark it in some way. It wasn't going to be melancholy or sad, just some people getting together and telling stories about him. By eight thirty, the house was full. Her mother was whizzing around, nagging, handing out appetisers and taking offense when people refused to sample them.

"Mom, stop forcing food on people. They're probably not hungry."

"But do they not know that I slaved all day.... all day to make them." Vittoria gesticulated wildly, her hands flailing above her head. She almost hit Brett, the sports anchor from the station as he passed by.

"I know, but it's fine. Leave them alone."

"Hey, babe." Brett came over and slapped Sam on the backside.

"Fuck off, Brett," she muttered, out of Vittoria's earshot or her mother would come down on her like a tonne of bricks about her language.

"Oh, come on. When are you going to come on a date with me?"

"Em, let's see. It's eight thirty now so....... never."

"You're such a cock tease, Sam," he grunted sulkily.

"No, you're just a cock, honey. Now go on and annoy someone else."

The guy was too stupid to take offense. He pursued her endlessly, but she was having none of it. She was sworn off men. And even if she did decide to start dating again, Brett would be the last man she would consider.

The doorbell rang and Sam ran to get it.

"Paul!" She threw her arms around him, as he stiffened slightly under her embrace. "I'm so glad you came. I know it was short notice."

"It's cool. Thanks for inviting me. I was chasing down near Alma when I got your text so I thought I'd pop in on my way home. Sorry I look such a mess."

"Of course. And you look fine. So who are you chasing with now?" She left the next part of her question hanging in the air.

"Jonah's still in France," he answered, picking up the unspoken.

Paul regaled her with the details of the new guys. They had a brand new Doppler radar built onto the truck that had cost a small fortune, so they were getting so much information about tornadoes now. Sam revelled in hearing his stories. It brought her back to last year. Some of the best days she'd ever had were chasing with Paul and Jonah. But it didn't bring her down anymore to think of it. She was in a better frame of mind these days.

"So, how is Jonah?"

"He's great. Settled in really well. Not only is he lecturing in meteorology, but they've asked him to stay on longer to help develop some sort of computer program for blind people. So he's very busy."

"Good. Good. I'm glad he's doing well."

"He asks for you, you know. Always likes to know how you are."

"That's nice. Now let's get you a drink. Come and meet my family."

After their awkward encounter the year before, when Sam had gotten herself into a drunken stupor and made a pass at Paul, they'd left it in the past, not spoken of it and become close friends. Sam sometimes felt that maybe he had feelings for her, but he never said and she wouldn't dream of confronting him. He looked out for her. She didn't see him often as he was busy lecturing and now that the season was in full swing again he was out on the road. She left him in the capable hands of Stacey, warned them not to start arguing and went to see how the other guests were for food and drink.

"Hey, Sam.... when are you gonna come chasing with me again?" Paul caught her hand as she walked past him, delivering a round of drinks.

"Some day, Paul. I will some day."

*

The envelope sat on her desk the next Monday morning. She stared at it for a while and considered opening it. No, coffee first, then envelope. Coffee drank, she picked it up and turned it over. She opened it slowly, almost afraid something would jump out and bite her.

The stamp on the front was its giveaway, telling exactly who it was from. Her stomach clenched as she pulled out the letter inside. It was from the head of the Meteorological Society. He wanted to invite her to speak at the annual conference in the Oasis Resort in Paris, Texas, under the heading "The Media's Role in Forecasting Extreme Weather." She would have to give an hour long lecture on the subject. Her stomach lurched as she thought of having to formulate an address. She could always decline the invitation but that would be counter-productive. It would be nice to be known, not only as GMO's weather girl, but as a serious meteorologist.

She picked up the phone.

"Paul? Hi, it's Sam."

"Hey! How are you? What's up? You gonna come chasing with me?"

"Eh, I will soon, I promise, but that's not why I'm calling you. I want your opinion on something... or rather, I want you to talk me into something. I've been invited to be a guest speaker at the AMS conference this year but I don't know if I want to do it. Talk me into it, Paul."

"Why do you need me to talk you into it? You know it's a wonderful opportunity. Are you holding back because of Jonah?"

"Yeah, I guess maybe on some level. I just worry that it's going to bring back so many memories and set me back. I've been doing so well, not getting drunk and feeling stronger, that I'm worried that something like this will make me undo all of that."

"Sam, you are stronger than this. You know you can do it. Jonah has moved on so you have to too."

She shook her head sadly, his words a wasp in her ear, thanked him for his advice and hung up. When he said Jonah had moved on, did he mean with someone else? She felt ill, thinking of him and

Sandrine or whoever, doing the things they used to do. Paul was right though, she had to move on or she'd never get anywhere.

That evening, sitting in her dining room, eating a microwave meal for one, she looked around, her eyes suddenly coming into focus. She was seeing things like she hadn't seen them for years, like she'd been wearing dirty glasses all along and had taken them off, cleaned them and replaced them, showing her how clear things really were. The house was a shrine to Bobby. There were photos of him everywhere, his baseball mitt and bat were still hanging on the hook in the hall. The Huskers poster was still tacked to the dining room wall, his hats still on the hook by the back door. It was as if she hadn't been able to see the wood for the trees but now someone had lifted her up so that she could see well above the canopy and could appreciate just how far the forest spread. Paul had been right - she needed to move on. She could always take down the posters and various things of Bobby's but the memories would always be imprinted in colour in the magnolia walls of the house. She needed a drastic change. Maybe moving on meant moving house too. A fresh new place that was hers and hers alone, no remnants of Bobby or Jonah holding her back in the past. She inhaled a breath of newly found purpose and opened her laptop. She had some work to do.

*

Standing in the garden of the little cottage type house she had seen on the realtor's webpage, her lungs filled with the scent of roses and honeysuckle. As the realtor told her why the owners were moving, they were retiring to Florida and how the house was in immaculate condition, Sam concentrated on imagining herself living here. The kitchen was cream with walnut finishes, modern but classic. The small living room with hardwood oaken floors was painted olive green, a colour that invited you in and promised to help you relax. Her house was big for one, and for a time, two people. Bobby and she had bought it before they got married, planning someday to raise a family, ensconced in its white picket fence. Maybe she'd meet someone and that would be a reality for her someday, after all she was only in her early thirties, but for now, she needed it to be just her and she couldn't do that in her existing home. This cottage was perfect: girly, not too small but not too big, a beautiful garden and not overlooked by houses or trees so she could sky-watch day and night without visual interruption.

"I'll take it," she said confidently. "I'll pay the asking price."

While the realtor wasted no time in making phone calls, Sam stood in the kitchen and smiled. She thought she could be happy here. There was just the arduous and possibly heartbreaking task of packing, which included packing up and getting rid of Bobby's things. She wouldn't get rid of everything, just his clothes and shoes, stuff that was taking up room. It wasn't going to be easy.

One stress that was taken from her was that her own house sold quickly. A family moving to the area from Wisconsin snapped it up a week after she put it up for sale. She got almost the asking price, which in itself, paid for the cottage with a little left over. She still had the money from Bobby's insurance policy - she'd used it to live on before she began chasing with Jonah and Paul but there was still enough left over to furnish the new house, leaving a fully furnished house behind her. It was some satisfaction that the bigger house would fulfill its potential and have a fully formed family in it. She imagined two beautiful dark haired children running down the stairs on Christmas morning, blowing out candles on birthday cakes, coming into the living room on the night of their Prom to the ooh's and aah's of their parents. It made her ache to realise they weren't going to be her children, coming to her and Bobby, or indeed Jonah. She'd always wanted children, but this was her life now and she wasn't afraid anymore. Dr. Levison had bestowed onto her, the skills to feel positive and to try and get the best out of life.

In between making phone calls to realtors, banks and insurance companies, she was also wading her way through research for her speech at the conference. It was coming together, although, she sighed many a time thinking how, if Jonah were here, he would be a real asset. But she could do it without him and she always had Paul to help.

*

Moving day was July the first and it was fast approaching, only a week away. It was time to pack. She took the day off work and started by making up boxes. The kitchen was the first room to be ransacked, as she figured leaving the painful rooms till last was best. If she started on Bobby's things, she'd spend the day crying and would get nothing done. Dish after dish and cup after cup were wrapped and carefully placed into boxes. Most of their kitchen ware had been wedding presents. She recalled taking note of everything, the day after the wedding, as Bobby and she sat in the living room, unwrapping gifts while writing down who had given what so they could thank them with cards after their honeymoon. If it hadn't been for their extremely generous guests, they'd have been eating off cardboard plates and drinking from plastic cups. Onto the living room, nothing much in there except DVD's, CD's and books. Surveying the tens of boxes at her feet in the hallway, she smiled satisfactorily. Downstairs was packed. Looking tentatively upwards to the top of the staircase, she sighed and made her way up, like a criminal towards the guillotine. She considered bringing a bottle of wine, but the last time she'd done that, she'd gotten into trouble with her boss and ended up back at the therapist's, so she refrained.

First the closet. She stood in it one last time, inhaling the musky, now fading, aftershave from Bobby's suits. Maybe she would keep one of them, just to keep his smell alive for another while. No. No, she had to get rid of everything. What had Dr. Levison said? 'A ship cannot sail if it's still tethered by rope to the dock.' Bobby's things, so present in this house, were the tethers, sucking her back to the past. Running her hand down the beautifully tailored Armani suits: grey, charcoal, navy and black, she inhaled one last time and placed them carefully into a black plastic bag, afraid that crumpling them would in some way disrespect him. His ties, a rainbow of colours and patterns, were placed in one sweeping motion into the bag for donation. She took one back out and put it into a moving box with her clothes packed into it, but then took it out again. 'A clean sweep and fresh start' was the mantra she was singing manically in her head, even if she didn't quite believe it.

The closet with no clothes, only memories, was the one she was truly dreading. For the next half hour, she sat Buddha-like on the floor, her wedding album across her lap and cried onto it. Her tears ran down the acetate covering the photos like little tiny streams down a flat mountain side. Bobby looked so happy. Her favourite was the one the photographer had taken of them at the altar as they said 'I do.' Bobby had tears in his eyes. Everyone had cheered when they kissed for the first time as husband and wife, then they practically ran down the aisle, hands clasped, to the open doors of their new life together. When she'd finished her wistful reminiscence, she closed the album slowly and placed it carefully in her packing box. No way would she get rid of it. She also kept some photos from holidays and their honeymoon and various items he'd kept that were close to his heart: his favourite watch, a peak cap that had been the first thing she'd bought him, and a mug that had a picture of them both printed onto it. She smiled when she found the first thing he'd bought her: a teddy bear that when pressed on the paw, said "I love you." It was his way of telling her that he loved her, before he'd ever had the guts to say it himself. She remembered crying and Bobby, thinking she was upset, took the teddy off her and went to leave, until she called him back to say they were happy tears, and that she loved him too.

In the back of the closet, was a box she had forgotten. Opening it slowly, her eyes began to fill with tears again. It was his 'little box of treasure' that he'd kept from his childhood. There were a few toy soldiers, a digital watch and some pebbles and shells, along with a grainy photograph of him with his parents and a collie dog. The day they'd moved in together, he'd showed it to her. She'd thought it was the cutest thing. As more tears fell, her eyes focused on a sheet of paper, stuffed into the bottom. She hadn't remembered that being there before. Her chest heaved as she opened it and saw Bobby's handwriting and the date. It was dated three weeks before the day he died, so he must have written it the day before he'd taken bad and was hospitalised.

My dearest Sammy,

The day I married you, I couldn't wait for us to begin spending our lives together, growing old together, playing with grandchildren together. Now this has been taken away. I know in my heart I don't have long left. This disease has robbed us of the happiness we deserve but I want you to know exactly how much I love you. Every night, I go to sleep and can't wait to wake up so I'll see you beside me. Those nights and days are numbered now but I will always cherish seeing your sleepy smile and squinty eyes in the first of the morning light. I love the way you grumble about having to go all the way downstairs in the morning to get coffee, how you look when you wear my clothes, how you stick your tongue out when you're concentrating on something. I love when you hold my hand because you hold it with such purpose, like we're never going to part. I love the way you smell. Sometimes I stand in your closet, just to smell the perfume you wear on your clothes.

And now the serious bit: if you're reading this, you're probably moving or clearing the place out, or maybe just feeling nostalgic. I don't know if you've moved on with someone else or if you're alone but either way, I want you to know that I'm happy for you, once you are happy. I want you to lead a life rich in health, happiness and success. You are a wonderful, special person and deserve the best of everything.

One last thing: whenever you catch a glimpse of the blue sky, feel a drop of rain on your skin or hear thunder rumbling in the distance - know that I am there behind it all, watching over you and loving you.

Love you always, Bobby

Her body heaved with giant sobs as she dissolved into a torrent of tears. Paul found her that way at lunchtime, letting himself in when she didn't answer the door. He went to her, wrapped his arms around her and held her tightly, rocking her until the sobs subsided and she could breathe normally again.

"Sorry," she sniffed.

"It's OK. It was always going to be hard."

"I found this." She handed him the letter and watched in surprise as tears spiked Paul's eyes while he read it. He smiled sadly at her.

"You know, I met Bobby a few times, once at a talk and twice or three times at dinners. He was a really nice guy."

"Yeah?" she sniffed, wiping her nose in her sleeve.

"Yep. He said he'd love to go chasing sometime so I told him if he ever wanted to come along, he just had to call."

"Yeah, that was something we wanted to do together too, but we never got the chance." She sniffed again.

"Now, don't you start again or I'll ruin my manly composure and cry with you."

"Sorry."

"It's OK. I need a good cry!" He feigned a sob while wiping his nose with his sleeve.

"Paul?"

"Yes?"

"Do you miss Jonah?"

"Yep..... I do. Do you?" He knew the answer without her having to open her mouth.

She bowed her head sadly. In a way, it felt nice to know she wasn't the only one who missed him. But today was a new day. She was beginning a new life of independence. Leaving this house meant leaving the tears, the lamenting and the breakdowns behind.

As Paul loaded up the truck with the packed boxes, she rifled through the last of her clothes. She found a checkered shirt that wasn't Bobby's. Jonah must have left it when he packed in such haste that day. She held it to her nose: Jonah smell, then folded it neatly and put it in the black bag for donation. But then, having a change of heart, she reached in, took it back out and put it in the box of her own clothes.

CHAPTER 16

That intoxicating aroma of rose, honeysuckle and twilight surrounded her as she sat in her garden, drinking wine and chatting the evening away with Stacey. She'd been a week in the new house and was unpacked and settled in. This warm, cosy little cottage felt more like a home than the other house ever had. It was hers and hers alone. She didn't have to argue with anyone about painting the bedroom lilac or putting little potted miniature roses in the sun room. When she had fallen apart after Jonah had left, she could never have imagined that being on her own would bring her any joy. But she could honestly say now, she was happy. She had her family, her friends and this beautiful new home. Maybe she'd get a cat. Yes, she was definitely going to get a cat, maybe two.

"So, do you still see Paul much?" Stacey asked, between gulps of wine.

"Yeah, actually, he helped me move in. He's great."

"He's a cutie, isn't he?"

"You've changed your tune. You couldn't stand the sight of him this time last year."

"Yeah, but we had a really good talk at your party and he explained that he'd been going through some stuff back then and that's why he was rude. He's actually a really nice guy."

"I told you, you were wrong about him. I don't know what I'd have done without him this past year. He's been a rock of strength to me."

"So why don't you get with him? I get the impression that he really likes you." She nudged Sam with her elbow.

"No, he doesn't. We're just good friends."

"Whatever. Well, I think he's divine. Those freckles and that Irish glint in his eye. He's adorable." Stacey swooned over her wine glass. "So are you nervous about the conference? When is it?"

"This weekend. I'm a bit nervous but I know it's going to be fine. Paul said he'd come with me. It'll be nice to have him there - a familiar face in the audience. My lecture is done, so it's just a case of practicing it now."

"Great, Sammy. Things are really taking off for you and you deserve it. I'm really happy for you."

"Thanks." She smiled at her friend. "By the way, you know how you're my best friend and you said you'd do anything for me?"

"Did I? I don't remember that but go on."

"My mother's coming tomorrow and I could do with a buffer. Could you stay and shield me from her insults?"

"I'd be happy to. I'm immune to Vittoria's vitriolic quips. Now, where do you keep the wine in this place?"

The next day, Sam was amazed that her mother had passed not one single negative comment. She loved her daughter's new house and was most complimentary. Stacey raised an eyebrow at Sam when Vittoria was admiring the bathroom, praising her choice of soft furnishings in the living room and marvelling at her kitchen. Either her mother was sick or had taken a Xanax.

That evening, after her guests had left, she was alone, feet up on her new biscuit-coloured upholstered couch, watching trashy TV. She stole her gaze away from the screen for a moment to take in and admire the work she had done. The room was warm and welcoming and she loved the way the green walls seemed to accentuate her framed photos more than they had ever done in the old house of cream and more cream. Her wedding photo took pride of place on the chimney breast. An enlarged photo of a tornado with a bolt of lightning behind it that Paul had taken on one of their chases together, hung on the recessed wall beside the chimney breast. It had been his house warming present to her and she loved it. A wooden frame with a picture of her with Stacey sat on the mantlepiece. She hugged herself with contentment. The scratchy wool of the checkered shirt wasn't the most comfortable thing to wear but she loved how it smelled. This would be the last time she'd wear it, she promised herself. But for one last time, she wanted to be close to Jonah.

Saturday morning dawned and the butterflies in her stomach came to life. The day of the conference was here. Nerves had eluded her all week but now they were here with a bang. She got up, showered and blow dried her hair. She'd gotten it cut for the occasion, so while it was still relatively long, it was thicker and healthier, falling into large bouncing waves around her shoulders as she blow dried it. She kept her make up muted, just foundation, mascara and lip gloss. Her trouser suit was black with a purple camisole underneath. She looked every bit the professional meteorologist. Paul was going to collect her and drive them both to the airport. When he arrived, he wolf whistled at her while she admired him in his suit: the first time she'd ever seen him out of his scruffy jeans and thread bare T-shirts.

The flight was short but her anxiety made it seem longer than it was. Not helped by the mild turbulence. Paul was too busy taking photos of the cumulostratus out the window to offer her any reassurances or comfort. As they had done last year, the conference organisers provided a car to take them to the venue. However, it was a town car this year.

"So this is how you famous people live," he quipped.

"I'm not famous. I'm just a simple weather girl from Omaha, Nebraska!" she said, hitting him playfully in the arm.

Walking into the lobby of the hotel, a flood of memories washed over her. The receptionist had changed, a different, equally smiley one in her place. Everything was the same, from the couches in front of the giant fireplace, to the artwork on the wall behind reception, to the Italian marble floors. She hesitated, then looked to Paul who flashed her a reassuring smile as they checked in. Not having time to go to her room, as their flight had been delayed, she left her bag in reception and made her way straight to the conference room. Opening the doors, a wall of chatter hit her. There were upwards of a hundred people in the audience. The conference organiser's assistant introduced himself to her with a weak handshake and thanked her for coming.

This was it..... the stage beckoned. Her stomach was somersaulting. Paul gave her a reassuring glance as she made her way to the podium. She couldn't see the audience, bar the first few rows with the lights shining in her eyes so that gave her some comfort. She cleared her throat and introduced herself. The rest of the speech just flowed. Before she knew it, she was reading her conclusion, thanking the audience and receiving a round of applause. Smiling shyly, she left the podium and went straight to Paul who gave her a friendly hug.

"You were amazing! And you said you were nervous. It didn't show one little bit."

"I need a drink!"

After a nerve-settling glass of wine, she felt almost herself again. Paul chatted happily about the new truck he was thinking of buying and she let his words wash over her, just like the warm wine fuzziness. Now that the speech she was dreading was over, she could concentrate on enjoying the dinner tonight and some lectures in the morning. Her heart sank as she remembered last year. Dancing in the corner with Jonah, the smell of his aftershave, the feel of his suit beneath her fingers, the sound of his whispers in her ear. Her skin erupted into goose-bumps as she recalled the feeling of his tongue running down between her breasts, down her belly button and on further down until he had her squirming and calling his name.

"Sam. Sam. Hello! You were miles away."

"Sorry."

"Reminiscing about last year, were you?"

"How'd you know?" She blushed under his questioning stare. Throwing a peanut at him and giving him a look of humoured derision, Sam excused herself to get ready for the dinner and told Paul she'd meet him at the bar at seven.

Closing her eyes to choke back tears, the familiar room stretched out in front of her. It was a different room on the same floor, however, they were all factory line designed and decorated: the same lamps, TVs and soft furnishings. She remembered Jonah's suit hanging on the door, the sight of him getting undressed, everything came flooding back. But she was stronger than this. She was her own woman now and wasn't going to be a slave to the past anymore. She stood up straight, took a deep cleansing breath, repeated her 'strong, confident woman' affirmations and set about getting ready.

After an hour, she stood admiring herself in the mirror. The purple, strapless gown made her tanned skin seem darker still, bringing out her eyes and framing her breasts, making them look bigger. Last year, the same reflection had been one of a waif-like, lost girl who was paler than she ought to have been with a bruise on her cheek and a broken spirit. This year, her skin had healed, her spirit was a little less broken and she was a healthy, more voluptuous version of herself.

Paul stood open mouthed at the bar as she walked in. He couldn't take his eyes off her.

217

"Sam.... you look..... I mean, you are.... you look gorgeous," he stuttered.

"Thanks. You scrub up well too. I didn't know you owned a tux."

"I rented one!"

"Ah."

"Listen, Sam. There's something I need to tell you," he began but was rudely interrupted by the conference organiser, the same big, burly man from last year, only this year he seemed bigger.

"Miss Di Matteo. What a wonderful speech. You had me hanging on your every word."

"Oh, that's so nice of you to say. I was very nervous and hoped it hadn't come across."

"Not at all. I have caught some of your bulletins and I must say, you were made for television. Now, let me walk you to your table."

She shot an apologetic glance at Paul who rolled his eyes, shrugged and had no choice but to trail behind like an obedient puppy. Their table was in the middle of the floor and was occupied with some people Sam had never met before, although after introducing herself, some of them recognised her from the TV.

She got chatting to a weather researcher who sat beside her, a handsome man in his early forties. He told her of his recent divorce and how he was finding being single lonely. It felt cathartic for her to hear it from someone else and to be able to reassure him that it will get better: she knew, she'd been left alone... twice. She excused herself to make a trip to the bathroom and as she got up, Paul grabbed her by the arm.

"Sam, I really need to talk to you. It's important."

"Can't it wait? My bladder can't take it anymore... I'll be back in two seconds."

He sighed and let her go. As she washed her hands and looked in the mirror, she recalled the women from last year, cooing over

Jonah. It made her smile. So many memories lived here. She dried her hands and left, making her way back to the table. Paul was chatting to a blonde woman in a red dress. He seemed pretty happy with himself. As she walked past a group of people at one table who were laughing uproariously, she felt a hand grab onto her left hand.

"Sam, is that you?"

She froze, afraid to look down. That gravelly, deep voice: the one that had whispered in her ear, called her name through the skirt tail downdrafts of a passing storm, the one that had uttered 'I love you' and 'I'm leaving.' From the corner of her eye, the figure took the napkin off his lap and rose from his seat. The six foot five frame dwarfing her as it always had done. She closed her eyes as tears blurred her vision.

"Sam?" he said again. How the hell would he recognise her? Of course, she was wearing the same perfume and never did change her shampoo. She liked to keep that little bit of him, that piece that meant she was always identifiable to him.

The lump in her throat grew to the size of an apple as she desperately tried to swallow it. What was he doing here? She watched Paul look on in horror. He mouthed 'I'm sorry' and raised his shoulders like he'd been trying to warn her. He had tried, but she'd brushed him off. If only she'd listened, she could have hidden in her room for the rest of the night. The confidence and contentment she'd felt earlier abandoned her, only to be replaced by pain and devastation again.

"How are you?" he continued, as if they were just old friends meeting up for the first time in a year.

"Jo..... Jonah?" was all she could manage to say.

"Yes. Are you OK? Do you want to sit down?"

He guided her to the chair next to him and she sat agape, taking him in. He was tanned, more so than usual and healthy looking. His eyes still had that twinkle in them. His tuxedo hugging him beautifully and she resisted the urge to run her hands down his shoulders, arms, up to his chest and into his hair.

"This is my assistant Sandrine, Sandrine this is Sam." The girl in red that Paul had been talking to held out her hand and smiled.

"Oh, Sam? The Sam? How wonderful to finally meet you. I've heard a lot about you and your speech was wonderful," she drawled in her exquisite French accent, like a vocal ballet, dancing on her tongue.

"You were there?" She ignored Sandrine, not out of rudeness but too mesmerised at Jonah's arrival to take anyone else in.

"Yup. Heard the whole thing. It was wonderful. Well done. You sounded great."

"Tha.... thanks." She shook her head. She just couldn't believe he was here.

"So, how've you been?"

"Good. You?"

"Great actually. France has been good to me. I came over for the conference and to visit Bella and the kids. Listen, do you think we could talk later?"

Sam was't sure how she should react.

"Of course, sure. I'd better go. Paul is over there. Did you see him?"

"Yeah, we talked earlier. We're going to get together for a drink later. Could we maybe talk between now and then, perhaps when the meal is over?"

The head of AMS came over and interrupted her, asking for her to come and meet his wife, who, he said, was a big fan of '*Good Morning, Omaha.*' She reluctantly agreed, never taking her eyes off Jonah.

"OK. That'd be good. Jonah..... It's good to see you."

"It's good to see you too, Sam. And by the way. You look great in purple."

"Thanks," she said as she was whisked away. "Wait, what?" She turned back to him but he was gone, swallowed up in the crowd, as she was embraced by a glamourous, geriatric woman dressed in black.

CHAPTER 17

"And I watch every morning while I'm putting my face on. You look so beautiful on the television, dear. I said to my Archie that you were a natural and I'm delighted to meet you."

"And you," Sam said, not listening to a word the woman was saying. Her eyes scanned the room for Jonah, but he was gone. His seat was vacant. She searched for Paul, who was still in his seat talking to Sandrine. So Jonah was alone. Where was he? Surely he couldn't get around without Sandrine. She escaped from the woman, said a hurried goodbye and made her way out to reception. There he was, coming out of the men's room. She ran up to him.

"Jonah? What did you say back there?"

"Come on, we need to talk."

He led her out to the garden while she tagged along beside him, oblivious to where they were going, simply staring hazily at him as he meandered his way through reception, out the main door and into the car park. The night air was warm and balmy, the stars twinkling like little fairy lights on a black wall. She didn't need to lead him. He knew where he was going. What was going on?

"Jonah. Can you see?" she asked as they sat on a bench. The little stream they had stood in only last year, trickled in the near distance.

"Yes, I can see."

"But, but.... how?"

"It's a long story but the short version is my boss at the university put me in touch with a friend of his who is something of a revolutionary neuroscientist. He has developed a new treatment for optic nerve damage using gene therapy. So I met with him and he asked if I'd like to be part of the trial. I said yes and that was eight months ago. My nerves began to regenerate about a month after the first procedure and it's been getting better ever since. While my sight is still pretty fuzzy, I can make out most things fairly definitely."

Realising she was staring open-jawed, she shook herself and sat up straight. She searched his eyes. They didn't appear any different, except that when he looked at her, they weren't directed vaguely at her, he was looking right into her eyes, through her pupil, right into her soul.

"That is..... incredible. I thought that technology was way off into the future."

"It's very new. My group was the first lot of human trials. It's worked on mice and rats for the last few years."

"Jonah, I can't believe it. What is it like to be able to see for the first time in seven years?"

"Amazing. I'm still trying to get used to it. It gets better every week. So anyway, we were supposed to talk."

"Yeah. We were. But I think it's a bit futile now. You can see... wow. I just can't get over it. Do I look how you thought I would?" She knew she was being narcissistic, but she had to know.

"Truthfully? You're much more beautiful. I'd a pretty good idea before, but I'd no idea your skin could be so sallow and I think your eyes are green, are they? It's still hard to make some things out."

"Yeah, they're green." She laughed. "Jeez, Jonah, I'm so happy for you."

"Thanks. Life's been good since I went to Paris."

She looked away sadly. Of course he was happy. He had everything he wanted: good job, sight, Sandrine. Looking back, his face was every bit the Jonah she dreamed of at night and thought about during the day. His blue eyes were the same, though not so vacant now. They bore into her like drills into the ground. His lips looked as delicious as they had done a year ago, when she had bitten them, kissed them and felt them on her tingling skin. His jaw was as strong, but now was clenched into a worried expression. He was unsettled, she knew by the look on his face. There were unspoken words behind those lips.

"So you said you never wanted to hear from me again? I was upset when you sent that mail, so I called Paul who said you were having some issues. I was going to come home, I'd even booked flights but he talked me out of it. He said he would sort it. Did he?"

Sam cursed silently. Paul certainly told Jonah every little thing. Had she known at the time, she'd have threatened to kill him.

"Yeah, he was great. I broke down a bit but he helped me through."

"So, are you guys.... together?"

"Jesus, no! What? No. We're just friends." A fleeting thought of the night she'd thrown herself at Paul crossed her mind. She debated whether to be honest with Jonah but thought it best to leave it.

"Sam. I've missed you so much. So many times I went to contact you but I was afraid to after you'd sent that mail. I worried that I'd mess things up for you again. Paul told me you were seeing a therapist."

She lowered her head. It was mortifying listening to him regale all of what Paul had obviously told him. Her face turned puce.

"I'm better now. I've moved house."

"Really? But you loved that house."

"I really didn't. I loved it when Bobby was there but it just became a permanent shrine to him. I felt imprisoned in it and needed to get out. So I packed up all my things, donated most of his and bought a little cottage two miles down the street. I'm really happy now."

"Good, I'm glad to hear it. I worry about you, you know." He tucked a stray strand of hair that was flapping across her lips behind her ear. The touch made her freeze, her gaze fixed onto his.

"No, you don't. You're living it up in Paris. You don't even think of me!"

"I do, you know. Say, why don't you come to Paris to see me?"

"I'm in Paris now and I'm seeing you."

"Don't be trite. You know what I mean. Come to visit me. Please, Sam? I fly home tomorrow and I'd love to show you around my new life."

Her heart sank again. His new life. He really had moved on. A little part of her was hoping he'd say he was coming home for good. She desperately wanted to be happy for him, and she was in a way, that he had his sight back but this was a different Jonah now. Not hers anymore. Maybe they could be friends or maybe it would be too painful. It remained to be seen. For now, they would share drinks as friends, she would say goodbye to him again tomorrow and they would probably email once in a while.

They joined Paul and Sandrine in the bar and chatted and laughed loudly until the early hours of the morning. It felt good for the three to be back together again and Sandrine fitted in well too, enjoying listening to their stories of chases. Sam watched Jonah move. He was more animated than usual, looking people in the eye rather than staring blankly at them, more energetic somehow, sure of himself. She wasn't sure about this new Jonah, she was almost afraid of him - he wasn't dependent anymore, didn't need her. The imperfection that was his blindness had made him beautiful to her. Now, he was perfect and she was intimidated.

When the bar closed, he got up, bent down to kiss her on the cheek, and retired to bed, leaving her emotionally spent and exhausted. She sighed deeply, feeling like she hadn't breathed all night and took herself to bed.

"You OK?" Paul asked as he walked her to her door.

"No." She sighed.

He smiled in weak sympathy at her and walked away.

She tossed and turned all night, as she'd expected she would. Had she said anything stupid? What did he think of her? Was he still attracted to her now that he could see what she really looked like? Everything had changed.

The next evening, lectures done, after exchanging hugs and promises of a visit to Paris, they parted and she and Paul spent the rest of the flight and trip home in silence. Paul knew she was shell-shocked and that she didn't want to talk. He hoped seeing Jonah wouldn't set her back again and vowed to keep an eye on her.

There was some consolation in returning to her new home. If she'd still been living in the old house, she'd have broken down again. That night, she rooted out Jonah's checkered shirt and slept in it.

In work, the next morning, her head was sleepy and non-functioning from two nights of restless sleep. One of the researchers kindly brought her a coffee and she drank it gratefully. Once the first hit of caffeine entered her bloodstream, she felt she had enough energy to open her computer and check her mail.

There was one from Paul, asking how she was. What a sweetie, she thought as she typed him a reassuring reply that she was fine and sober. There one from Jonah. She hesitated before opening.

Dear Sam,

I hope you got home safely. I've just arrived in the door after the long flight. Very tired! I can't tell you how wonderful it was to literally see you in Texas. You look incredible, although, I always knew that. And I'm thrilled your life is going so well for you.

I want to reiterate my invitation to come over to visit me here in Paris. I'd love to show you around and spend some time with you. Please consider it and let me know what you decide.

Love, Jonah. x

She read it fourteen times. Reaching up to the screen, she touched the little 'x' he had put after his name. The first thing he had done when he got home after his transatlantic flight was to email her. He was practically begging for her to go and visit. Did he still love her? Who knew? She needed to decide if it was a good idea or not to go. If she went and he wanted to be just friends, it would tear her apart, like dangling a lollipop in front of a child and then taking it away. But if he wanted more, it would be equally devastating as he would be all the way over in Europe and she would have to come back to Omaha. For a fleeting second, she thought maybe she could get a job over there but dismissed it immediately. She loved her new life, house and job and she couldn't just give it all up, like that, after such a short time. A twinge of pain twisted in her stomach, a reminder of the agony of Jonah leaving. She couldn't risk going through that again. Paul would know what to do. She sent him a text asking if he was free for lunch.

"Wow, he's really keen for you to go over, isn't he? Did you guys sort everything out the other night?" Paul asked, as he sat opposite her in the café across from the station that lunchtime. He was out chasing today but was staying local, so agreed to meet her. He had his own secret ulterior motive: he wanted to make sure she was OK. She hadn't said more than two words on the journey back from Texas. Seeing Jonah had hit her hard.

"Well, depends what you mean by sort out. We talked about his procedures, his work everything but the obvious thing we should have discussed. I'm not even sure if there was chemistry. I was just so shocked to see him and to hear his news. It was like he was a different Jonah."

"He might be different to you, because you never knew him before his accident, but to me, he's the same old Jonah."

"Really? Didn't you know about his sight returning though?"

"No, I didn't. Well, I knew he was going through with the trials, but he never said anything about the results. I guess he was afraid to mention it in case it didn't work."

"So, what do I do about Paris? Should I go over?"

"It depends what you want out of it. What do you want to happen?"

She thought about it for a moment while she sipped her coffee. It was a good question.

"Well, I want him back more than anything but it's become far too complicated now. We've moved on so there's more at stake."

"Look, the way I see it is, it can only go two ways: you go over and he wants more, you've to come home and he's to stay there. Or else, he just wants to be friends so you come home. Both ways you end up heartbroken. But then, option C is, you don't go over at all, remain email buddies."

"So you think option C is what I should do?" She felt a little disappointed. She'd wanted Paul to talk her into going, to tell her that she and Jonah would meet under the Eiffel Tower and fall back in love.

"Try to think of yourself in ten year's time. Will you look back and think '*I was right not to go to Paris that time, I wonder what Jonah's doing now*?' or will you regret every day that you didn't take your heart in your hands and go after the man you love. It might not work out, you've both changed but can you honestly tell yourself that you don't want to give it a chance and see what happens?"

She shook her head, trying to make the tears reabsorb before they fell. Paul was right, as always. She got up, kissed his forehead and paid for lunch. Walking her to her car, he hugged her and told her that whatever decision she made would have to be right for her and nobody else.

Sinking onto her couch that night, pizza in one hand, phone in the other, she decided she needed one more opinion and dialled Stacey's number. Regaling the weekend details and email, Stacey swooned on the other end of the phone.

"Sammy, if you don't book a flight to Paris tonight, I will fucking book it for you. Imagine both of you, walking hand in hand down the banks of the Seine, eating croissants and drinking wine, kissing under the Eiffel tower and sipping coffee on the street side. You have to go, Sam. What if you don't? You'll never know what could have been."

"That's what Paul said. But what if I go and he just wants to be friends, or we realise we still love each other and I've to come home alone again, leaving him there? I can't do that, Stace."

"But you'll never know...... You need to do this, Sam. Don't let him slip away again. Do you love this man?"

"Yes, I love him more than anything."

"Then fucking go to Paris. Go! Hang up now and book the flights. If you haven't emailed me proof of your booking within half an hour, I'm going to come over there and lock you in a room until you do."

She said her goodbyes to Stacey and before she had time to think, looked up Jonah's email, and seeing the number on the bottom of his signature, dialled it into her phone. It was early morning there so she hoped he wouldn't still be asleep. It rang twice and he was there, his sleepy, gravelly voice speaking French. Her stomach clenched as dizzying anxiety enveloped her.

"*Bonjour?*"

"*Bonjour.... Jonah, est cela vous?*"

"*Oui, c'est moi. Sandrine?*"

"*Non, c'est Sam.*"

"Sam! I didn't know you spoke French."

"*Oui.* I'm just practicing for when I come to Paris."

"What, really? Oh that's great. When are you coming?"

"It's up to you. Whenever suits you. I could take next week off work and come over then."

"Great, great! I'll cancel my plans for next week. Let me know your flight and I'll have a car sent out for you. I still can't see well enough to drive so I hope you don't mind me sending someone to collect you."

"Not at all. I'll mail you the details. I'm looking forward to it, Jonah."

"Me too. You've made my day."

"*Au revoir.*"

She hung up and hugged herself. The fabric of his well-worn shirt was rough on her arms, but she didn't care. She would see him next week. The smile plastered to her face refused to budge and she slept like a baby that night.

CHAPTER 18

Standing clutching her bag in Charles De Gaulle, she felt self-conscious being alone. She looked around at people hugging and embracing warmly. It made her teary, made worse by the fact she felt so out of place. There were some men with name signs, waiting for travellers unknown to them, but none with her name. She began to panic. Where was the driver? She followed the crowd and made her way outside to the taxi rank where scores of cabs and limousines were situated. There was a queue for the taxis so she decided to go back in to have one more look. The crowd had dissipated and in its place stood a family with two little girls, an older couple and Jonah. Jonah? He must have been there all along and she'd missed him. She walked up behind him, suddenly feeling shy. Gingerly, she placed a hand on his shoulder.

"Guess who?"

"Oh, I'd recognise that perfume anywhere."

He turned around and scooped her into his arms, twirling her around. She prayed he would kiss her, but to her disappointment, the hug seemed to be it.

"I thought you were sending someone?"

"Did you really think I'd leave you to come through the airport on your own? I've a cab waiting outside. Come on."

He brought her out to where the taxis were whittling down the long queue and brought her to a waiting Mercedes.

"Would you like to go to your hotel first to freshen up?"

"Yes, that would be nice. *L'Hotel de Rivière, s'il vous plait.*"
The driver nodded and pulled out into the traffic, whisking them
Paris bound.

They sat in relatively awkward silence, except for the low hum
of the DJ on the radio, blabbering away in incomprehensible
French. Her first sight of Paris was a depressing one: endless
kilometers of industrial estates and motorways. Then, the scenery
changed: the architecture became more classical, opening up streets
swarming with stylish Parisians rushing about through their busy
day while the tourists were evident, sauntering, map reading and
pointing at the various points of interest. The cab pulled up outside
a large Baroque style building, with an impressive flight of steps up
to a golden doorway.

The driver handed out her luggage and Jonah paid him. She
made her way up the steps, briefly taking in the sounds and smells
of the city on her short journey to the door of the hotel. When she'd
checked in, she looked around for Jonah, who was stationed at a
pillar nearby.

"I'll get a coffee in the bar while you freshen up."

"Or you could come up to the room, if you like." Was that being
too familiar, she wondered? After all, they had been lovers, but he
might misconstrue the invite as a blatant come on.

"No. No, that's OK. I'll wait here."

So, he was on the page that said it wasn't appropriate. She was
surprised to find herself a little disappointed by his coyness. This
was a bad sign. He wasn't exactly demonstrating that he wanted to
patch things up with her. He was bordering on cold, business like.

Her room was everything she would expect from a 5 star
Parisian hotel: large, theatrical brocade curtains, big bed in the
same fabric and classic, elegant marble bathroom. A small part of
her wished Jonah had come up to see it. Her primeval self wanted
to ravage him: his familiar scent, his broad shoulders and his new,

almost fashionable dress sense. However, she knew that wouldn't be the way it should happen, were it to happen at all. They had a lot of issues to address first.

She showered and changed quickly, not wanting to leave him too long. He was still in the café/bar sipping on an Americano when she came down thirty minutes later. He looked........ beautiful, his hair slicked back, a side effect of his nervously running a hand through it. It took her breath away to see him, waiting for her. Butterflies flew desperately around her stomach and she swallowed the bubble of sick.

He smiled when he saw her approach and she sat down, ordering a coffee from the waiter cleaning the table beside her.

"So, what's your room like?"

"It's really luxurious. Thank you for booking it. Beats those motels we used to stay in on chases." She smiled a half smile and turned her gaze toward the window.

"This one was Sandrine's idea. It's her favourite."

Sam's lip curled. The mention of the woman's name pulled on a nerve. She managed to turn it into an insincere smile directed at Jonah.

"I'm still getting used to seeing you. It's very strange."

"Yeah, it must be weird. I keep thinking I need to help you up steps and stuff."

"I'm still not great at getting around and reading small fonts is difficult, but hopefully I'll get there. And if it doesn't get any better than this, then that's OK. It's so much better than not being able to see anything but bright and dark blurs."

"I'm happy for you, Jonah."

"So what do you want to do first? Tower? Champs Elysees? Shopping?"

"You tell me. Have I got you for the whole week?"

"Yes, indeed. I've cancelled my plans and lectures so I can be your own personal tour guide."

She smiled weakly. 'Tour Guide?' Was that all he was going to be?

"Might as well start at the Tower then." She sipped her coffee and tried to suppress the feeling that this trip wasn't going to be any more than meeting up with an old friend who *wasn't* going to declare his undying love for her nor insist they marry on the top of the Eiffel Tower. She tried to talk herself into thinking more positively and just enjoying the trip - after all, it was her first time in Paris. She inhaled deeply and stood, beckoning him to join her. They walked out into the Parisian afternoon sun and Jonah led her in the direction of the tower.

Despite her feelings of disappointment, she was surprised to find how emotional she felt as they stood at the bottom of the Eiffel Tower and gazed up along its colossal iron lattice. It was a thing of beauty, and much bigger than she'd imagined. Under its formidable shadow, it compounded her feeling that she should embrace the trip and make the best of it. If she and Jonah were going to just put a patch on the breakup and be friends, then that would have to be OK.

After a dizzying ascent, the top pier revealed the city of Paris below and around them. Not great with heights, Sam kept herself well back from the barrier. Jonah held the same look he'd had that first time she'd witnessed a storm with him: revelling in the wind on his face. This time, his eyes were taking in everything the tower was showing him.

"Hungry?" he asked.

"Actually, yeah. I didn't eat much on the plane."

"Well, I know a great little place."

As they sat on the street front, eating Croque Madames and drinking Sancerre, she studied him. He was still Jonah, but he looked different. His stare wasn't empty and broken, it was definite and purposeful. His clothes were different too. Gone were the combats and oversized T-shirts. Instead, he wore black, slim fit trousers with a white shirt and grey sweater. He'd been Parisian'ised.

"You're smiling." He wiped the melted gruyére from his mouth with a napkin, which made a change from wiping Big Mac sauce off with his sleeve.

"Am I? Sorry. I'm just amused by how.... civilised you are."

"Is that an insult or a compliment?"

"Oh, a compliment. You're not really 'storm chaser Jonah' anymore. You're more, 'French intellectual Jonah' now."

"Oh. I hadn't realised. Is it my clothes? Sandrine said my clothes were too casual so she brought me shopping for a new wardrobe. I didn't take much notice to be honest, of course I couldn't see so just wore what she gave me. The thought did strike me that she could have been putting anything on me. I did notice a pink shirt in my wardrobe last month. I dread to think I was wearing that at some stage."

On hearing her name again, Sam felt like he had taken the fork resting on her plate and stuck it straight into her chest. That was it. That was the reason he was being coy and friend-like. He was with Sandrine. Tears pricked the corners of her eyes, but she sniffed them back and necked her glass of wine with little feminine charm.

"You OK?"

"Yes. Sorry, I thought I was going to choke on a crumb. I'm fine. So anyway, how is Sandrine?"

"She's great. I'd be lost without her."

That's what you used to say about me, she thought sadly. She bet Sandrine never stood in a stream or listened to thunder storms with him. She shook her head to get rid of any thoughts of Sandrine. She was a nice girl who didn't deserve Sam's negative thoughts. She would just have to try to find a way to be happy for them. Positive thinking, Sam, positive thinking... she repeated it in her head until the words lost all meaning.

They spent the rest of the day sightseeing and then had a perfectly amicable and civilised dinner near the hotel, until Jonah walked her to the foyer. He kissed her on the cheek, told her he was delighted she was here to visit and that he'd collect her in the morning to show her around the University campus.

After breakfast the next morning, she treated herself to a massage in the hotel spa by the stunningly handsome Hans, a Swedish masseur, all blonde hair, muscle and hands. She was thoroughly relaxed and at one with the world when Jonah arrived, looking ridiculously suave: black jeans, a white T-shirt and black pinstriped dinner jacket. She couldn't help but silently swoon.

The university was exactly that: a university. He showed her around the lecture halls, labs and then dropped the bomb that they would be meeting Sandrine for lunch, after which they would head back into the city for a surprise. Was Sandrine going to be part of this surprise, she wondered bitterly? She hoped not.

Lunch was ... pleasant. Sandrine was nice, but they had nothing much to talk about. Sam watched obsessively for signs that they were together: hand holding, a kiss, a look - but nothing was evident. It was all very friendly and cold. It gave her some comfort.

Thankfully, Sandrine said she had work and embracing Sam with a kiss on both cheeks, told her to enjoy her surprise. She smiled and winked at Jonah who reciprocated. Sam was eaten alive with jealousy at the thought of Sandrine and Jonah sharing a secret.

"So let's do some shopping before.... well, before later."

Back in the city, they pottered around the stores and Galeries Lafayette, where Sam treated herself to a new handbag, bought a purse for Stacey and some cloud shaped cuff links for Paul. Shopping done, Jonah brought her back to her hotel and told her to change into something nice, not too formal, but nice. Again, he waited for her in the bar. Up in the room, she threw on a blue cowl necked dress, pulled the bobbin from her hair, letting it tumble down her shoulders and touched up her make up. Jonah whistled when she arrived back down, ready to face whatever this 'surprise' was. He held his arm out for her to link and the touch of his dinner jacket against her bare arm sent a shiver down her spine. He smelled like he always did - Eau de Jonah. At least some things hadn't changed.

As they walked along the Seine riverbank, Sam inhaled the air. It was so... well, it smelled bad but the atmosphere more than made up for it. Artists sketching, writers writing, lovers kissing. How Jonah could not be in the mood for love here was beyond her. He stopped at a gangway that led onto a large cruise barge.

"Your dinner awaits, Ma'am." Taking her hand, he stepped onto the boat, helping her step down and greeted the waiting member of staff, who showed them to a riverside table.

"Is this my surprise? Dinner on the Seine?"

"Yes, do you like it?"

"It's beautiful."

The Eiffel Tower looked down over them, twinkling with a myriad of fairy lights, which reflected off the water and into Jonah's eyes as he stared at Sam. Uncomfortable, she looked away out over the river, thinking she should pinch herself as it didn't feel real. The rest of the boat filled up with diners and soon they were on their way, cruising down the Seine, gourmet food served and exquisite champagne drank. The conversation was light and informal until Jonah became quiet.

"You OK?"

"Sam, we should talk."

There was her stomach doing a bungee dive again. She looked anxiously at him and shifted in her chair, hitting accidentally off his foot. He looked solemn, staring into his champagne flute.

"I'm sorry," he continued, not meeting her gaze.

"Oh no, that was *my* foot, sorry."

"What? No." He looked up, amusement and confusion in his face. "Not that. I'm sorry for leaving you. I regret it every, single day. I'm so sorry I hurt you."

"But...it wasn't your fault. I drove you away. I should never have messed up like that. And anyway, you'd never have gotten the opportunity to do the medical trial if you hadn't left."

"I know, but even still, I ran away when I should have stayed and worked it out with you. I can't blame you for not mentioning I was your boyfriend. It was an awkward situation you were in and I should have been more sensitive to that. I realise now I overreacted. I knew deep down you weren't ready to be with someone again so soon but I should have stayed and helped you through it rather than bolt like I did." He looked out over the river. She watched his reflection in the window as Paris sailed by. He was staring at nothing in particular, his expression a mixture of guilt and wistfulness.

"Look, maybe we did get in too deep, too soon. What's happened has happened. And, maybe it happened for a reason. If you hadn't left, you wouldn't be where you are now: in Paris, being able to see, great job. I've changed for the better too. I've had lots of therapy and really feel like I'm in a good place."

"That's great, I'm happy for you." He smiled a half smile. She gazed into his eyes. Time to get down to brass tacks.

"So, why did you invite me here, Jonah?"

He cleared his throat. "I had an ulterior motive." He coughed again, twirling the empty champagne glass between his fingers. "When I saw you at the conference, my heart almost leaped from my chest. I didn't know you'd be there, I just saw this beautiful woman standing at the podium and when they announced it was you, I felt dizzy. You were so beautiful and everything I had imagined you would look like: dark, petite, pretty. Regaining my sight was wonderful, but it culminated in that first view I had of you. If the doctors had told me after that, that I'd have to lose my sight again, I wouldn't have cared. I'd seen the only thing I needed to. I saw your face. Nothing else mattered to me and all my old feelings for you came flooding back. I never stopped loving you, Sam and seeing you there almost floored me, especially knowing I had to come back here."

"But you and Sandrine...?"

"Huh? Me and Sandrine what? You think we're together? She's my PA, Sam. Nothing more. Although, she did try to kiss me once on a department night out, but I couldn't do it. I couldn't think of anyone but you, haven't been with anyone since."

Sam nodded, not raising her gaze from her glass. Her stomach flipped as she fought the smile that was trying to spread itself across her face.

"So, have you thought about me much?"

"Jonah, I've thought of nothing else since the day you left. I..." She hesitated, thinking of the kiss with Paul. Should she tell him? Yes, she needed to be honest if nothing else. "I kind of went through a breakdown after that. I just wasn't able to cope anymore and the only solace I could get was by drinking to numb it all and.... and I kissed Paul." As the words poured out like a verbal oil spill, she waited for him to blow up. Braving a glance at him, told her otherwise. He just nodded.

"So, was it a one off?"

"Yes, a mistake. I was overcome and very drunk. If it weren't for Paul and Stacey, I would never have gotten through it. But I did and I'm here."

Jonah pulled his face into a painful grimace.

"Jesus, I did that to you?"

"No, not you, life did it to me - losing Bobby, you, my stupidity and fear of what people thought of me."

"So where do we go from here?" He raised his eyes to meet her gaze and their blueness pierced her.

"Where do you want to go, Jonah?" She didn't want to commit to anything until she knew exactly what he wanted to do. Just then, the waiter arrived. They ordered another bottle of champagne and waited until he returned before continuing their conversation. The wait was excruciating. He poured two glasses, amid the deafening silence between Sam and Jonah, and retreated quickly, sensing the electrifying atmosphere.

"Where can we go, Sam? I'm over here and you're all the way across the Atlantic. Long distance would be too hard."

She knew this and while the distance thing was problematic, mostly she was hearing that he still loved her. She couldn't see a solution but she made a decision.

"Well, we can't help the distance between us next week, but right now, I'm here and you're here. So why don't we make the most of our time?"

"You know what? I'm regretting booking this dinner cruise."

Her stomach sank again. "Why?" she muttered, not sure she wanted to hear the answer.

"Because if we were on dry land, I'd have dragged you out of the restaurant and back to your hotel and made love to you all night long."

She fought very hard to suppress the urge to jump up and down, shrieking with pure, honest joy. But she didn't, choosing instead to raise a coy eye brow and smirk at him.

"Well, we'll be docking again in an hour. We'll just have to wait, won't we?"

He groaned as he reached for her hand, telling her it would be the longest hour of his life. They were well marinated in champagne and feeling brave. Sam took her foot from her shoe and ran her toes up his leg.

He inhaled sharply and closed his eyes. Opening them slowly, he looked deep into hers, squinting in the candlelight, searching for her thoughts. He knew them by the way she looked back. Dessert was eaten while their eyes locked on each other. A stray piece of cream found itself on Jonah's bottom lip. She reached up, took it onto her finger and put it to his lips, parting them just a tiny bit until he could taste the sweet morsel. He took a strawberry half off his plate, dipped it in the chocolate drizzle and held it to her mouth. She went to take a bite but he pulled it away from her, smiling smugly. Holding it back above her lips, she took another attempt and he again pulled it away. It reminded her of the night she had watched him sleeping and how she had longed to kiss his lips, but had been afraid to wake him from his much needed sleep. On her third try to catch the strawberry, he let her have it, savouring watching her bite down on it, juice dripping onto her chin.

Eventually, the boat docked and they were some of the first people off. In a quiet corner of the street, he stopped walking, turned to her and without saying a word, tipped her chin up with his finger and pressed his lips to hers while Paris happened around them. He inhaled slowly, gathered himself and took her by the hand. They walked back to the hotel speedily, hand in hand, not speaking. She fumbled with the key card as she tried to unlock the door. They burst into the room, he took her head in his hands to kiss her, then shut the door with his foot and they began the task of removing each other's clothes. Their mouths never parted, items of clothing dropped to the floor in their wake and both sank onto the bed and made love twice, fast, hungry, needy, sweaty. Almost a year of missing each other, loving distantly, pain and grief was expressed through their bodies. Afterwards, they lay facing each other. He stroked her hair while mapping her face with his eyes.

"I never knew your eyes could be so beautiful. They were the one thing I couldn't read with my hands."

"I am so happy that you have your sight back, Jonah, but I used to love when you felt my expression with your hands. It was so..... so intimate."

He smiled and closed his eyes. He ran his hand down her face, touching his thumb briefly off her bottom lip, then down her neck, stopping at her breasts before running down to her hip, where he pulled her into him, so she could feel how aroused he was. He kissed her lightly, eyes open, locked onto hers.

"I've never loved anyone like I love you, Sam."

She squinted, trying to keep tears from falling. She had to make sure that every second of this trip counted. To waste it being sad that she had to leave would be pointless. She'd save her tears for the flight home. His declaration hung in the air. She couldn't say it back to him without crying so left it there, unrequited. Instead, she kissed him and they spent the next few hours gazing at each other, broken only by the odd kiss, eventually falling asleep in each other's arms.

The next morning, she awoke, her body stiff and her arm asleep. No longer did she wake up in the mornings looking for Bobby or Jonah, she woke knowing she was alone and that it was OK. So it was a surprise to see Jonah's face. As she moved under his grip, her arm began to wake up and tingle. Her wriggling caused him to stir. He blinked and tried to focus, looking surprised at where he was.

Smiling sleepily, he touched her face and kissed her. "Good morning," he croaked.

"Hey. What's the plan for today?" she said, climbing out of bed and pulling his shirt from the day before over her head.

"Can we stay in this room all day?" he asked, stretching and yawning.

"No, we're going to sight see."

"But I've seen it all. There's only one thing I want to see." He grabbed the end of the shirt and dragged her back onto the bed. She squealed, trying to scramble away from him but he persisted and held her down, kissing her on the neck until her arms relaxed and she lay, completely succumbed to him. "You look so hot in my clothes." He growled, turning her legs to jelly. His hair flopped down as he crouched over her. She tried to stretch up to kiss him, but he was holding her down and was too strong for her to resist. Eventually, she resorted to begging.

"Please kiss me, Jonah."

"If you want me, you have to come up to me."

She struggled again but it was no use. He was far too strong. She groaned under his weight, his muscular shoulders holding her in place, eyes shining with mischief. He lowered his face slowly, retreating when she reared up to meet him. She complained again and he relented, touching her lips with a feather light kiss. She longed for him to take her again, to make her feel satiated but he jumped off the bed, stretched and yawned. His sinuous back rippled and folded as he moved, his backside was tight and hot. She ogled him and felt absolutely unapologetic about it.

"Let's have some coffee and decide what to do."

"OK. I suppose we can go out. I need to stop by my apartment and change clothes anyway."

After a breakfast of croissants and coffee in a quaint little café near the Arc de Triumphe, they got a cab to Jonah's apartment. It was a small, modern two bedroom flat on the university campus, with plain, student-esque furniture and an old leather couch. Sam supposed it hadn't mattered to him when he'd first arrived anyway.

"Hey Joe, where were you last night?" Sandrine purred as she walked out from one of the bedrooms, wearing nothing but a thigh skimming negligee.

Sam stared at her, open mouthed. 'Joe?'

"I stayed with Sam. Did you leave any hot water?"

"Yeah, I haven't showered yet. You go ahead."

He pulled his shirt off over his head, threw it on the couch and was shower-bound. Sam sat awkwardly on the couch watching Sandrine move about the kitchen, her pert, twenty something year old bottom almost on show under the minuscule negligee

"So, do you stay here much?" Sam asked, her voice almost so high pitched that only dogs could hear it.

"I live here. Didn't Jonah tell you?" Her French accent caused the words to roll seductively off her tongue. Sam wanted to punch her.

"No.... he didn't." Her teeth were gritted so hard that they almost crushed away to dust.

"Here's your tea. He's finished in the shower so I'm going to hop in. Make yourself comfortable."

"Oh, like you did?" Sam muttered bitterly.

"*Desolé?*"

"Oh, I just said thanks."

Sandrine shot her a suspicious look and walked out.

"So, you didn't tell me Sandrine lives with you?" she spat at Jonah as he emerged, wrapped in only a towel, drying his hair with another.

"Oh, didn't I? Yeah, we've shared since I moved here. She's great, isn't she?"

Sam's lips curled into an insincere, saccharine smile. Whatever about them sharing a flat, but her walking around in skimpy little underwear was inappropriate.

"You're not jealous, are you?" He winked at her and tickled her chin like he would one of his nieces or nephews.

"Nooo. Just surprised, that's all."

As soon as Jonah was dressed, they were getting the hell out of there.

"Sandrine's a bit...... upfront, isn't she?" Sam commented as they walked along the Champs Elysees, carrying shopping bags full of presents and clothes for her to bring home to Jonah's family.

"Really? I hadn't noticed. I guess she got used to not having to hide anything because I was blind when we first began living together. She could have been walking around stark naked and I wouldn't have known."

"Isn't it weird?"

"No, I don't notice really. I guess I just don't look at her in that way."

"I think she's trying to get your attention, Jonah." Sam was getting annoyed at his naivety. The woman was practically throwing herself at him. He sensed her apprehension and put his arm around her, pulling her tight to him.

"Relax. I told you, I've only got eyes for you."

"But what about when I go home?"

His face darkened. "Let's not talk about that now, OK? Come on, I've a great idea for lunch."

They lay on the banks of the Seine, near to a busker who was playing quintessential French peasant music on a violin which added beautifully to the atmosphere. Jonah had stopped along the way at his favourite bakers, bought a quarter loaf of sour dough, then stopped at the cheese shop for brie and finally, bought a bottle of Merlot. This was their rustic, picnic type lunch. He tore chunks of bread, picked off a piece of brie and fed it to her as she lay on the grass, absorbing the sun. The wine was complex and rich in berry flavours when taken with the sharp, smooth brie. It was the nicest food ever, simple, fresh and nourishing. When they finished, he lay down beside her, leaning on his elbow.

"What could be a better city to regain your sight in than this one?" she said, as the beauty of the river and the surrounding buildings gave her a feeling of contentment.

"Yeah, although, the only thing I was interested in seeing was you."

She blushed under the intensity of his gaze. His eyes bore into her like they wanted to see what they had never seen before, into her soul.

"So, why didn't you come home?"

"A few reasons but mostly I was afraid. I was worried firstly, that you just wouldn't want to speak to me at all. Then I was also worried that if you did speak to me, that it would be different somehow because I'm not the Jonah that you were in love with."

She understood that. He was right in a way. She'd loved blind Jonah. Not because he was blind but because of how it made them closer to each other than anyone else could ever be. The times where she tried to be in the darkness with him were some of the most amazing and special times in her life. Now, he was still Jonah but didn't need her like he used to. She wasn't sure how she could explain that to him or how she even felt about it.

They stayed on the river bank for the remainder of the evening, blending into the Parisian landscape, becoming part of the romance of it all: watching the boats sail by, lovers kiss, artists sketch and listening to the buskers.

CHAPTER 19

"Oh god, I can't do this. It's too hard." Jonah clung to her, hugging her so tightly that she couldn't inhale fully. When she pulled away, standing on her toes, she took his face in her hands, kissed him and told him she'd see him soon. Maybe he could come home to visit or she'd come back in a few months.

"A few months," he whispered, like the words were a knife in his chest. "I'm going to miss you so much, Sam. This week has been... amazing."

"Yes, it has. It's been wonderful. But I have to go, Jonah. I love you. I'll call you as soon as I land."

"I love you too." She peeled herself away from him, his head bowed as she took her luggage and walked away. She stole a glance as she went through the gate and the sight of him broke her heart: staring at the ground, shoulders hunched, a lonely figure cut into the crowd.

*

She felt refreshed and relieved that she'd slept the entire flight over the Atlantic as the plane made its final descent. She couldn't have coped with the hours of being trapped in a steel tube having Jonah thoughts running like Olympians through her head. They never discussed what would become of them when she had to go home. It was too painful and remained the elephant in the room following them around. Were they going to have a long distance relationship? Were they going to remain friends, who occasionally had sex, but saw other people? The elephant had shrunk when they weren't together, but now it had split in two: they had one each following them.

She was never so glad to see a familiar face as she was to see Paul's when she landed back in Nebraska, emerging from the arrivals' gate. He held her tightly in his arms.

"What are you doing here?" she asked, sleepily.

"I figured you'd need a ride and a hug."

His kindness made a lump form in her throat and as he took her luggage, she kissed him on the cheek and told him how much it meant to her. It would have been twice as upsetting to arrive back to the airport alone, watching families and lovers embrace happily. Then having to drive home to an empty house. She loved him for his thoughtfulness.

"You hungry?" she asked, as Paul pulled into her driveway. The midnight moon lit their way.

"Starved. Will I get take out?"

"I'll get it delivered, you've done enough."

"No, it's fine. Anyway, they don't deliver this late. I'll go get it and get some chocolate too. You look like you need it."

"Thanks Paul. You're such a good friend."

When he left, Sam picked up the phone. It was morning in France so Jonah should be up. Sandrine told her he had left for work, but that she'd pass on the message. When Sam asked her if he was OK, she said he was fine and said her goodbyes before hanging up. Sam felt let down. He had been devastated at the airport. What had changed? She imagined him getting up, dressing with a spring in his step and heading out to work, smiling at the sunny Parisian morning. Was he over her again already?

Paul returned with Chinese food and a giant slab of chocolate. Sam filled him in on all things Jonah and Paris.

"So didn't you sort anything out? Are you back together or what?"

"Well, I don't know. We did some...... you know, stuff but we never actually talked about it." Her phone rang, interrupting her from explaining further, not that she could as she didn't even know herself. It was Stacey calling to ask how she'd gotten on. Sam told her to call over, that Paul was here and they were having food.

Ten minutes later, Stacey was bear-hugging her at the front door. She regaled the details a second time, this time including the romantic bits that Paul wouldn't have been interested in when she'd told it the first time around. He looked suitably bored now, while Stacey was enthralled. She too asked where they were relationship-wise only to be told the same as Paul.

"Guys, I'm kinda zapped. Do you mind if I go to bed? You can stay here and finish the food, there's wine in the fridge. You're welcome to stay over, there's the spare room and the couch."

She kissed them both goodnight and thanked them for being there for her, saying how lucky she was to have such wonderful friends. She slept so solidly, that when the phone woke her at 6 a.m, she thought she was dreaming it. Jonah's number popped up. He apologised for missing her that morning, he'd gone to work early. He sounded fine, she thought. Upbeat and in good form. It made her feel like crap. It would have been nice to know she wasn't alone in pining.

He signed off telling her he'd talk to her soon. She dragged her heavy head out of bed and threw on her robe. Paul and Stacey's cars were still in the drive. The couch was empty so she wondered where he was, presuming that Stacey had taken the spare bed and he the couch. The smell of the coffee brewing woke her up some more and she set about making eggs and bacon. By nine o'clock, there was no sign of either of her friends so she became curious. Tip toeing up the stairs, she cursed as she forgot to avoid the creaky one. She slowly opened the door to the spare room and shut it immediately, clasping her hand over her mouth. Stacey and Paul were fast asleep, wrapped in each other's arms. She couldn't suppress a giggle. Paul and Stacey..... together. She wanted to tell someone. The only person was Jonah but she didn't want to phone him back. Talking to him was too raw.

She acted nonchalant when Stacey came into the kitchen, looking sheepish and shy, an hour later.

"So.....?"

"OK! Don't grill me. Paul and I slept together last night."

Sam burst out laughing, her friend's face was a picture of guilt and self-reproach.

"Aren't you mad?"

"Why would I be mad? I think it's lovely."

"Really? Isn't it weird for you?"

"No. Not at all. My two best friends together? I'm thrilled."

"Hold on. We only slept together. It's not like we're getting married or anything."

"Not yet, anyway! So, what happened?"

"OK, after you went to bed, we started talking about the row we'd had in your house that time. He explained how he hadn't been himself and that he'd been getting over someone. He seemed so sweet and vulnerable. I said I forgave him and went to give him a peck on the cheek, but he turned just before I could and kissed me really gently on the lips. Sam, he is a good kisser." She feigned a dramatic swoon. "I was weak by the time he'd finished. Anyway, you know I've always had a thing for red heads."

"Have you?" Sam was amused watching her highly animated friend.

"Well, yeah. Ever since Dr. Owen Hunt came into Grey's Anatomy."

"Oh right, so ever since last year?"

Stacey punched Sam playfully in the arm but still had an unrelenting smile like a crescent moon knocked on its side.

"So then what happened?"

"Things got hot and heavy after that and we ended up in bed together. I know I was a little drunk but I remember everything. He was so sexy. Really tender and when he......"

"That's enough! Too much information. I don't want to hear about Paul that way," Sam protested. She was reminded of the awkward, fumbling encounter they'd had of their own.

She teased Paul when he eventually surfaced, carrying the same tussled hair and sheepish look of his partner from the previous night. They left later, heads down, not saying a word to each other, walking to their respective cars. Sam gathered the presents Jonah had bought for his niece and nephews and putting them into the back of the car, drove the familiar route to Bella's house. On opening the door, Bella shrieked and threw her arms around Sam, almost knocking her over. Bella hadn't changed, although the children had grown up a bit. The two women sat, sipping coffee and talking about everything but Jonah. The children delighted in opening their presents from their favourite absent uncle. Finally, she cut to the quick.

"Do you miss him?" There was genuine concern in Bella's voice.

"Yes. More than anything. I wish he'd never left. It was really hard saying goodbye yesterday."

"Do you know he almost came back from Paris after the first week? We had to talk him into staying. He couldn't leave you, even though you'd broken up, he didn't want to be so far away, in case you came looking for him."

Sam winced with guilt, knowing he had almost given up his new job and the chance to get his sight back so he could come back to Omaha in case she got in touch - after telling him not to call her again. Bella looked at her with pity.

"Don't worry, Sam. If you guys are meant to be together, it will happen. Keep some faith. Jonah was so in love with you. I know I shouldn't say this, but I never saw him happier than when he was with you. Not even when he was married."

"I don't see how it can work, but thanks for saying that." Bella hugged her as she left and told her it would work out. Sam wasn't so sure.

Several days passed, and Sam and Jonah talked or emailed every day. But in recent days she felt he was quieter and more distant. During their last phone call, she was dragging the words out of him. When she asked if he was all right, he mumbled that he was fine and offered no further explanation. On a Wednesday morning, a week after returning from Paris, she was in work so made sure no one was around to see her reading his latest mail. As her eyes scanned the brief but sucker punch text, she felt a knot form in her stomach. She read it again, more slowly, making sure she was absorbing every syllable. A researcher interrupted her, asking her something about synoptic charts. She dismissed him with a snappy retort to ask someone else, that she was busy.

Dear Sam,

Saying goodbye to you again was so hard. Too hard. I need to go away for a while, need to get out of this place for a bit, sort my head out, get a change of scene. You won't be able to contact me. I'm sorry but I'll be in touch soon.

Jonah.

She stared at the screen in disbelief. Was he serious? She typed a lengthy, emotional reply and sent it. A half hour she waited but got no word from him. She felt hurt at his instruction not to contact him. Thankfully, it was time to go home. Head down, she didn't say good bye to anyone, just made her way to her car, cursing Jonah for ever setting foot on the earth and she drove blindly home. When home, she tore his checkered shirt to shreds and stuffed it into the bin.

After her initial reaction of painful anger, she calmed. Was Jonah going through a breakdown similar to the one she'd had? Maybe the events of the past year were too overwhelming? Maybe after he had time to think, he'd call her and beg her to come back to Paris where they could rekindle whatever this romance was. Her heart was still broken and her stomach sick, but she gave him the benefit of the doubt. He was a tempestuous man. He needed time.

Two days passed without as much as a text from him. Flitting between empathy and anger, she'd been tempted many times to drink a bottle or two of wine but she knew it would only end in her either back in therapy or phoning Jonah and drunkenly ranting to his voicemail. Paul phoned to see if she wanted to go on a chase. She refused and when he asked her what was wrong, she told him everything. He agreed with her when she called Jonah a bastard, but asked her to be patient, to give him time and insisted she come along on the chase to take her mind off it. She tried to refuse, but he was so insistent that she relented. It would be good to take her mind off Jonah and anyway, there was some really good potential for supercells. It had been too long since she'd chased. It might be just what she needed.

On Saturday morning, she checked the charts and radar and felt a little flutter in her stomach. Conditions were perfect for a big day, like storm season wanted to end with a bang. They were sticking close to home, eastern Nebraska was going to come alive with storms in the early afternoon. She took out her comfy jeans and a white tank top she hadn't worn since starting her new job and put them on, strangely excited about the day ahead, despite her stomach churning at the hurt caused by Jonah. Pouring the coffee into her travel mug, she felt a jab of sadness as memories of last summer with him flooded her mind. She shook them off and went to answer the door as Paul knocked.

"Ready?"

"Yup." She pulled the door behind her and skipped to the truck, eager to spend the day doing something other than thinking about Jonah.

Paul had a big stupid grin on his face. Sam decided he'd probably spent another night with Stacey. There was another head in the truck. She laughed, thinking of her best friend being dragged on a chase with Paul. It was Stacey's worst nightmare. At least they'd have a bit of fun along the way.

"We have another chaser with us today." Paul grinned impishly.

"Don't tell me it's Stacey?"

Paul shrugged.

"Do you know what you're getting yourself in for, bringing her? She is gonna spend the entire time giving out about her hair being blown to pieces," Sam joked as she put her bag in the trunk.

"Morning Stace! So he bribed you to come wi......." She stopped dead.

"Sam."

In the split second it had taken for her brain to register who she was seeing, her mouth had dried up and her hands had begun to shake, all while an overwhelming dizziness overcame her. She realised she hadn't blinked when her eyes began to water furiously.

"Jonah? What are you doing here? I thought....."

"I know what I said. I went to the airport, was going to catch a flight to Spain to stay with my cousin, just to clear my head and get some perspective. When I got to the airport, I realised the only flight I wanted to catch was to home. I didn't need to clear my head, I needed to come home to you."

"But I was worried about you. I didn't know where you'd gone, how you were feeling."

"I'm sorry. I guess I could have found a better way of going about it. I should have let you know."

"Yes, you should have. I was mad and angry and mad some more. How long are you home for?"

"Forever Sam. I've ditched my job and have come home for you. If you'll have me." He was out of the truck now, standing with his hands in his pockets, begging her with his eyes.

Sam closed her eyes and shook her head. If she re-opened them and he was gone, then this was all a horribly teasing dream or hallucination. If he was still there, then it was really happening. Almost afraid to find out, she slowly opened one eye. He was still there, looking at her pleadingly. The past few days had been lonely and she'd spent the time thinking, mostly worrying, about him. She wasn't sure if she wanted to kill him or hug him. But one look into his hypnotic blue eyes and her anger dissipated.

"You really should have told me."

"I'm sorry, Sam. I just....." His forlorn face broke her heart. She couldn't be mad. He was here, offering himself to her. How could she refuse? She walked over, stood on her toes and kissed him like she'd never kissed him before. Paul smiled smugly as he watched on in awkward silence. Sam caught him.

"You were in on this?" She slapped Paul playfully on the arm, as he nodded, looking guilty and she turned back to Jonah. "What about your job? Surely you can't just leave?"

"Yeah, I did. As soon as I landed in Omaha, I knew I was never going to go back so I called and told them I was leaving. They were great about it."

"Wow. I can't believe it. I just can't believe you're here, Jonah. When did you get back?"

"Yesterday. I was going to call you but Paul said you were going chasing today so I thought I'd surprise you in person instead."

"I just can't believe it," she reiterated, stroking his face.

"Guys, this is touching and all but can we go, please?"

They jumped into the back and Paul sped towards Fairbury, Nebraska where a supercell was exploding over the fields. Sam couldn't take her eyes off Jonah and he off her, not believing they were together again.

"I can't get over the fact that you're here..... I was so afraid you'd never want to see me again."

"No.... no, not at all. I was just.... I was in a bad place when you left and....Paul, I'm terrible at this, can you explain?"

"No, it's all you Jonah." Paul shrugged.

"Sam, listen, I came all the way from Europe to be with you. I quit my job, left my home, everything to be here. Please don't be upset."

How could she be, when he was looking at her with those blue eyes, searching and pleading like a starving puppy? She moved across the seat and snuggled into him, smiling up into his face. His countenance changed from worry to relief as he hugged her close to him. Paul groaned something about getting a room. They drove through Fairbury town and out into the suburbs, driving into the epic storm before them. Lightning crackled and split the sky on the horizon, the cloud turning the late summer sky to darkness, looming like a mothership from a far off planet. Sam looked up at Jonah who was like a child seeing Santa. Awe, excitement, electricity were written all over his face. This was the first storm he'd seen with his eyes in nearly seven years.

"You know what makes it better?"

"No, what?" she asked, gazing up at him adoringly.

"Seeing it with you."

She reached up to kiss him and he reciprocated, their lips touching in the lightest of ways: just a taste.

"So, is anyone gonna check the radar or are we just going to take shots?" Paul's sarcastic tongue was in full flight today.

"Sorry, boss. I think Sam should read the radar because I'm not used to these new ones. I studied them a bit in France, but I think Sam's probably more used to them."

She opened the laptop. "We need to head north east, Paul. It's going to avoid the town, which is good, but it's highly unstable. There's a really good hook echo here, boys. There's definitely rotation." She looked at Jonah again who wasn't listening. He was hypnotised by the storm.

"Should we deploy a sensor pad, Jonah?"

"Have you still got some?"

"Yeah, I modified them slightly to give them better grip on the ground. But they're pretty much still the same."

"Yeah, let's do it then." The boys whooped. Sam laughed at their child-like excitement.

Paul drove at speed to get north of the storm, and as he passed it, Sam noticed not only a rotating funnel cloud, but stirring on the ground.

"Paul, move it. We've contact on the ground."

Just as she said the words, a snake dropped from the cloud and whipped up debris high into the air. Paul pulled the handbrake, the truck swerved to a stop and he jumped out to get the sensor pad. Jonah and Sam got out too, the twister sashaying back and forth in the field beside them.

"Sam, I need to ask you something."

"Jonah, is this the best time?" she asked, and clapped her hand over her mouth as Jonah got down onto one knee on the ground before her. The twister was coming closer but she didn't know where to look, at it or Jonah.

"Oh, this is the perfect time. Samia Di Matteo, will you marry me?"

He produced a little purple velvet box from the pocket in his combats. In it, was nestled a platinum ring with a circular solitaire diamond and little amethysts climbing up the side to it.

"Jesus, Jonah, you're mad! Yes, yes I'll marry you but for god's sake, can we get out of here? There's a tornado closing in on us."

He grabbed her, put the ring on her finger, his hands shaking wildly and picked her up, swinging her around, burying his head in her shoulder.

"You've just made me the happiest man alive. The day I met you, I knew I wanted to marry you and I knew I'd propose in front of a twister."

"Seriously, you're mad!" Her head swam both with happiness and panic as she looked over his shoulder to see the tornado inch closer. Debris began to fly at them and Paul shouted that they needed to move. Sam heard something among the sounds of branches hitting the ground and whistling wind. It sounded like a cat in distress. She walked slowly around the truck, trying hard to listen. She called to Jonah, he'd be able to hear it better than she.

"Sam, we really need to go."

"No, Jonah listen. I hear an animal or something."

"Fuck, Sam, seriously?"

"Jonah, just listen," she shouted.

He moved around the truck to her and stood still for a second. Then he darted to a gap in the ditch, and disappeared briefly before reappearing with a tiny grey kitten in his arms.

"Hurry guys, hurry!" Paul had the engine running and was white as a sheet. The tornado was baring down on them.

Jonah and Sam jumped in, narrowly avoiding being hit by a branch and Paul reversed up the road, not having time to turn the truck. They watched the twister cross the road in the exact spot that Jonah had gotten down on his knee.

"Are you videoing this Paul, it's huge!"

"I'm too busy trying to save your ass.... here, you do it," Paul said, still driving as he threw the video camera at him. Jonah didn't know whether to catch the camera or drop the kitten. Luckily the camera landed on his leg, undamaged and he handed the kitten to Sam.

"This is fucking awesome! We're back in business, Paul!"

"Woo hoo!" Paul shouted as the twister ran straight over their sensor pad, shifting it slightly on the road, but not picking it up.

They watched for another five minutes as the tornado snaked over the opposite field and then dissipated, leaving a shower of debris falling from the sky. Paul ran to collect the sensor. Sitting in the back of the truck, Jonah turned to Sam, took her head in his hands and kissed her until she had to stop to catch her breath. The kitten wriggled between them, crying to be freed from the passionate embrace.

"So, you'll marry me then?"

"Yes. I'll marry you."

"That makes me so...... so happy. You have no idea." Jonah rolled his eyes theatrically.

"I have every idea. I love you."

"Oh, god, I love you, baby. So, what are we going to do with this little guy?"

"Keep him. When you went away, one of my plans was to become a 'crazy cat lady,' so this could be the start."

"There is one more homeless person who needs looking after."

"I guess seeing as we're getting married, we'll need to live together at some point."

"Should we start looking for a house?"

"You know what Jonah, I love my little cottage. Why don't you move your stuff in there?"

"Will there be room with you and little fur ball there too?" He rubbed the kitten's head.

"We'll try to squeeze you in!"

He kissed her once more. Her diamond ring glinted in the sun that was breaking through the dying storm cloud as she stroked his face.

THE END

EPILOGUE

"To the newly crowned, Mrs. Mason." Jonah clinked his champagne flute to Sam's as the fizz escaped from the glass, leaving little sparkling bubbles on their hands. Her engagement ring, now kept company, nestled next to a diamond encrusted band, reflected the hazy moonlight.

"And to you."

She inhaled the crisp, fresh air. It smelled like lavender, water and grass. She shivered slightly as its dampness settled around her shoulders, biting her skin.

Jonah wrapped his arm around her, pulling her tighter. The water lapped the upright posts of the jetty underneath, making her feel sleepy.

She heard him inhale and followed his gaze. He was staring at the moon that, before now, had been shrouded in cloud. It had broken free from the suffocating veil, to reveal its silvery disc body, cutting a path across the lake as it broke through the dark, straight to Jonah, greeting him once again.

"It's so beautiful," she purred into his ear, comforting him.

"Thank you for this. I just don't know what to say."

She smiled with self-satisfaction. From the moment he'd told her he could see again, she knew she would bring him back to Vermont to the lake. All through the wedding preparations, she'd managed to keep the honeymoon destination a secret. Not liking being kept in the dark, Jonah had sulked but he trusted her. Thanks to Bella helping her plan, they were here now, just the two of them, looking upon his favourite sight in the world.

Jonah sighed happily and yawned. He rose to his feet, pulled Sam up by the hand, then hoisted her up into his arms. He bid farewell to the moon and carried his wife back to the fire-lit cabin.

"Don't you want to stay a while longer?" she asked, wrapping her arms around his warm neck.

"I've found something I like looking at more." He kissed her, until her cold toes curled as he opened the cabin door and carried her inside, shutting it against the cool moonlight.

Made in the USA
Charleston, SC
03 August 2013